Over the Garden Wall™

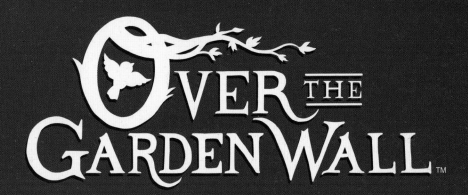

VOLUME TWO

OVER THE GARDEN WALL Volume Two, August 2017. Published by KaBOOM!, a division of Boom Entertainment, Inc. OVER THE GARDEN WALL, CARTOON NETWORK, the logos, and all related characters and elements are trademarks of and © Cartoon Network. (S17) Originally published in single magazine form as OVER THE GARDEN WALL ONGOING No. 5-8. © Cartoon Network. (S16) All rights reserved. KaBOOM!™ and the KaBOOM! logo are trademarks of Boom Entertainment, Inc., registered in various countries and categories. All characters, events, and institutions depicted herein are fictional. Any similarity between any of the names, characters, persons, events, and/or institutions in this publication to actual names, characters, and persons, whether living or dead, events, and/or institutions is unintended and purely coincidental. KaBOOM! does not read or accept unsolicited submissions of ideas, stories, or artwork.

BOOM! Studios, 5670 Wilshire Boulevard, Suite 450, Los Angeles, CA 90036-5679. Printed in China. First Printing.

ISBN-13: 978-1-68415-006-9, eISBN: 978-1-61398-677-6

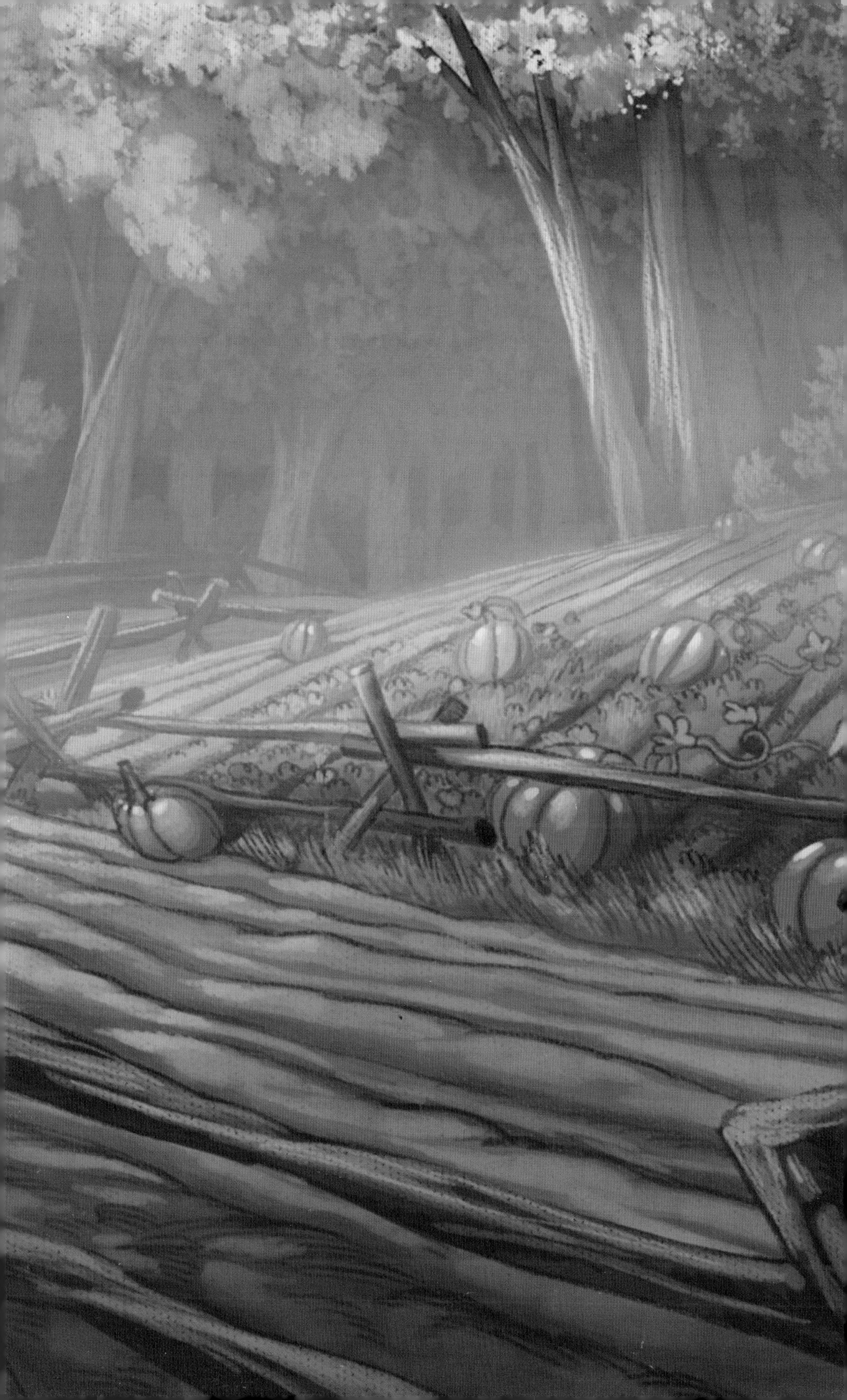

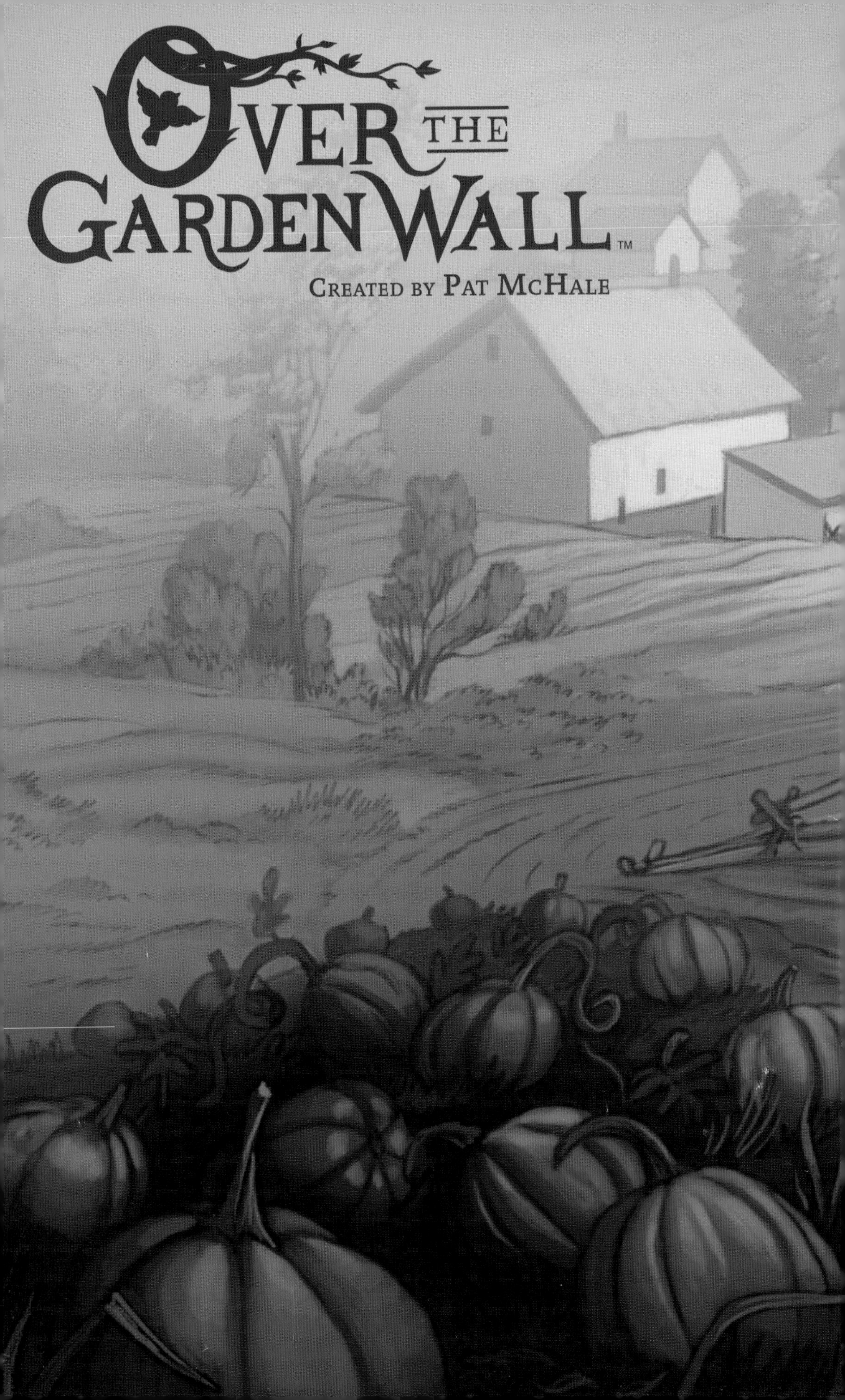
Over the Garden Wall™
Created by Pat McHale

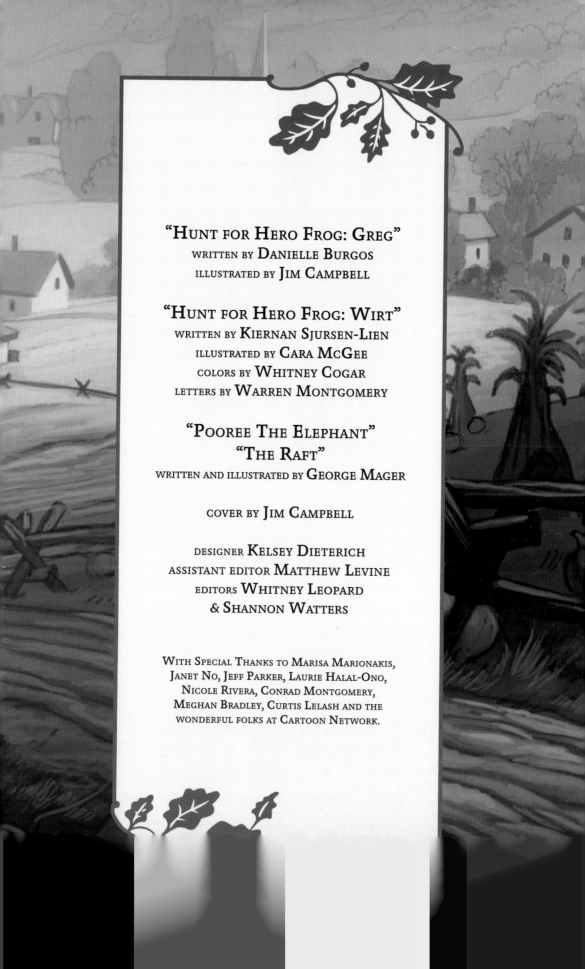

"Hunt for Hero Frog: Greg"
written by Danielle Burgos
illustrated by Jim Campbell

"Hunt for Hero Frog: Wirt"
written by Kiernan Sjursen-Lien
illustrated by Cara McGee
colors by Whitney Cogar
letters by Warren Montgomery

"Pooree The Elephant"
"The Raft"
written and illustrated by George Mager

cover by Jim Campbell

designer Kelsey Dieterich
assistant editor Matthew Levine
editors Whitney Leopard
& Shannon Watters

With Special Thanks to Marisa Marionakis,
Janet No, Jeff Parker, Laurie Halal-Ono,
Nicole Rivera, Conrad Montgomery,
Meghan Bradley, Curtis Lelash and the
wonderful folks at Cartoon Network.

Hunt for Hero Frog

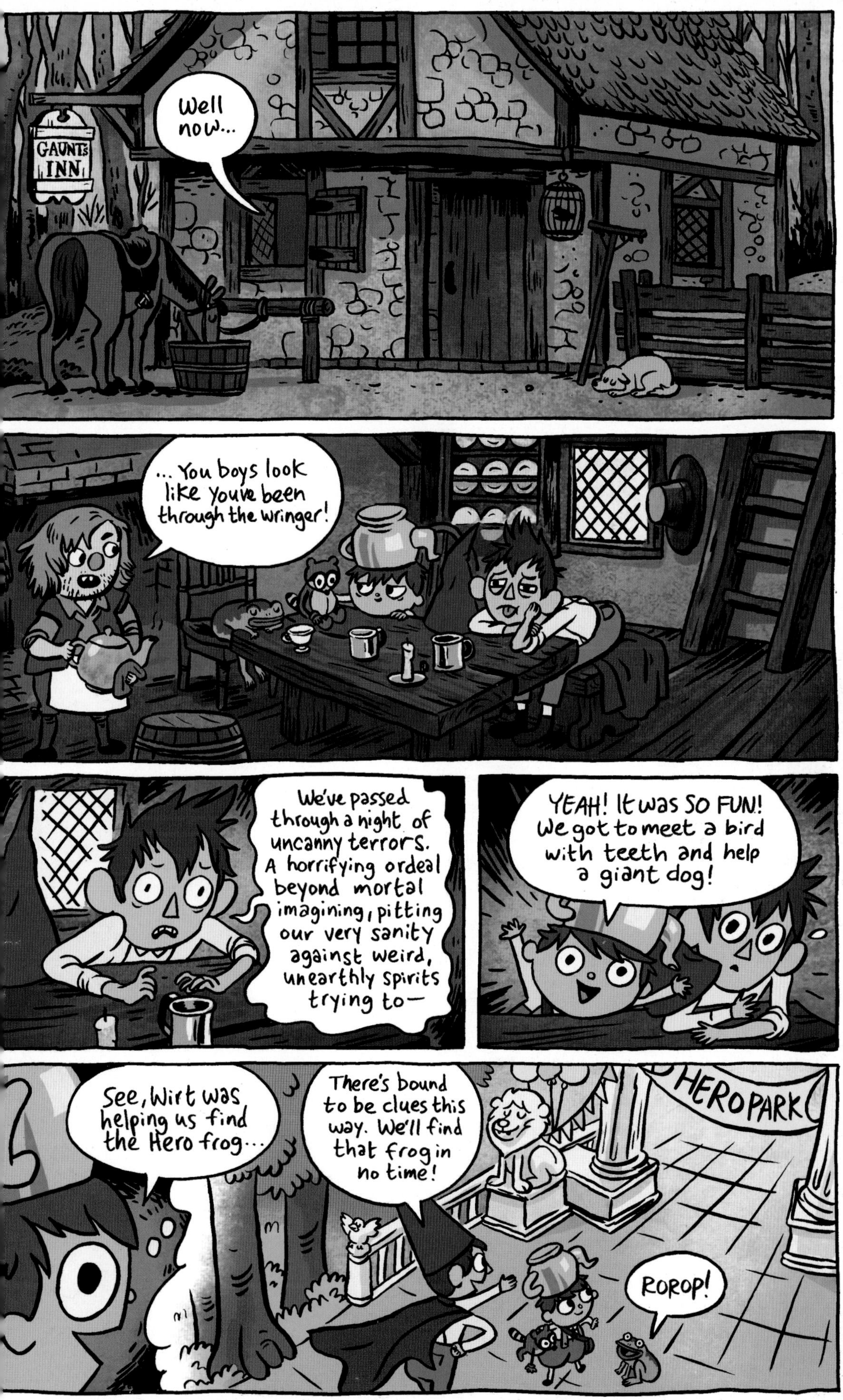
GAUNT's INN
Well now...
... You boys look like you've been through the wringer!
We've passed through a night of uncanny terrors. A horrifying ordeal beyond mortal imagining, pitting our very sanity against weird, unearthly spirits trying to—
YEAH! It was SO FUN! We got to meet a bird with teeth and help a giant dog!
See, Wirt was helping us find the Hero frog...
There's bound to be clues this way. We'll find that frog in no time!
HERO PARK
ROROP!

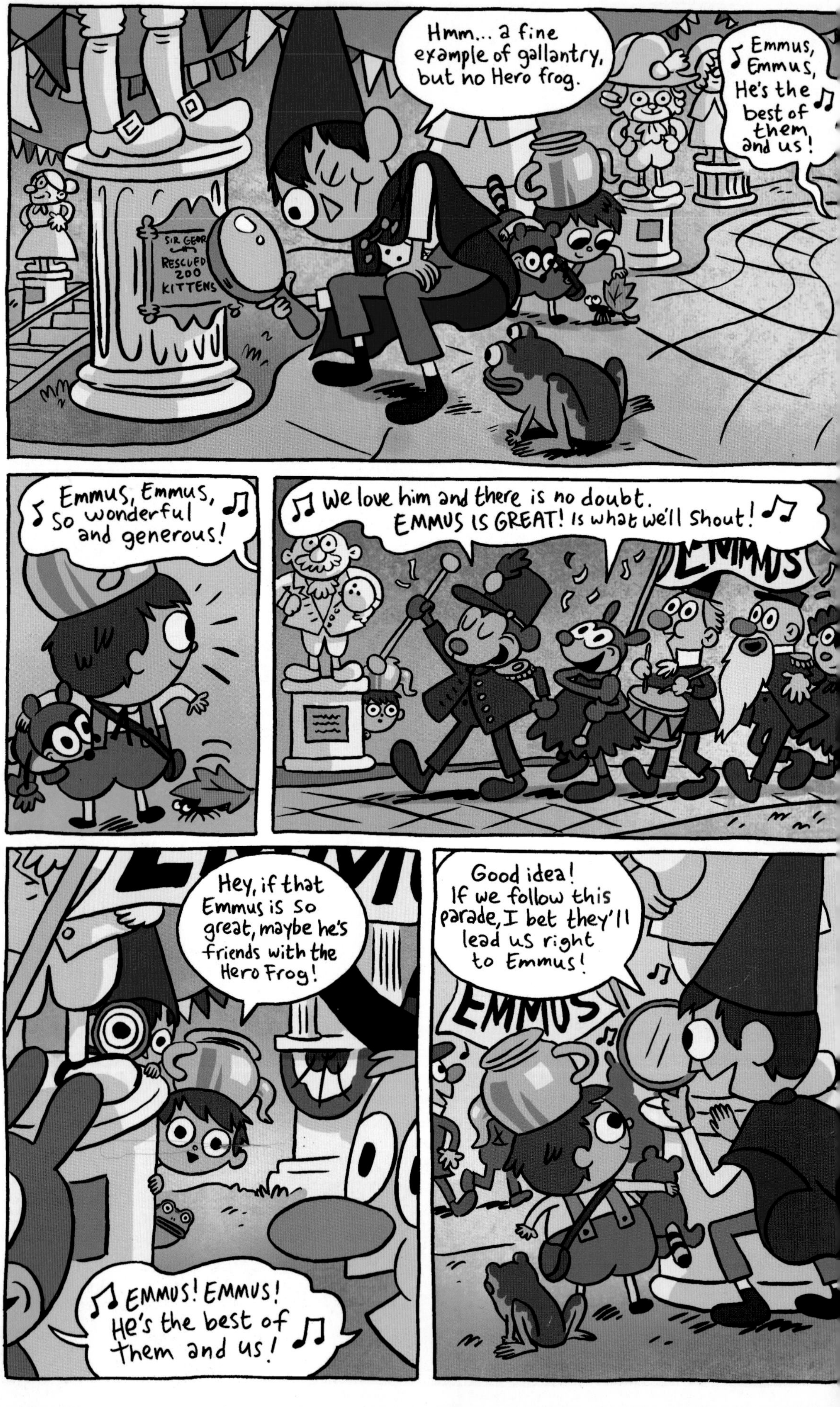
SIR GEOR
RESCUED 200 KITTENS
Hmm... a fine example of gallantry, but no Hero frog.
♪ Emmus, Emmus, He's the best of them and us! ♫
♪ Emmus, Emmus, So wonderful and generous! ♫
♫ We love him and there is no doubt. EMMUS IS GREAT! Is what we'll shout! ♫
EMMUS
Hey, if that Emmus is so great, maybe he's friends with the Hero Frog!
♫ EMMUS! EMMUS! He's the best of them and us! ♫
Good idea! If we follow this parade, I bet they'll lead us right to Emmus!
EMMUS

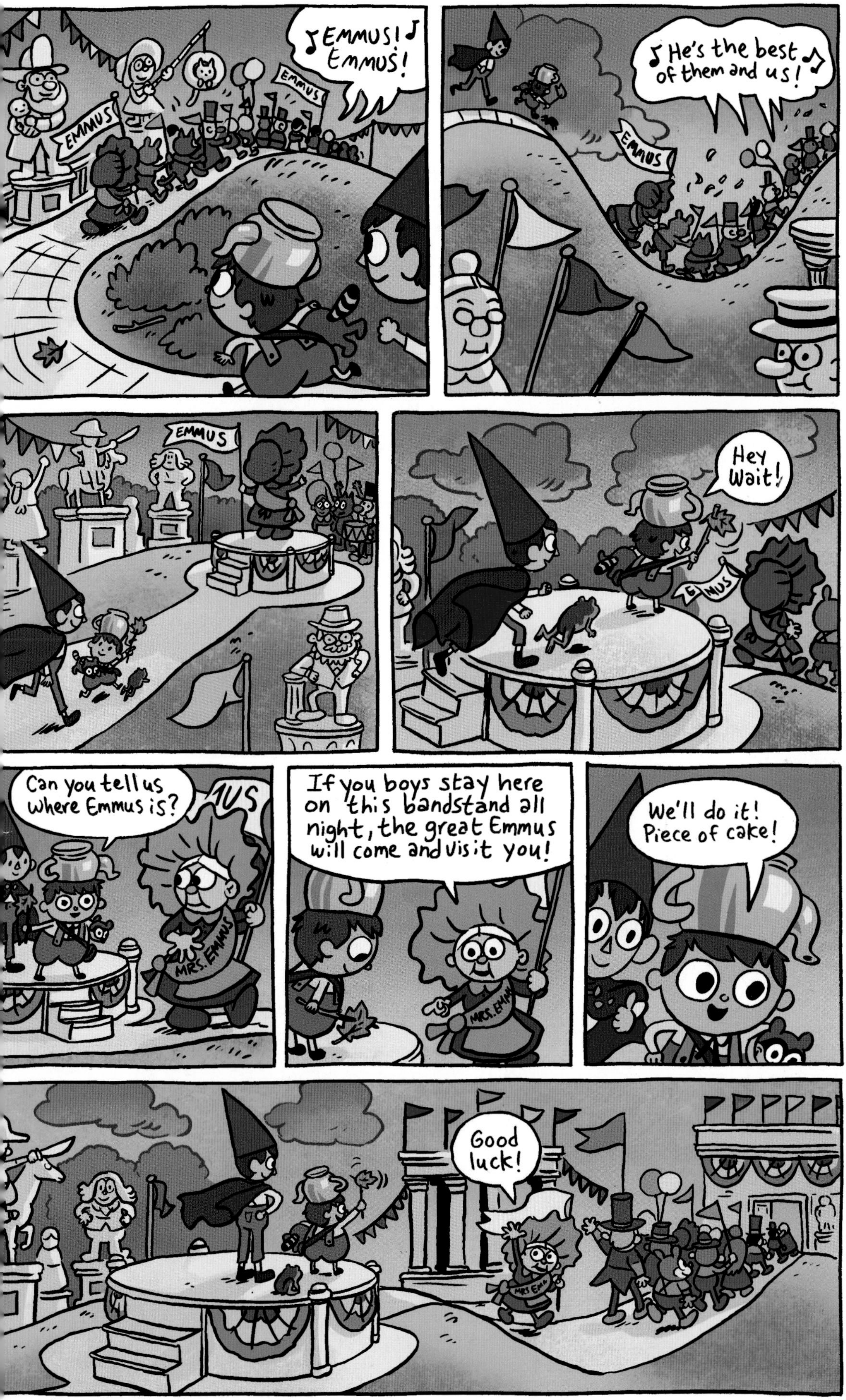
♪EMMUS! ♪
Emmus!
EMMUS
EMMUS
♪He's the best of them and us! ♪
EMMUS
EMMUS
Hey Wait!
Can you tell us where Emmus is?
MRS. EMMUS
If you boys stay here on this bandstand all night, the great Emmus will come and visit you!
We'll do it! Piece of cake!
Good luck!

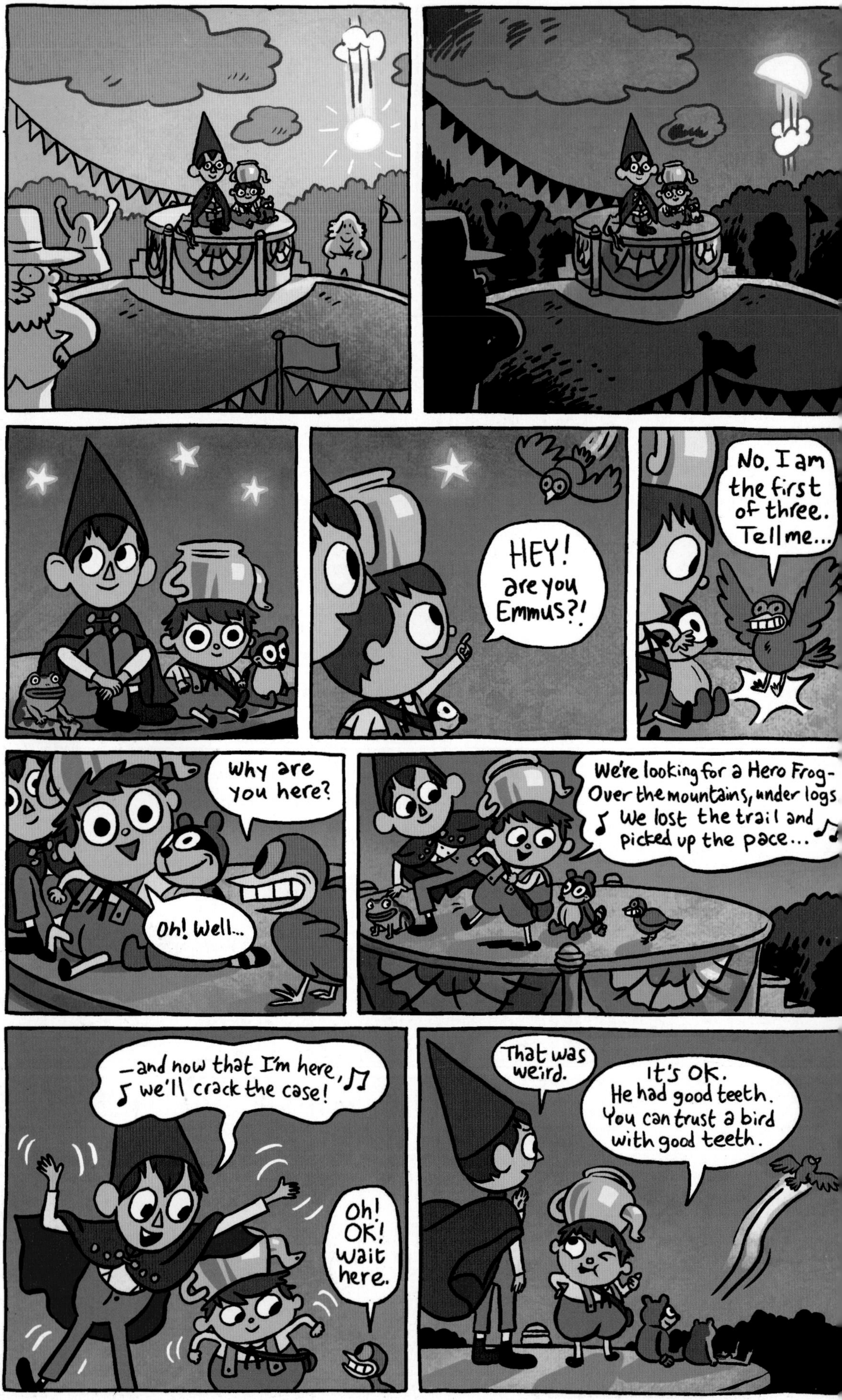
HEY!
are you
Emmus?!
No, I am
the first
of three.
Tell me...
Why are
you here?
Oh! Well...
We're looking for a Hero Frog-
Over the mountains, under logs
We lost the trail and
picked up the pace...
—and now that I'm here,
we'll crack the case!
Oh!
OK!
wait
here.
That was
weird.
It's OK.
He had good teeth.
You can trust a bird
with good teeth.

AWOO-WOO-HOO-HOOOOO!

Emmus?

AWOoo-HOoo-HOO-HOOO!

AAOOOOOH! I have a terrible toothache!

Well...

there are a number of symptoms and reasons...brushing too much - not brushing enough...

Oh, that's awful! Let me take a look!

...poor flossing technique...

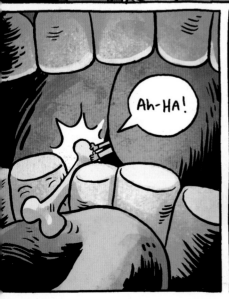

Ah-HA!

...One school of thought says a water pick is the answer, but...

POP!

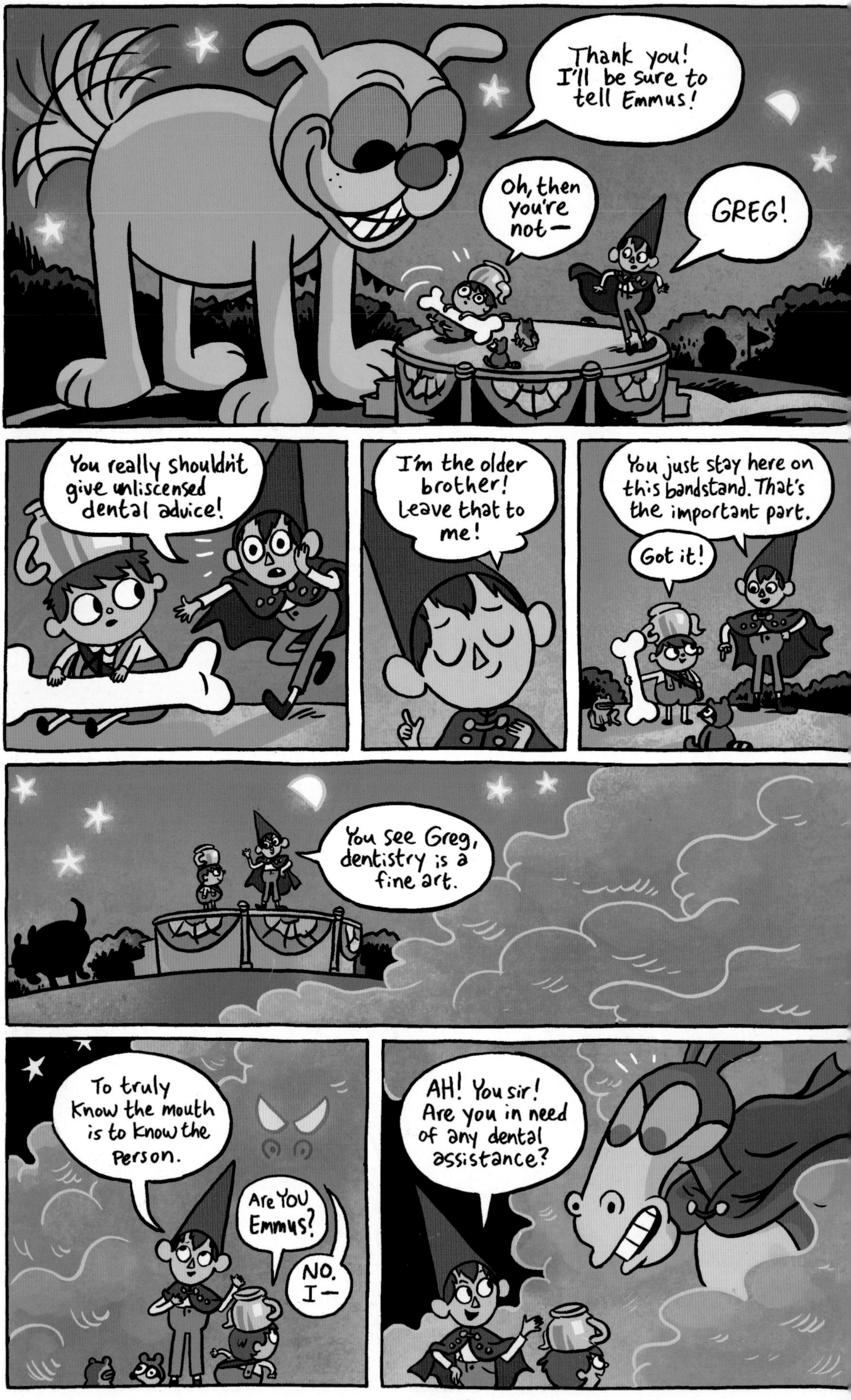

Thank you! I'll be sure to tell Emmus!
Oh, then you're not—
GREG!
You really shouldn't give unliscensed dental advice!
I'm the older brother! Leave that to me!
You just stay here on this bandstand. That's the important part.
Got it!
You see Greg, dentistry is a fine art.
To truly know the mouth is to know the person.
Are YOU Emmus?
NO. I—
AH! You sir! Are you in need of any dental assistance?

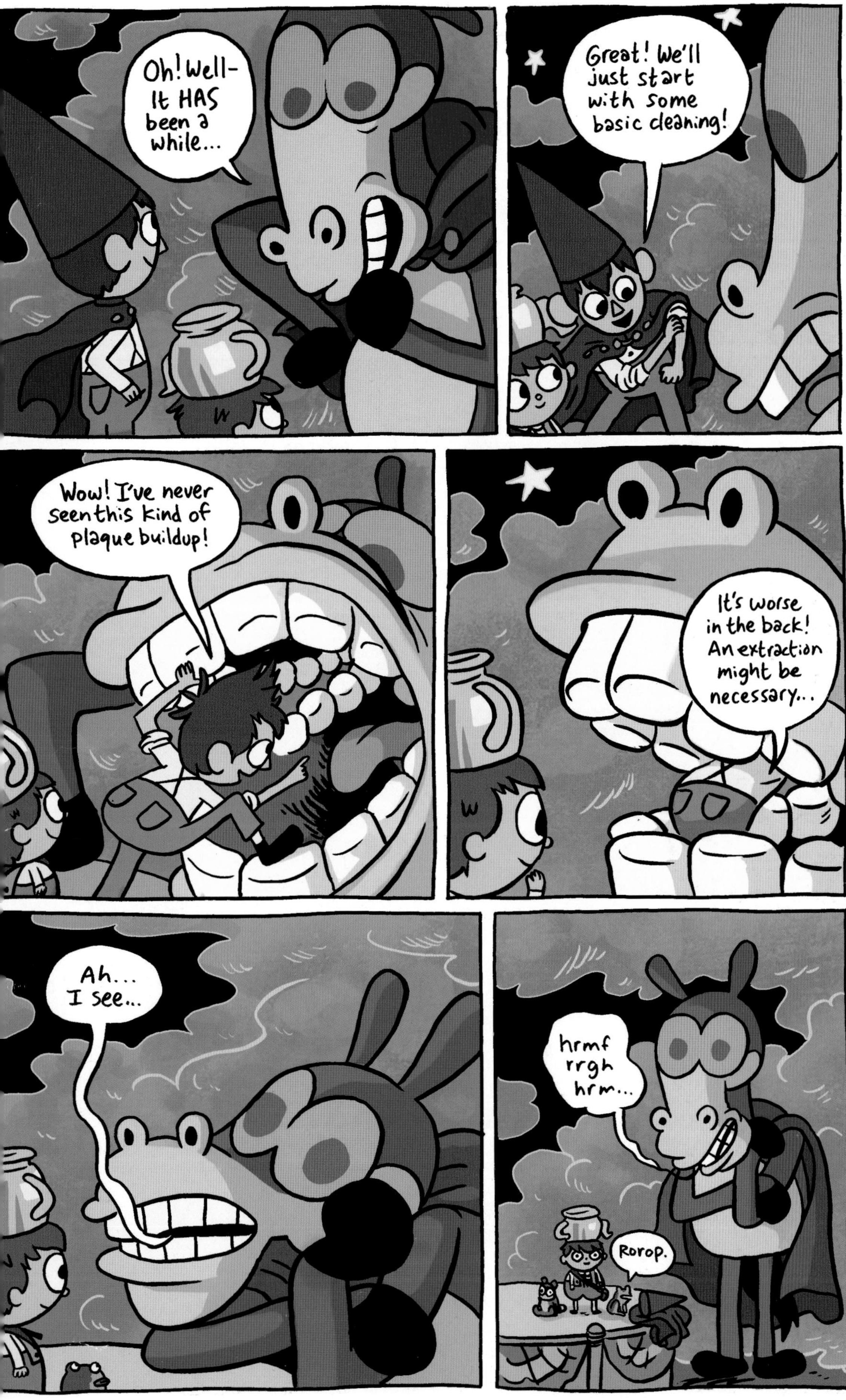
Oh! Well-
It HAS
been a
while...
Great! We'll
just start
with some
basic cleaning!
Wow! I've never
seen this kind of
plaque buildup!
It's worse
in the back!
An extraction
might be
necessary...
Ah...
I see...
hrmf
rrgh
hrm...
Rorop.

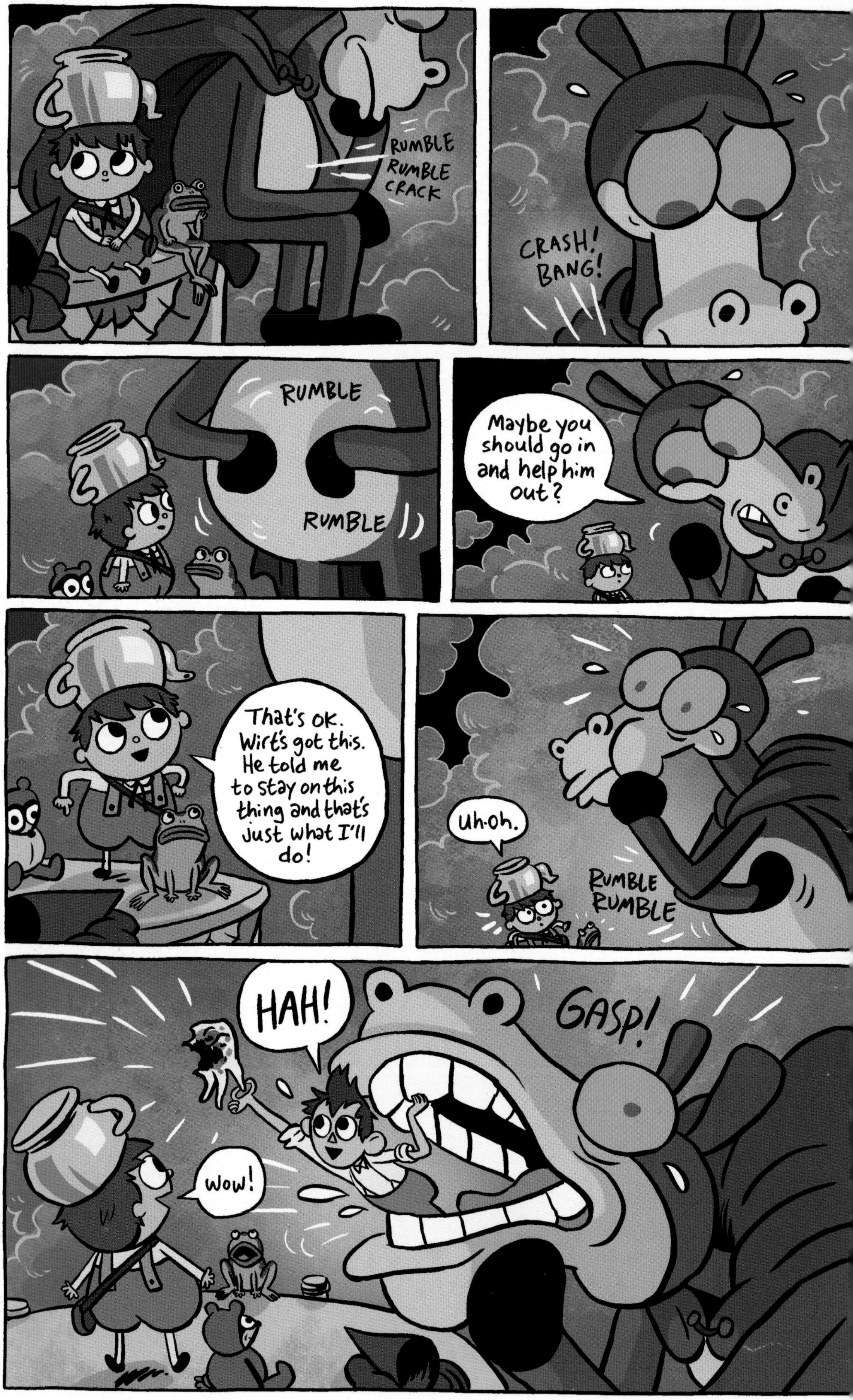
RUMBLE
RUMBLE
CRACK
CRASH!
BANG!
RUMBLE
RUMBLE
Maybe you should go in and help him out?
That's OK. Wirt's got this. He told me to stay on this thing and that's just what I'll do!
Uh-oh.
RUMBLE
RUMBLE
HAH!
GASP!
WOW!

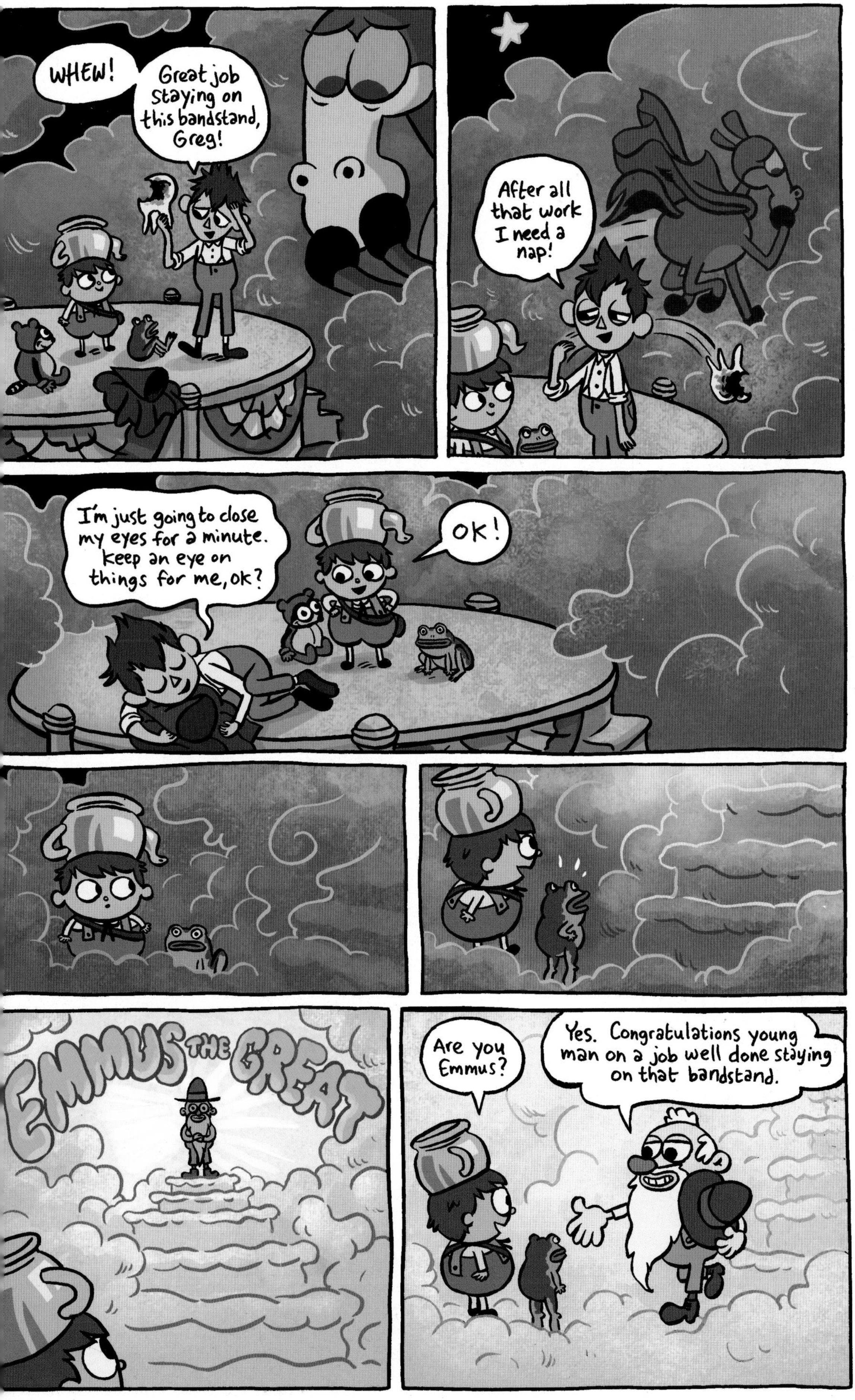
WHEW!
Great job staying on this bandstand, Greg!
After all that work I need a nap!
I'm just going to close my eyes for a minute. Keep an eye on things for me, ok?
OK!
EMMUS THE GREAT
Are you Emmus?
Yes. Congratulations young man on a job well done staying on that bandstand.

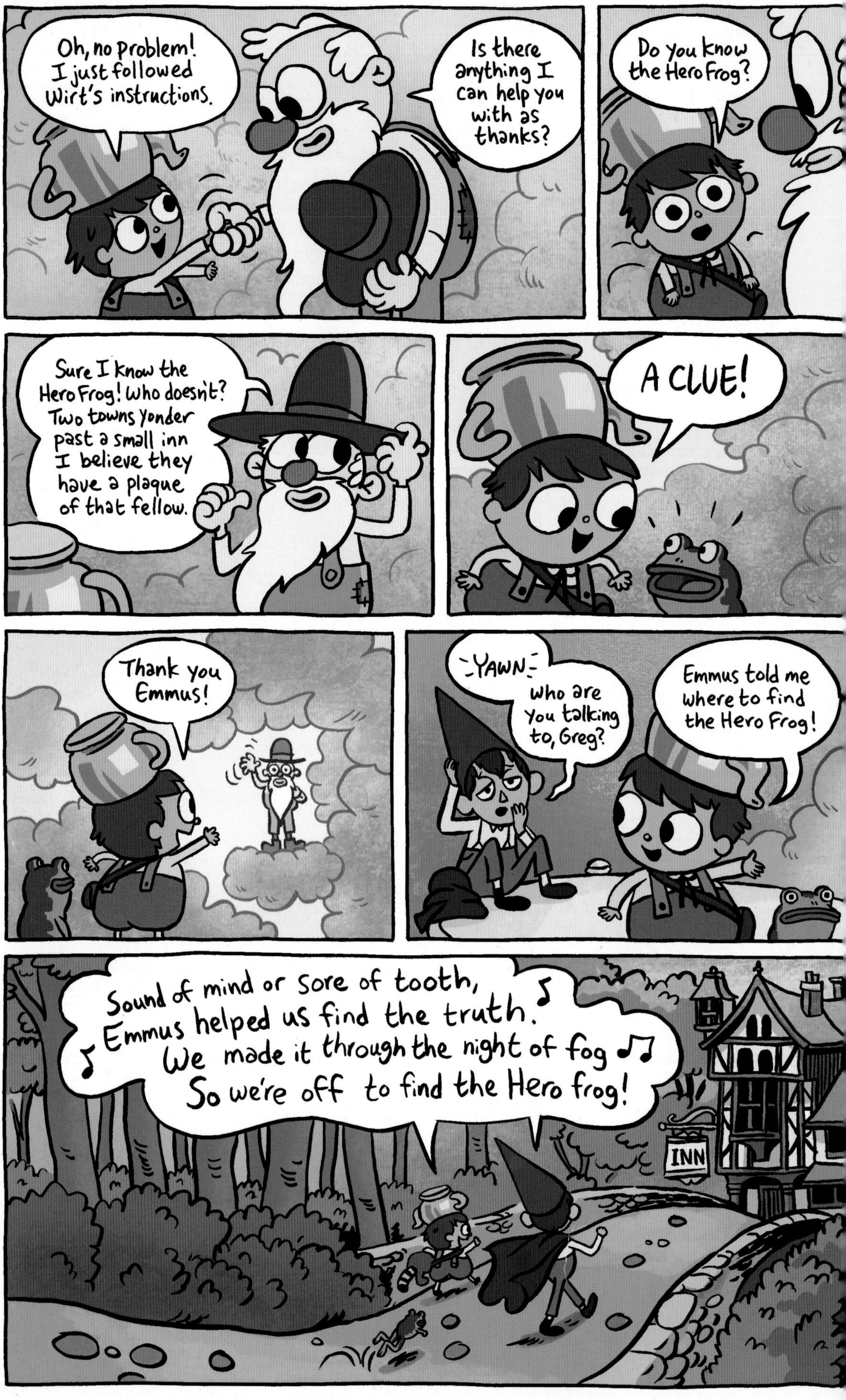
Oh, no problem! I just followed Wirt's instructions.
Is there anything I can help you with as thanks?
Do you know the Hero Frog?
Sure I know the Hero Frog! Who doesn't? Two towns yonder past a small inn I believe they have a plaque of that fellow.
A CLUE!
Thank you Emmus!
YAWN
Who are you talking to, Greg?
Emmus told me where to find the Hero Frog!
Sound of mind or sore of tooth, Emmus helped us find the truth. We made it through the night of fog So we're off to find the Hero frog!
INN

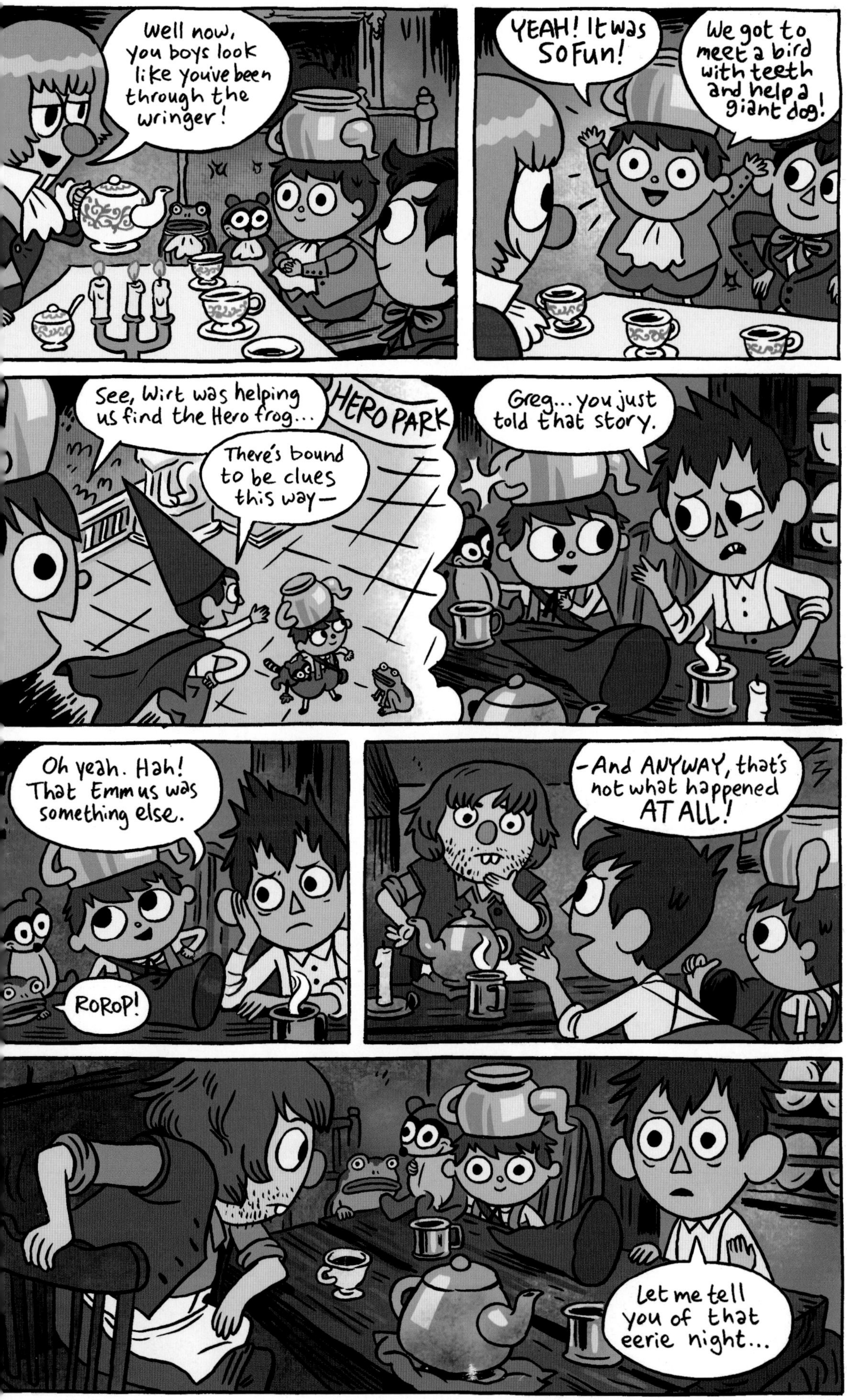

Well now, you boys look like you've been through the wringer!
YEAH! It was SO FUN!
We got to meet a bird with teeth and help a giant dog!
See, Wirt was helping us find the Hero frog...
HERO PARK
There's bound to be clues this way—
Greg... you just told that story.
Oh yeah. Hah! That Emmus was something else.
ROROP!
—And ANYWAY, that's not what happened AT ALL!
Let me tell you of that eerie night...

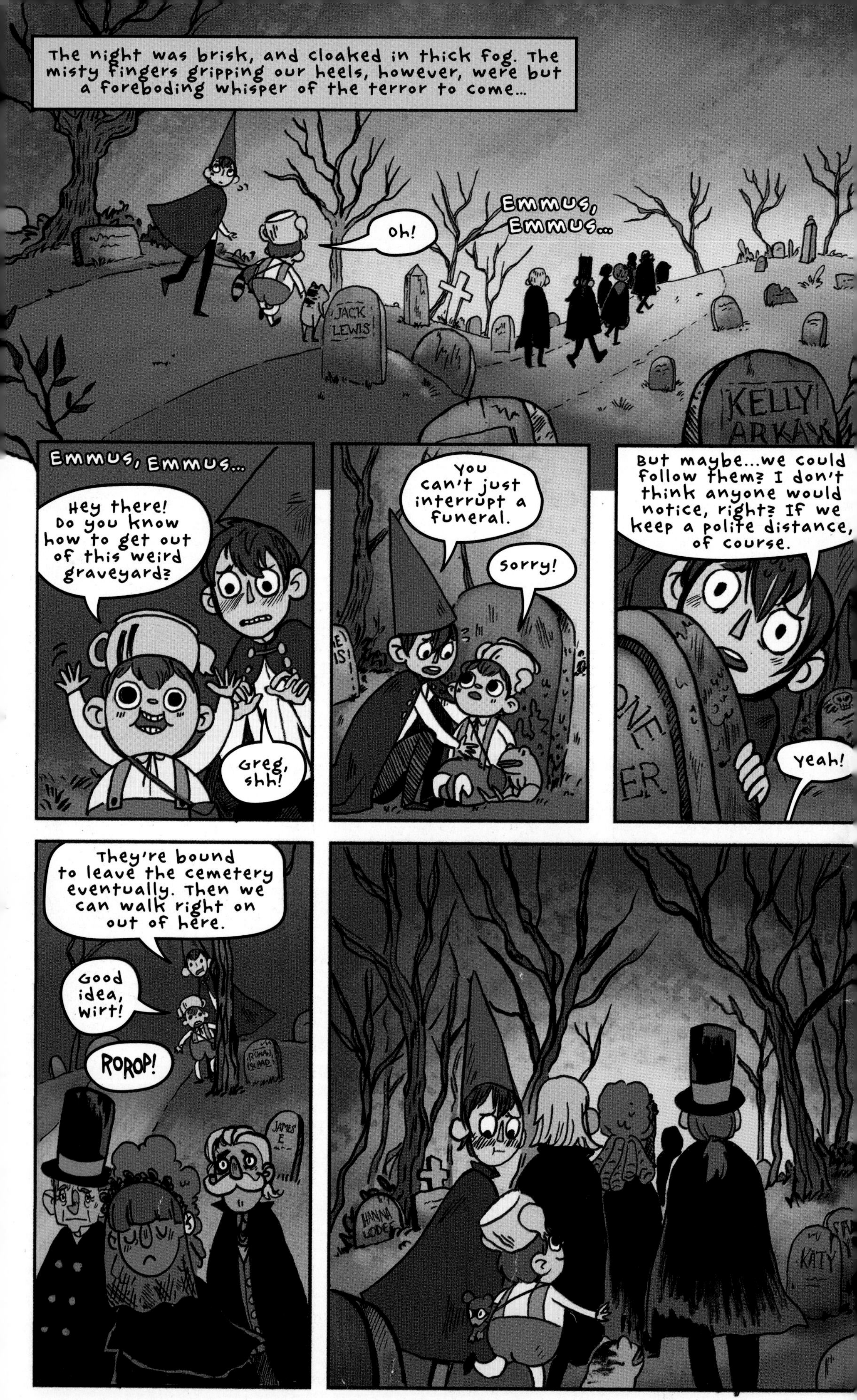

The night was brisk, and cloaked in thick fog. The misty fingers gripping our heels, however, were but a foreboding whisper of the terror to come...
Oh!
Emmus, Emmus...
JACK LEWIS
KELLY ARKA
Emmus, Emmus...
Hey there! Do you know how to get out of this weird graveyard?
Greg, shh!
You can't just interrupt a funeral.
Sorry!
But maybe...we could follow them? I don't think anyone would notice, right? If we keep a polite distance, of course.
Yeah!
They're bound to leave the cemetery eventually. Then we can walk right on out of here.
Good idea, Wirt!
ROROP!
RONAN ISLBAD
JAMES E
HANNA LODEE
KATY

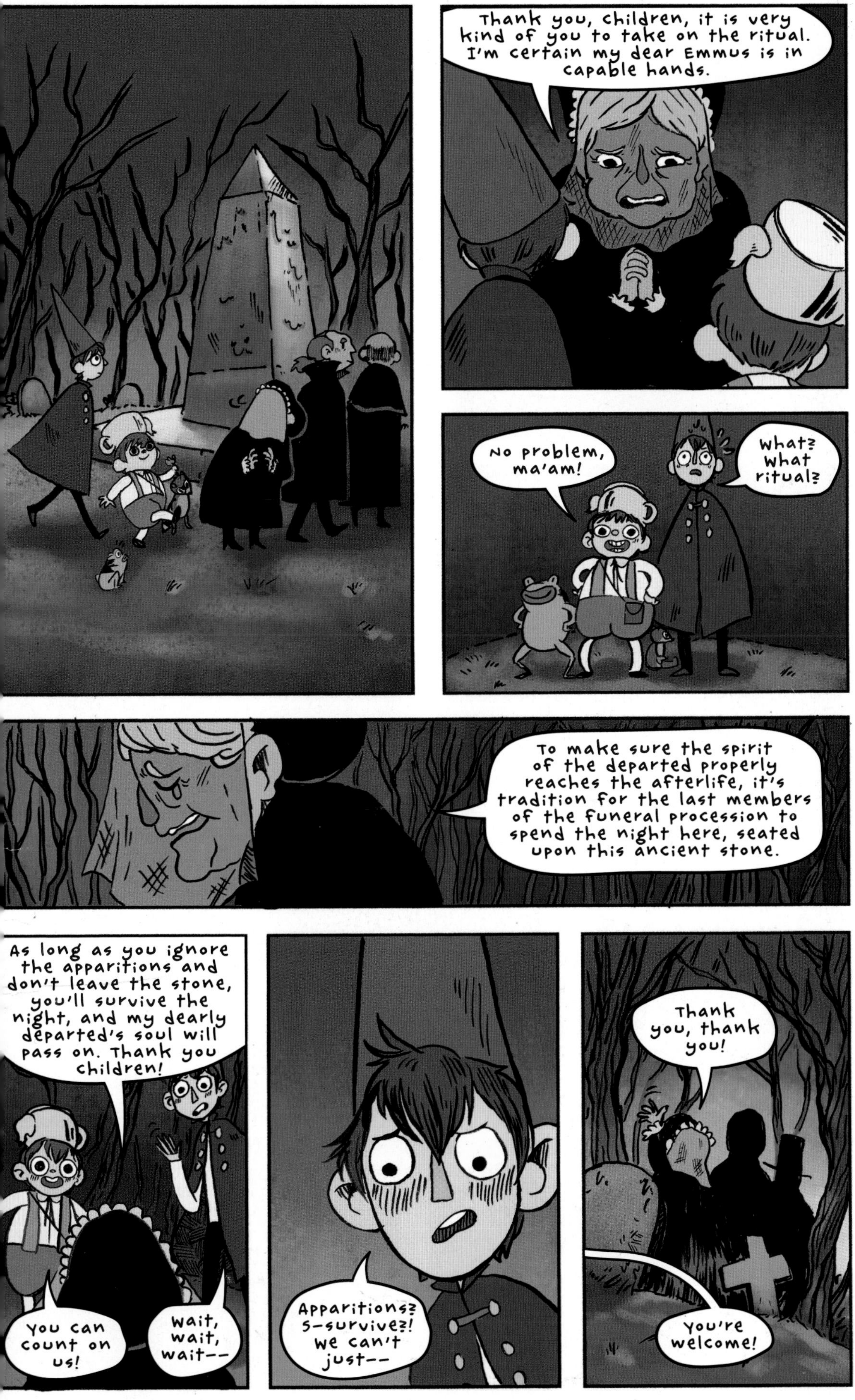

Thank you, children, it is very kind of you to take on the ritual. I'm certain my dear Emmus is in capable hands.
No problem, ma'am!
What? What ritual?
To make sure the spirit of the departed properly reaches the afterlife, it's tradition for the last members of the funeral procession to spend the night here, seated upon this ancient stone.
As long as you ignore the apparitions and don't leave the stone, you'll survive the night, and my dearly departed's soul will pass on. Thank you children!
You can count on us!
Wait, wait, wait--
Apparitions? S-survive?! We can't just--
Thank you, thank you!
You're welcome!

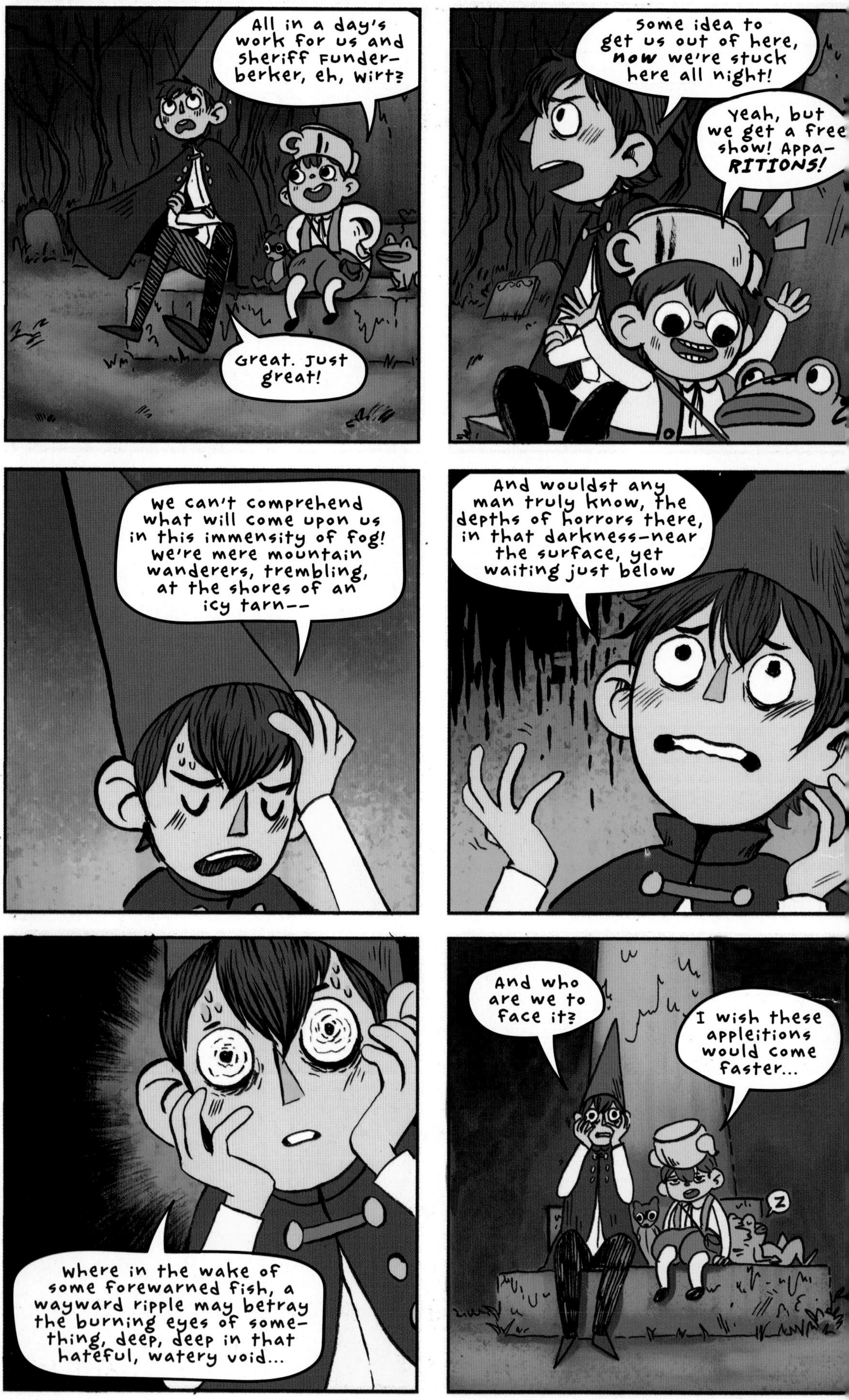
All in a day's work for us and Sheriff Funder-berker, eh, Wirt?
Great. Just great!
Some idea to get us out of here, now we're stuck here all night!
Yeah, but we get a free show! Appa-RITIONS!
We can't comprehend what will come upon us in this immensity of fog! We're mere mountain wanderers, trembling, at the shores of an icy tarn--
And wouldst any man truly know, the depths of horrors there, in that darkness-near the surface, yet waiting just below
Where in the wake of some forewarned fish, a wayward ripple may betray the burning eyes of some-thing, deep, deep in that hateful, watery void...
And who are we to face it?
I wish these appleitions would come faster...
Z

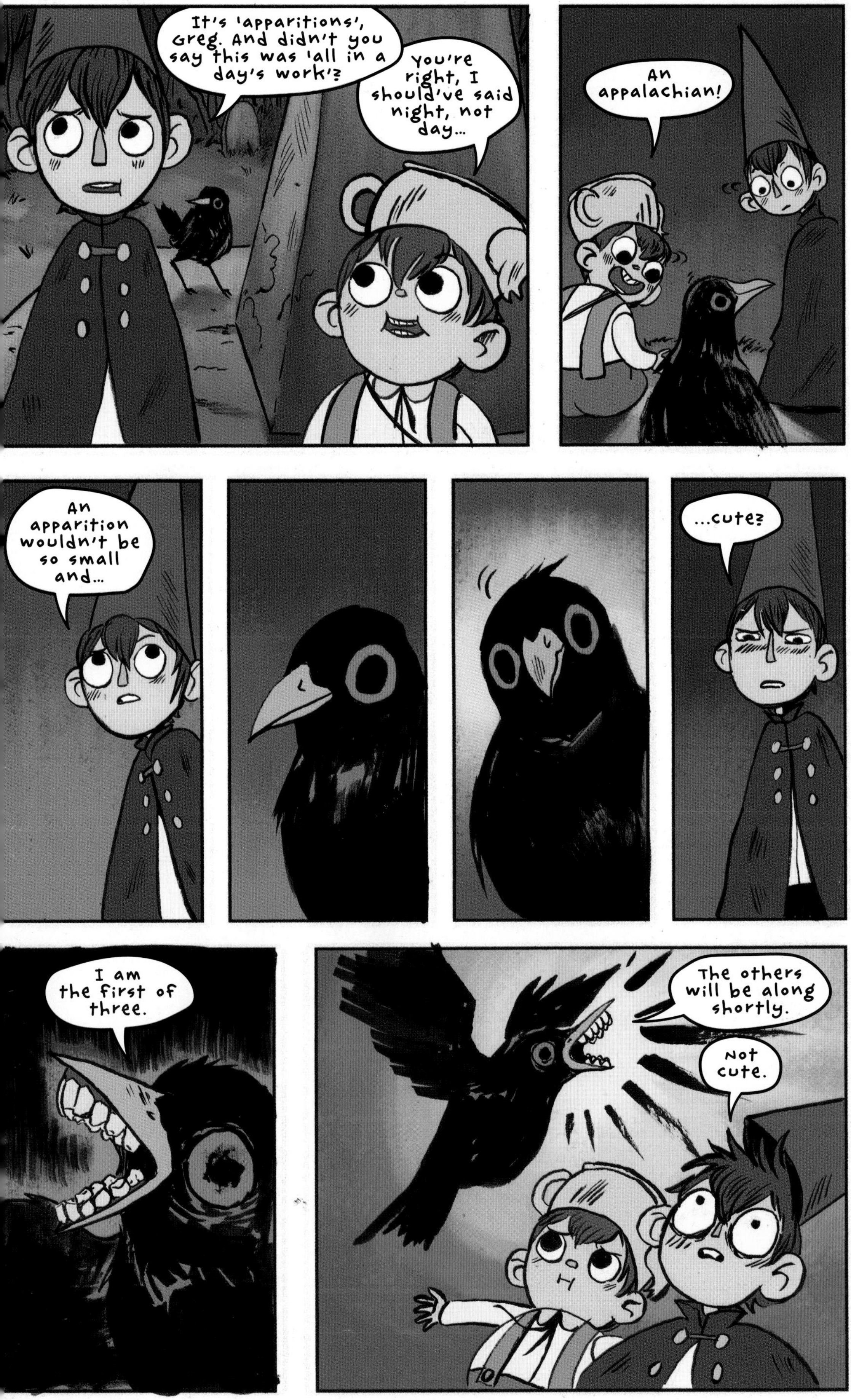
It's 'apparitions', Greg. And didn't you say this was 'all in a day's work'?
You're right, I should've said night, not day...
An appalachian!
An apparition wouldn't be so small and...
...cute?
I am the first of three.
The others will be along shortly.
Not cute.

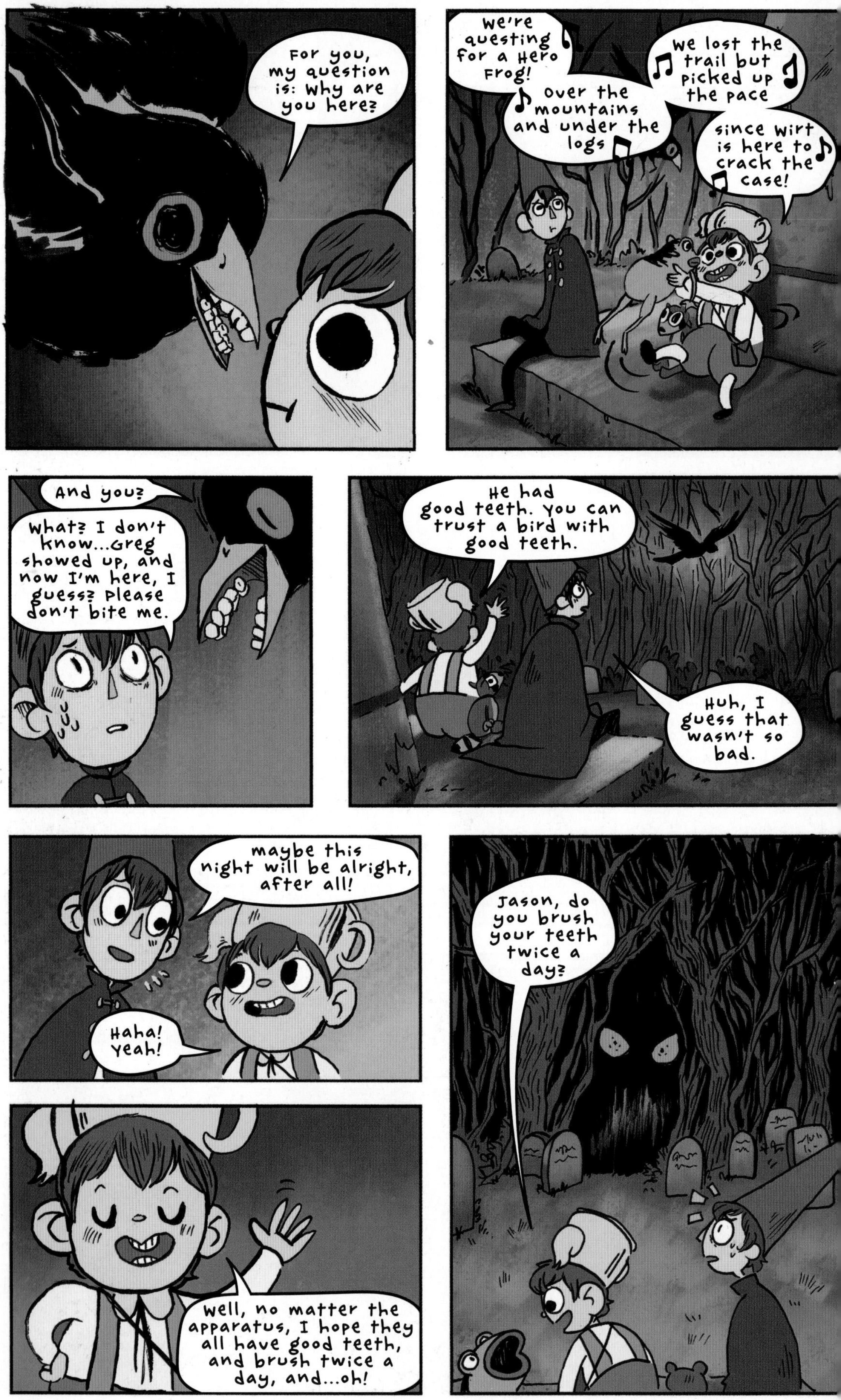
For you, my question is: Why are you here?
We're questing for a Hero Frog!
Over the mountains and under the logs
We lost the trail but picked up the pace
since Wirt is here to crack the case!
And you?
What? I don't know...Greg showed up, and now I'm here, I guess? Please don't bite me.
He had good teeth. You can trust a bird with good teeth.
Huh, I guess that wasn't so bad.
Maybe this night will be alright, after all!
Haha! Yeah!
Well, no matter the apparatus, I hope they all have good teeth, and brush twice a day, and...oh!
Jason, do you brush your teeth twice a day?

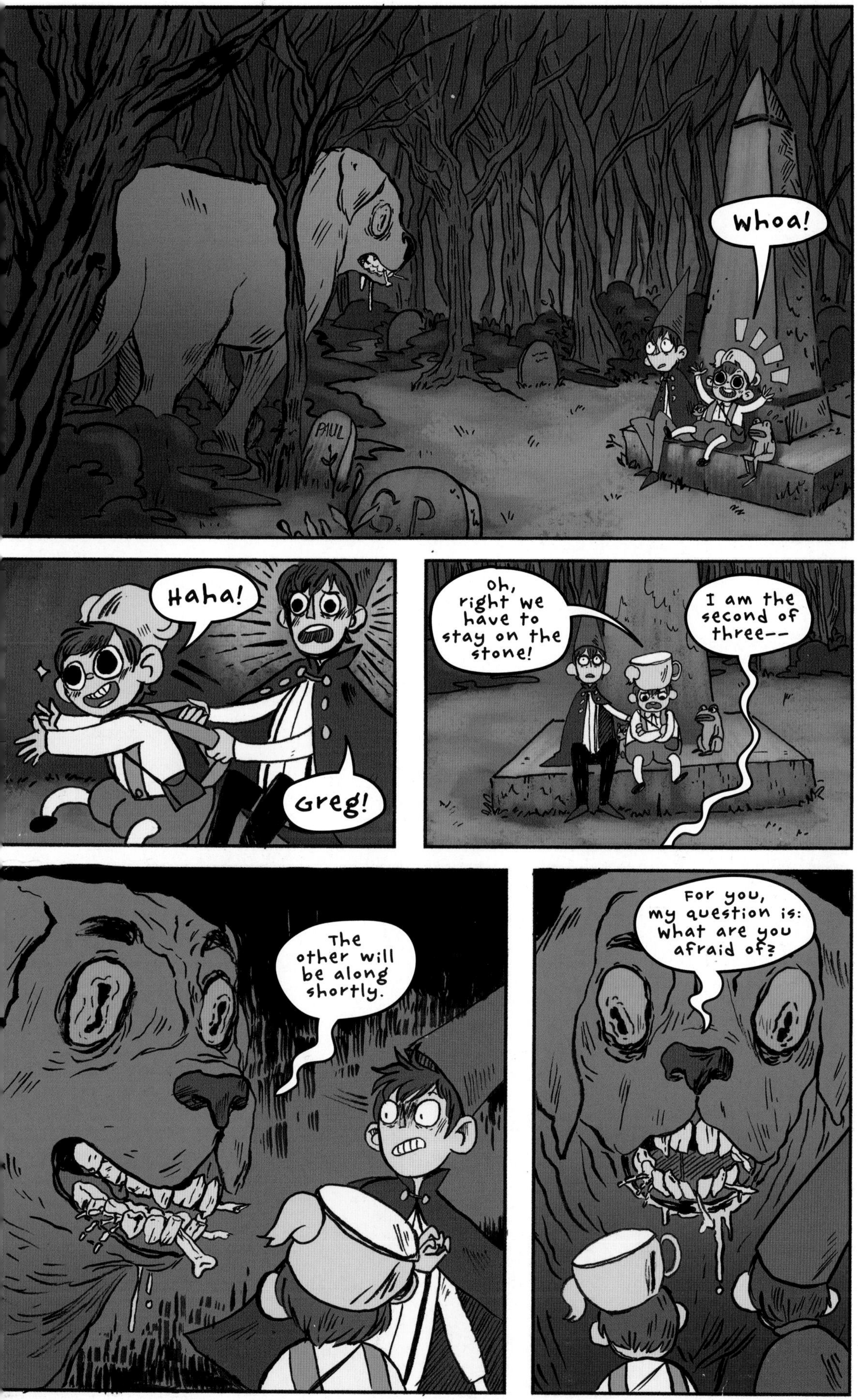

Whoa!
Haha!
Greg!
Oh, right we have to stay on the stone!
I am the second of three--
The other will be along shortly.
For you, my question is: What are you afraid of?

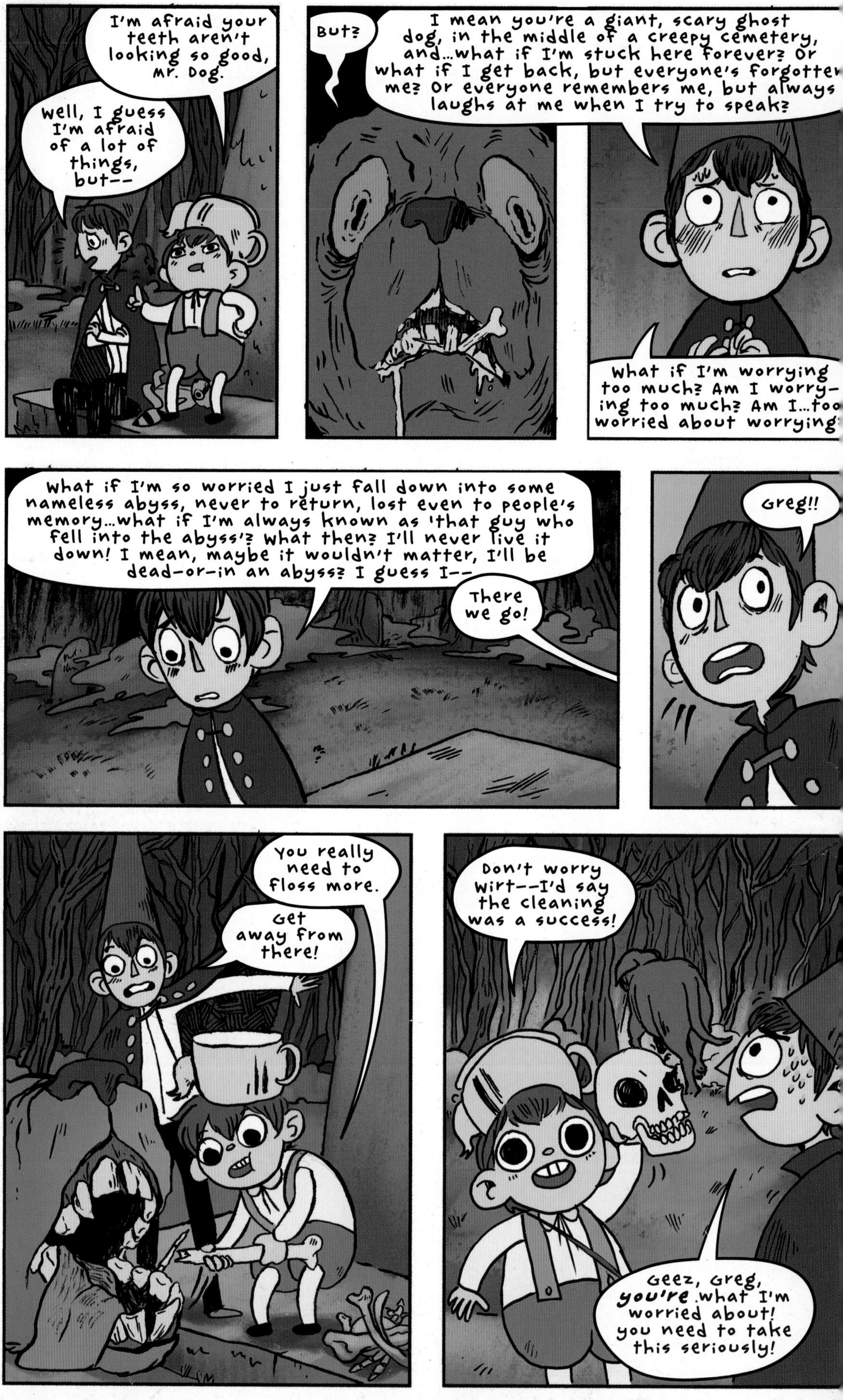
I'm afraid your teeth aren't looking so good, Mr. Dog.
Well, I guess I'm afraid of a lot of things, but--
But?
I mean you're a giant, scary ghost dog, in the middle of a creepy cemetery, and...what if I'm stuck here forever? Or what if I get back, but everyone's forgotten me? Or everyone remembers me, but always laughs at me when I try to speak?
What if I'm worrying too much? Am I worrying too much? Am I...too worried about worrying?
What if I'm so worried I just fall down into some nameless abyss, never to return, lost even to people's memory...what if I'm always known as 'that guy who fell into the abyss'? What then? I'll never live it down! I mean, maybe it wouldn't matter, I'll be dead-or-in an abyss? I guess I--
There we go!
Greg!!
You really need to floss more.
Get away from there!
Don't worry Wirt--I'd say the cleaning was a success!
Geez, Greg, you're what I'm worried about! you need to take this seriously!

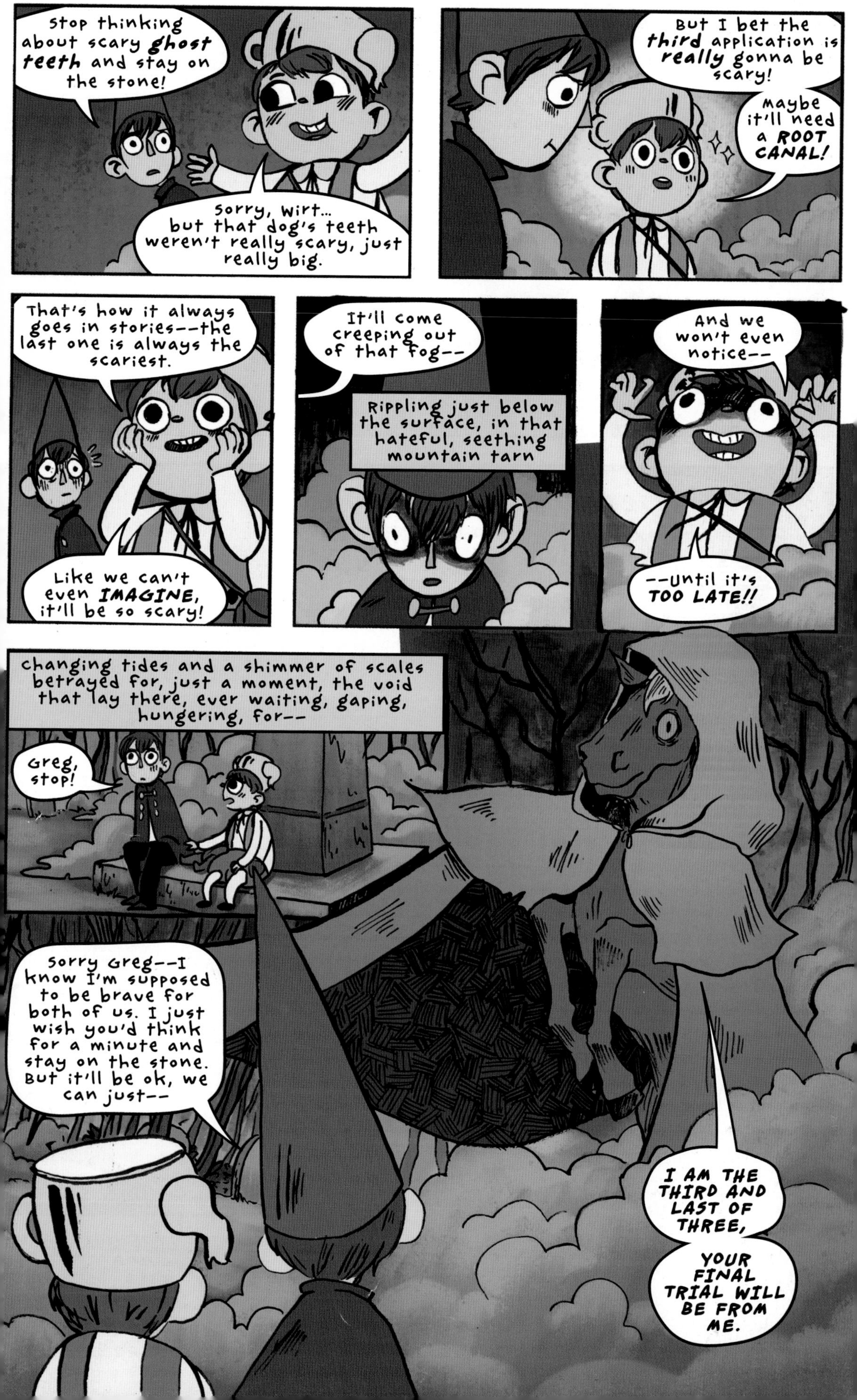
Stop thinking about scary ghost teeth and stay on the stone!
Sorry, Wirt... but that dog's teeth weren't really scary, just really big.
But I bet the third application is really gonna be scary!
Maybe it'll need a ROOT CANAL!
That's how it always goes in stories--the last one is always the scariest.
Like we can't even IMAGINE, it'll be so scary!
It'll come creeping out of that fog--
Rippling just below the surface, in that hateful, seething mountain tarn
And we won't even notice--
--Until it's TOO LATE!!
Changing tides and a shimmer of scales betrayed for, just a moment, the void that lay there, ever waiting, gaping, hungering, for--
Greg, stop!
Sorry Greg--I know I'm supposed to be brave for both of us. I just wish you'd think for a minute and stay on the stone. But it'll be ok, we can just--
I AM THE THIRD AND LAST OF THREE,
YOUR FINAL TRIAL WILL BE FROM ME.

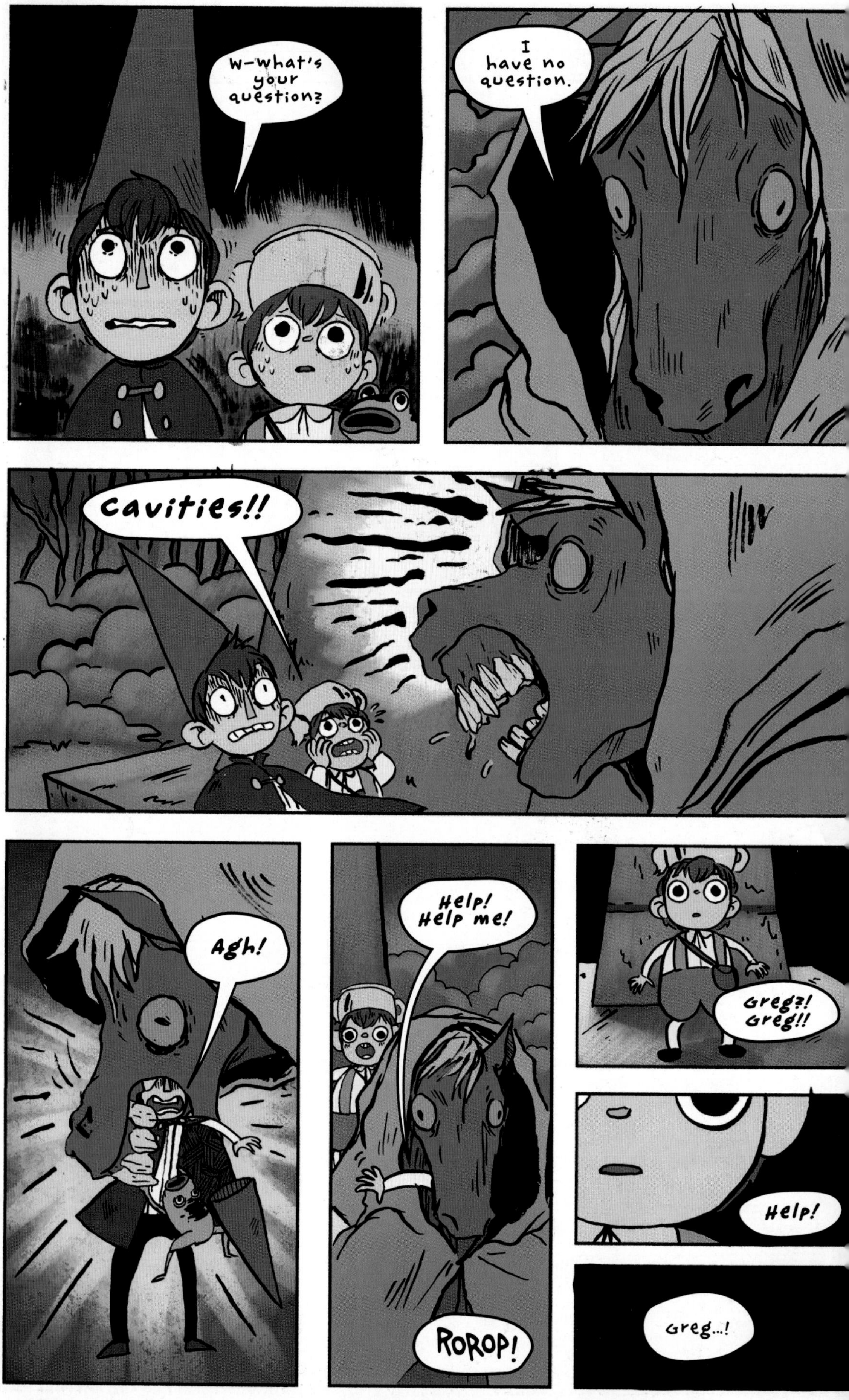
W-what's your question?
I have no question.
Cavities!!
Agh!
Help! Help me!
ROROP!
Greg?! Greg!!
Help!
Greg...!

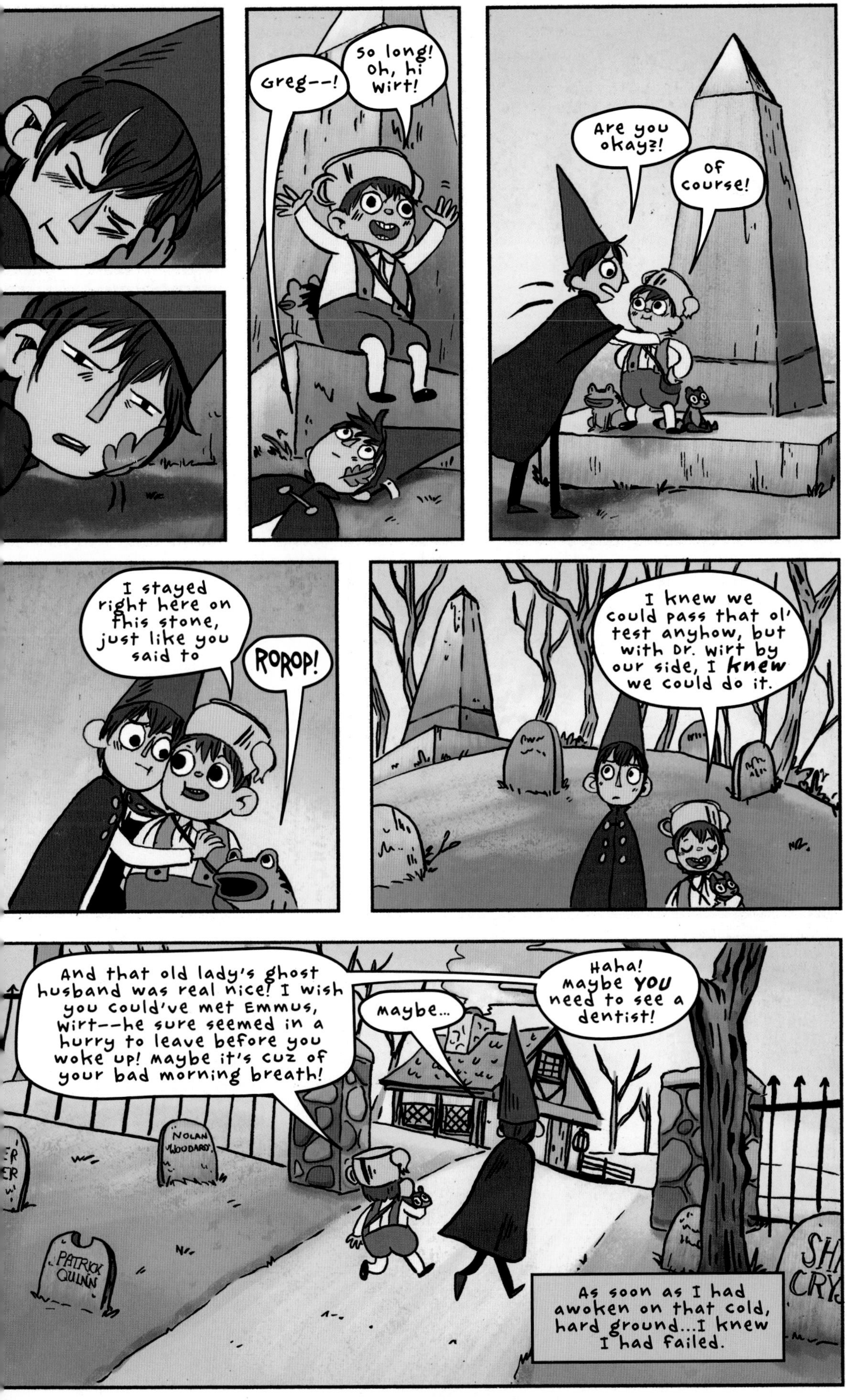
Greg--!
So long! Oh, hi Wirt!
Are you okay?!
Of course!
I stayed right here on this stone, just like you said to
ROROP!
I knew we could pass that ol' test anyhow, but with Dr. Wirt by our side, I knew we could do it.
And that old lady's ghost husband was real nice! I wish you could've met Emmus, Wirt--he sure seemed in a hurry to leave before you woke up! Maybe it's cuz of your bad morning breath!
Maybe...
Haha! Maybe YOU need to see a dentist!
NOLAN WOODARD
PATRICK QUINN
As soon as I had awoken on that cold, hard ground...I knew I had failed.

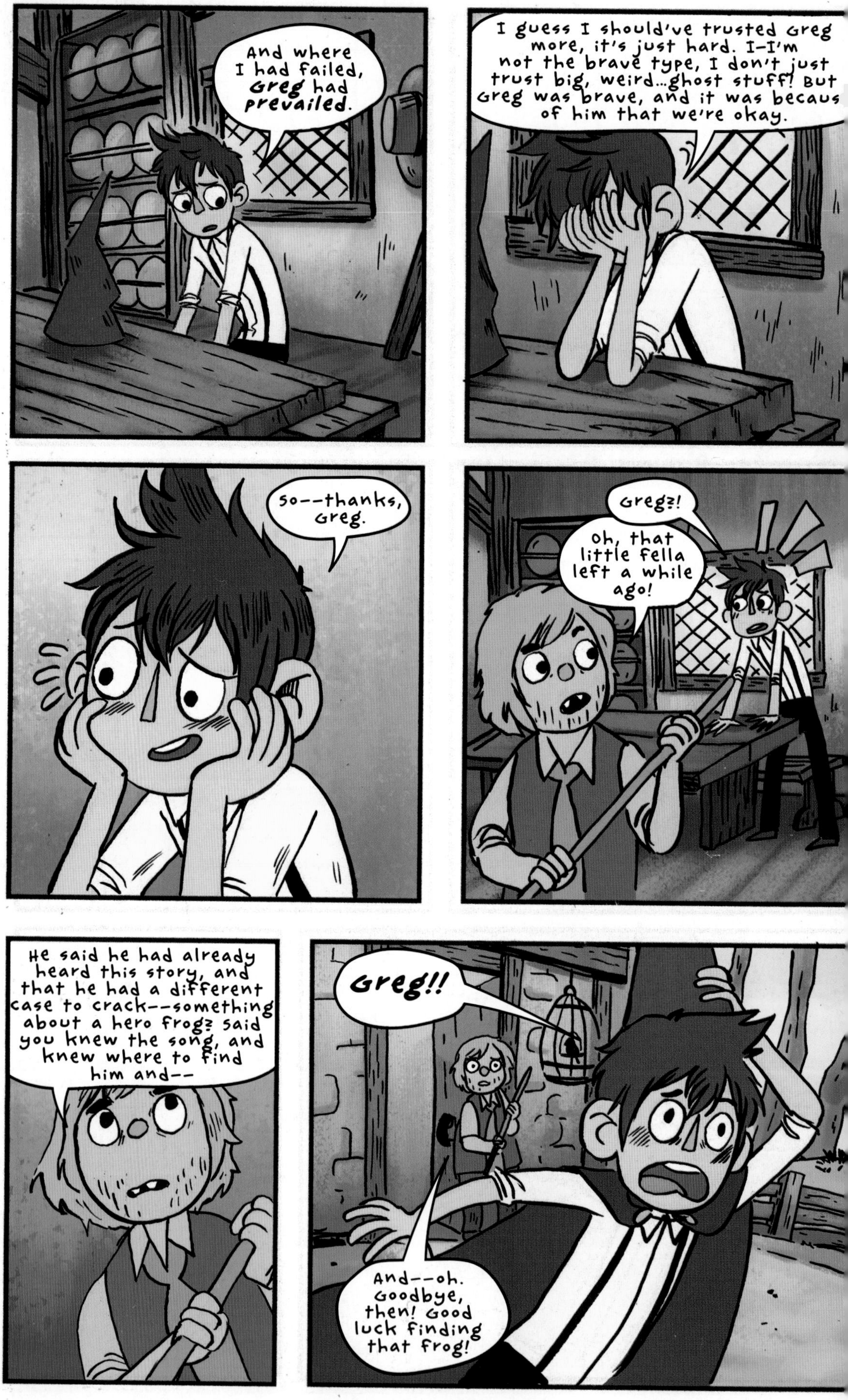

And where I had failed, Greg had prevailed.
I guess I should've trusted Greg more, it's just hard. I—I'm not the brave type, I don't just trust big, weird...ghost stuff! But Greg was brave, and it was becaus of him that we're okay.
So--thanks, Greg.
Greg?!
Oh, that little fella left a while ago!
He said he had already heard this story, and that he had a different case to crack--something about a hero frog? Said you knew the song, and knew where to find him and--
Greg!!
And--oh. Goodbye, then! Good luck finding that frog!

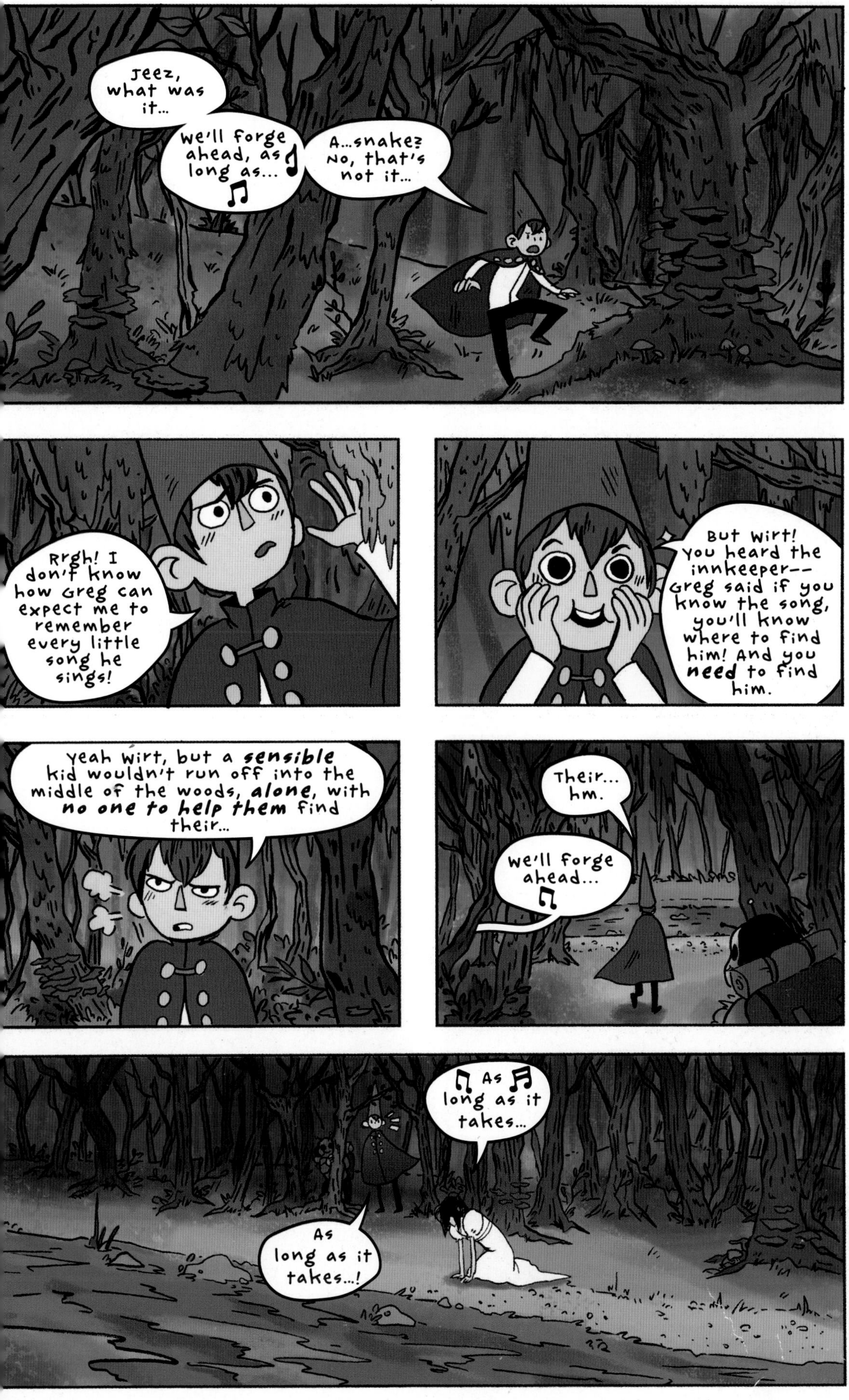
Jeez, what was it...
We'll forge ahead, as long as...
A...snake? No, that's not it...
Rrgh! I don't know how Greg can expect me to remember every little song he sings!
But Wirt! You heard the innkeeper-- Greg said if you know the song, you'll know where to find him! And you need to find him.
Yeah Wirt, but a sensible kid wouldn't run off into the middle of the woods, alone, with no one to help them find their...
Their... hm.
We'll forge ahead...
As long as it takes...
As long as it takes...!

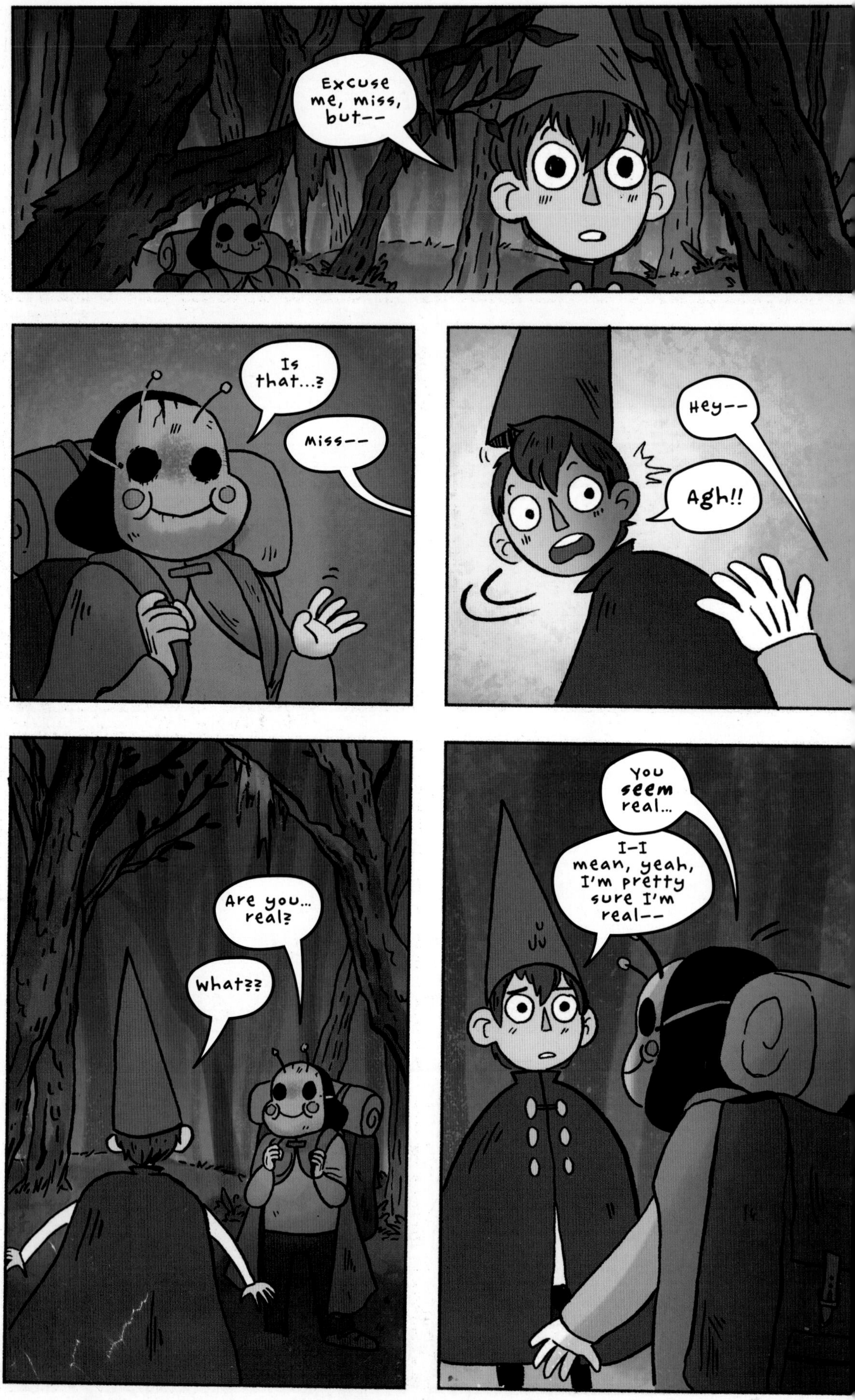
Excuse me, miss, but--
Is that...?
Miss--
Hey--
Agh!!
Are you... real?
What??
You seem real...
I-I mean, yeah, I'm pretty sure I'm real--

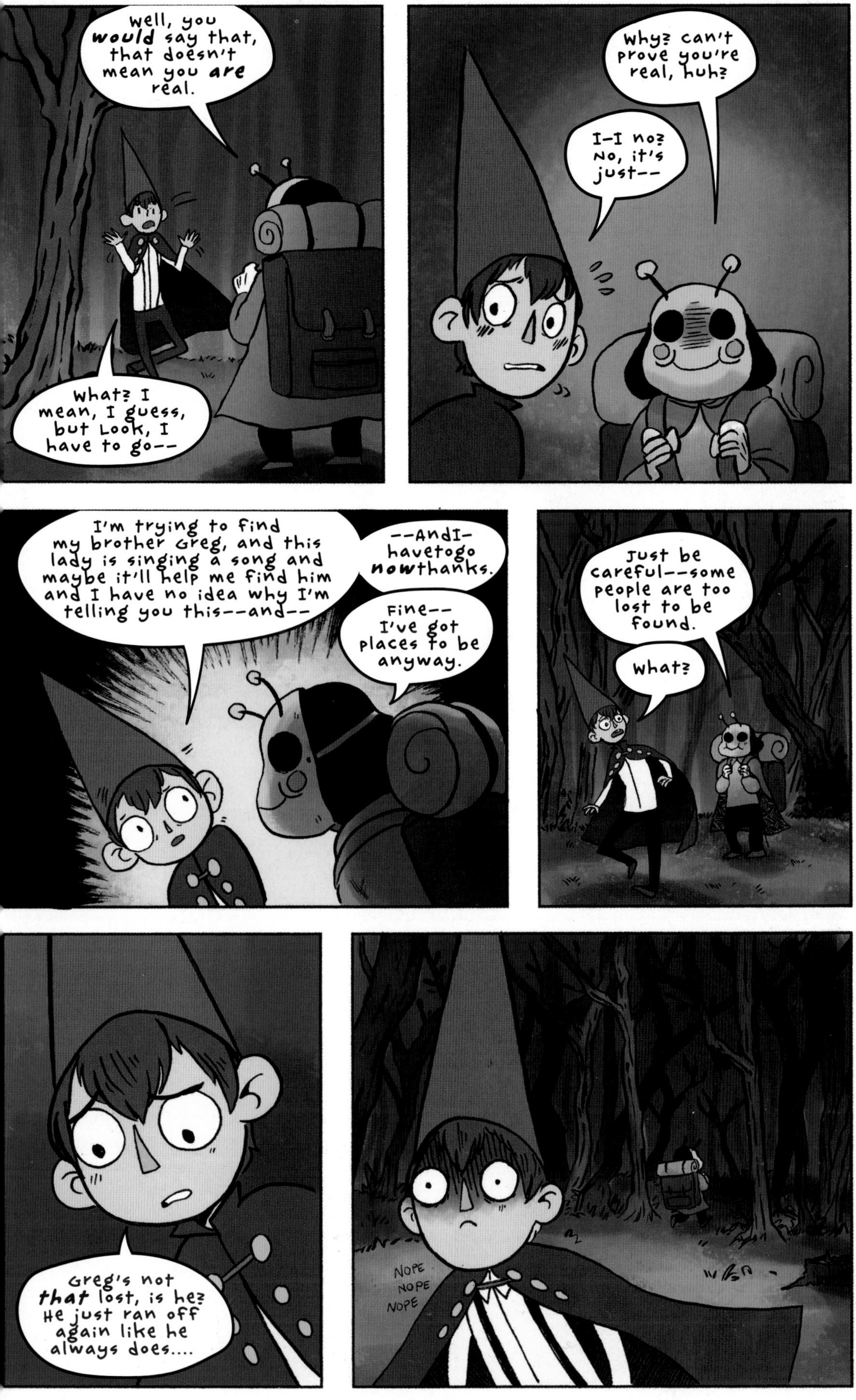
Well, you *would* say that, that doesn't mean you *are* real.
What? I mean, I guess, but look, I have to go--
Why? Can't prove you're real, huh?
I-I no? No, it's just--
I'm trying to find my brother Greg, and this lady is singing a song and maybe it'll help me find him and I have no idea why I'm telling you this--and--
--AndIhavetogo *now*thanks.
Fine-- I've got places to be anyway.
Just be careful--some people are too lost to be found.
What?
Greg's not *that* lost, is he? He just ran off again like he always does....
NOPE
NOPE
NOPE

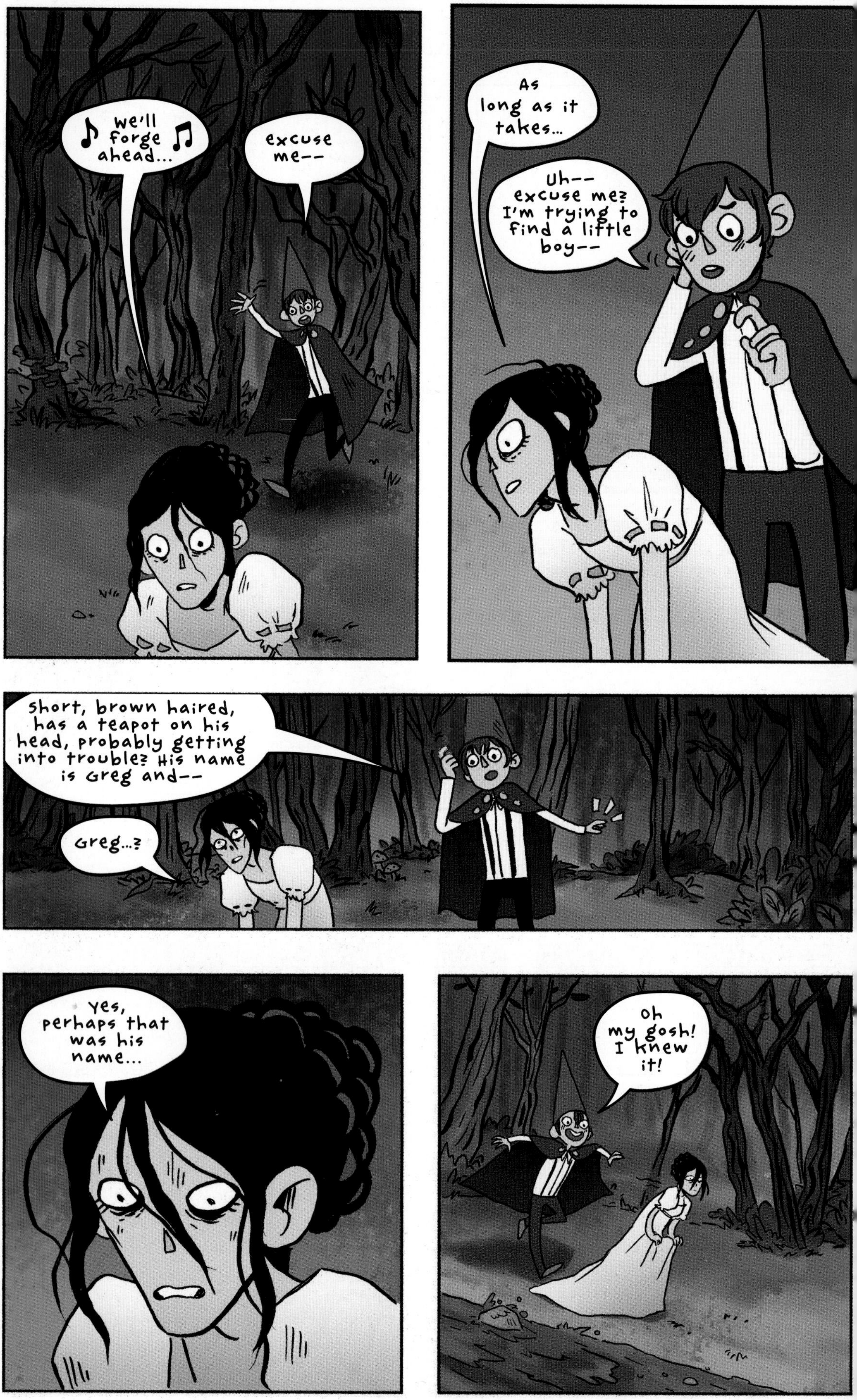
♪ We'll forge ahead... ♫
excuse me--
As long as it takes...
Uh-- excuse me? I'm trying to find a little boy--
Short, brown haired, has a teapot on his head, probably getting into trouble? His name is Greg and--
Greg...?
Yes, perhaps that was his name...
Oh my gosh! I knew it!

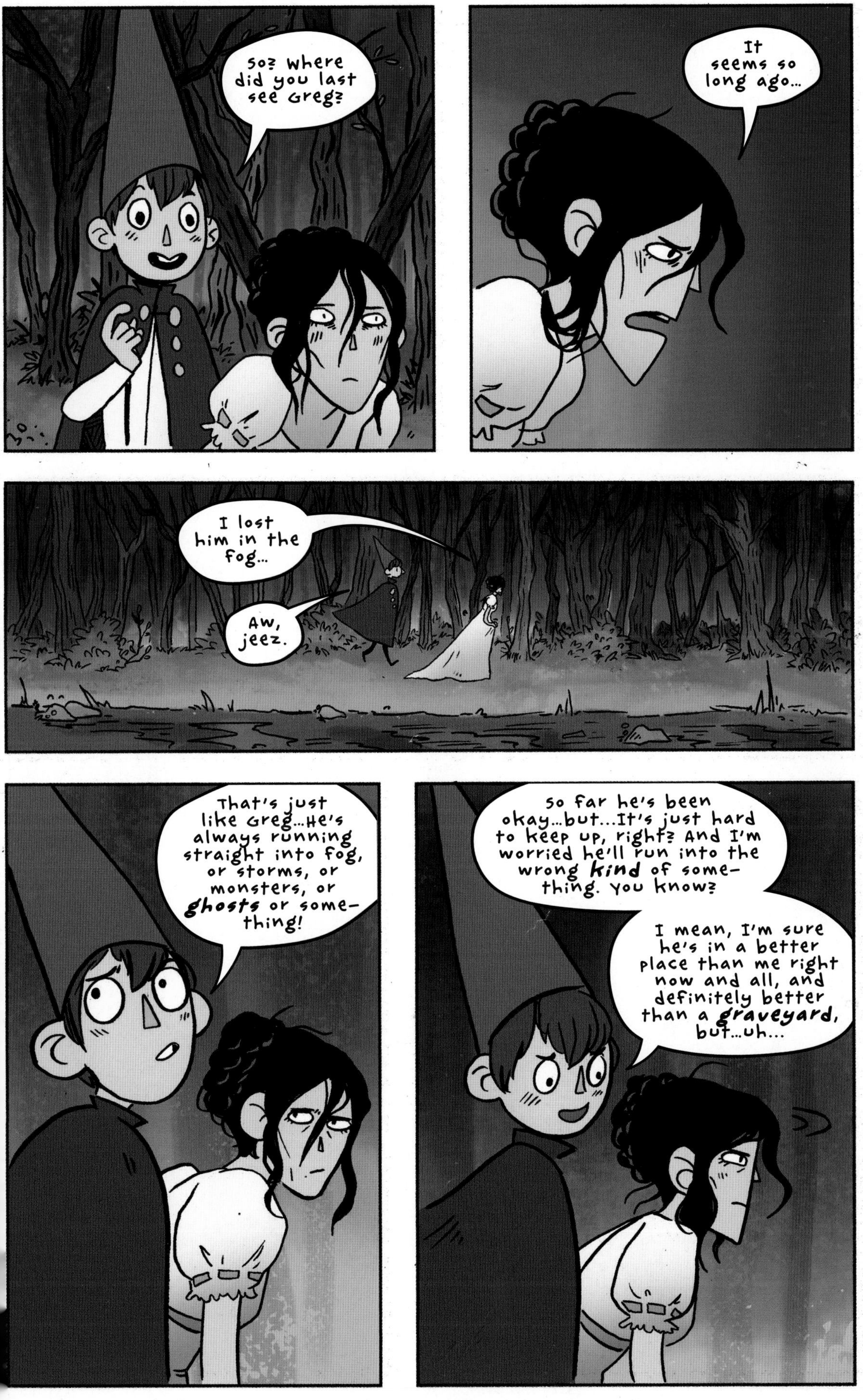
So? Where did you last see Greg?
It seems so long ago...
I lost him in the fog...
Aw, jeez.
That's just like Greg...He's always running straight into fog, or storms, or monsters, or *ghosts* or some-thing!
So far he's been okay...but...It's just hard to keep up, right? And I'm worried he'll run into the wrong *kind* of some-thing. You know?
I mean, I'm sure he's in a better place than me right now and all, and definitely better than a *graveyard*, but...uh...

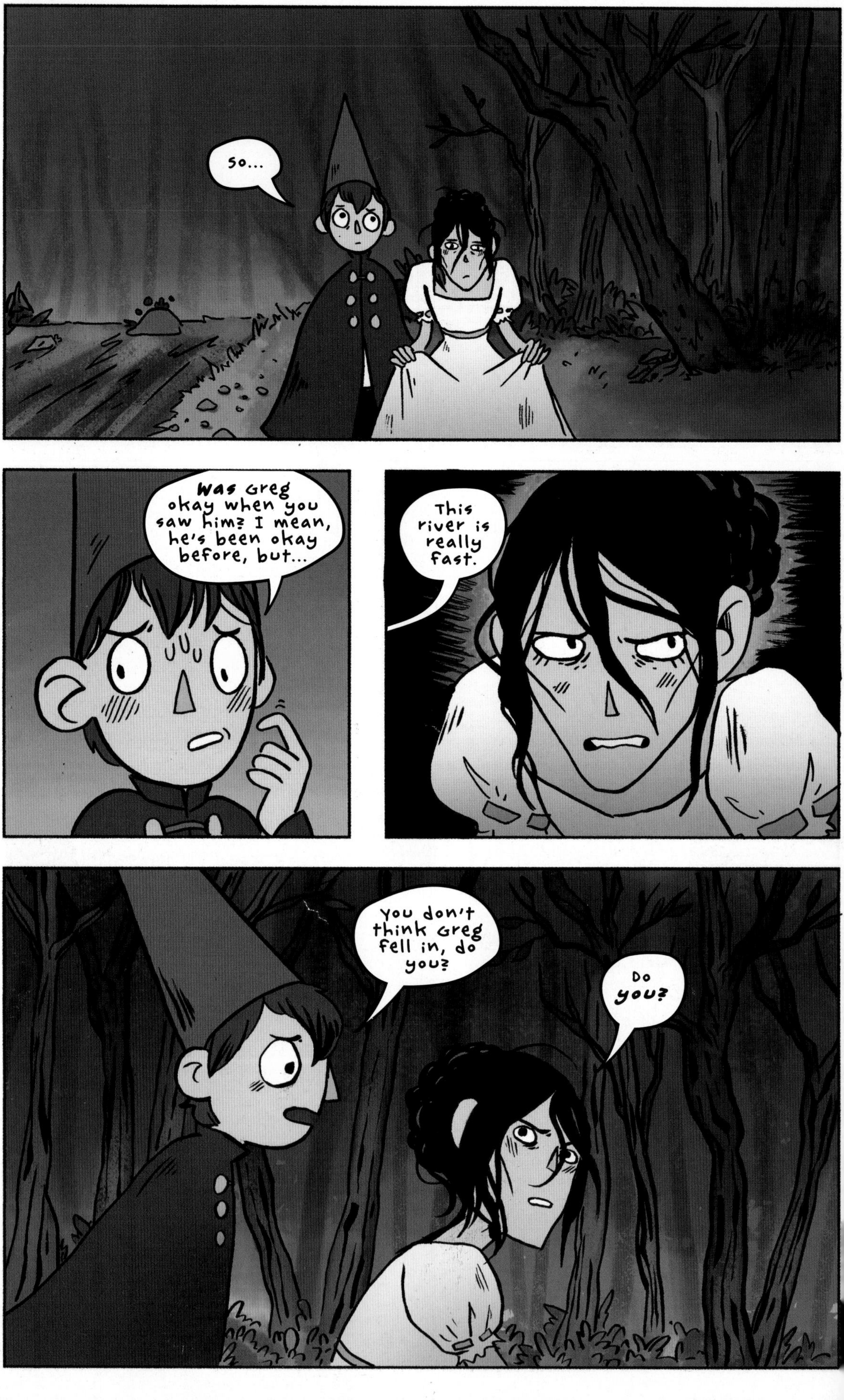
So...
Was Greg okay when you saw him? I mean, he's been okay before, but...
This river is really fast.
You don't think Greg fell in, do you?
Do you?

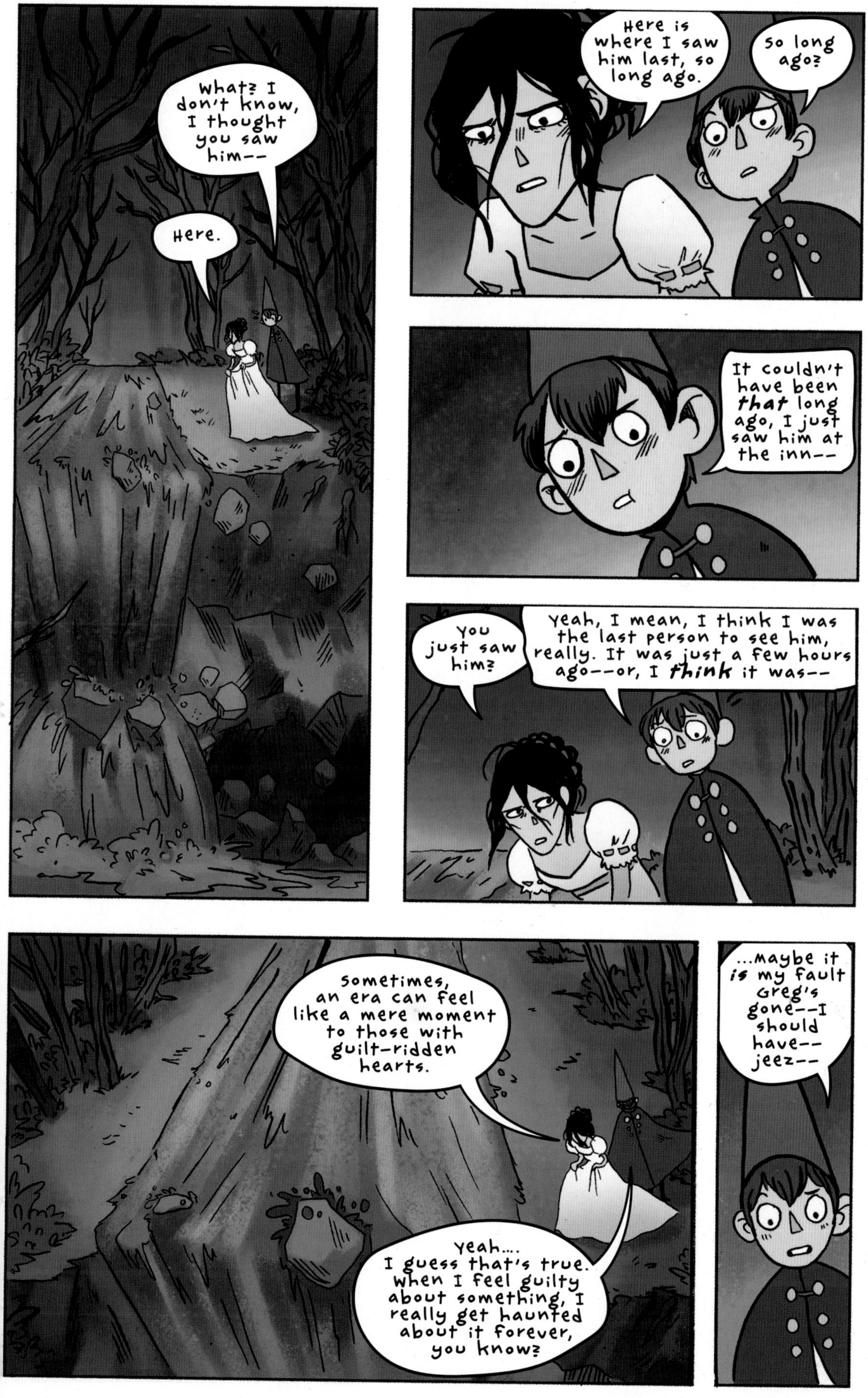
What? I don't know, I thought you saw him--
Here.
Here is where I saw him last, so long ago.
So long ago?
It couldn't have been *that* long ago, I just saw him at the inn--
You just saw him?
Yeah, I mean, I think I was the last person to see him, really. It was just a few hours ago--or, I *think* it was--
Sometimes, an era can feel like a mere moment to those with guilt-ridden hearts.
Yeah.... I guess that's true. When I feel guilty about something, I really get haunted about it forever, you know?
...Maybe it *is* my fault Greg's gone--I should have-- jeez--

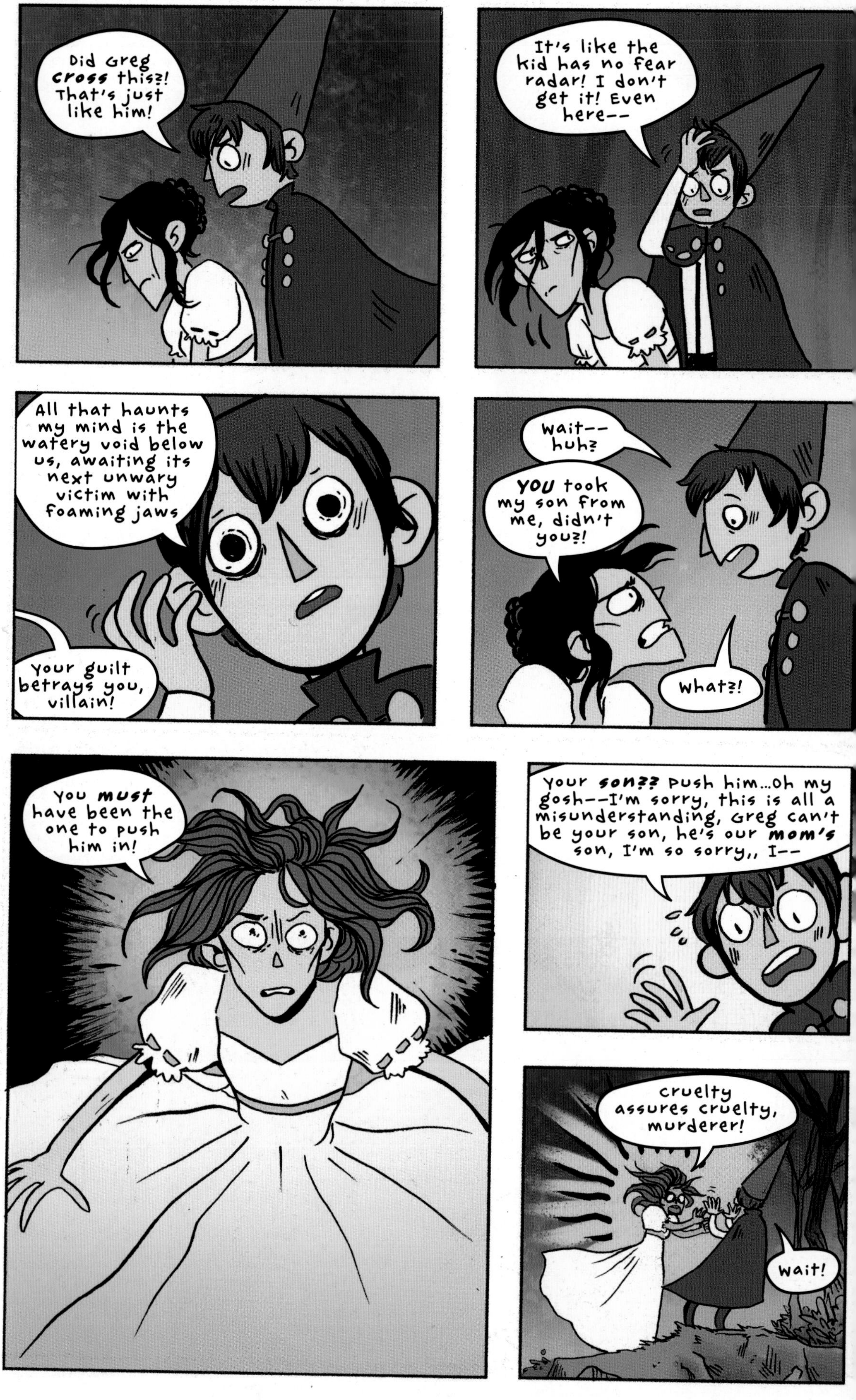
Did Greg cross this?! That's just like him!
It's like the kid has no fear radar! I don't get it! Even here--
All that haunts my mind is the watery void below us, awaiting its next unwary victim with foaming jaws
Your guilt betrays you, villain!
Wait--huh?
YOU took my son from me, didn't you?!
What?!
You must have been the one to push him in!
Your son?? Push him...oh my gosh--I'm sorry, this is all a misunderstanding, Greg can't be your son, he's our mom's son, I'm so sorry,, I--
cruelty assures cruelty, murderer!
Wait!

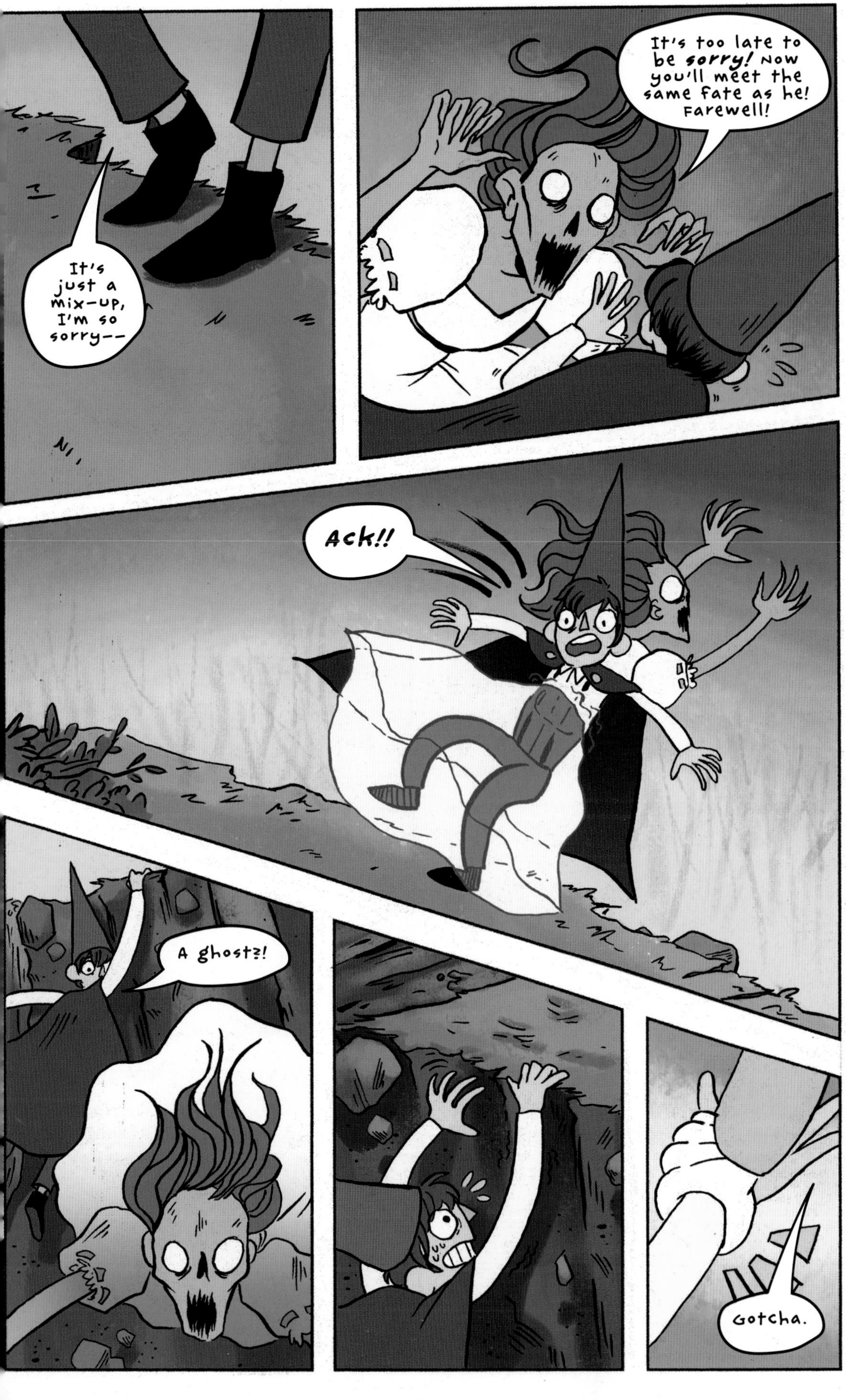
It's just a mix-up, I'm so sorry--
It's too late to be sorry! Now you'll meet the same fate as he! Farewell!
Ack!!
A ghost?!
Gotcha.

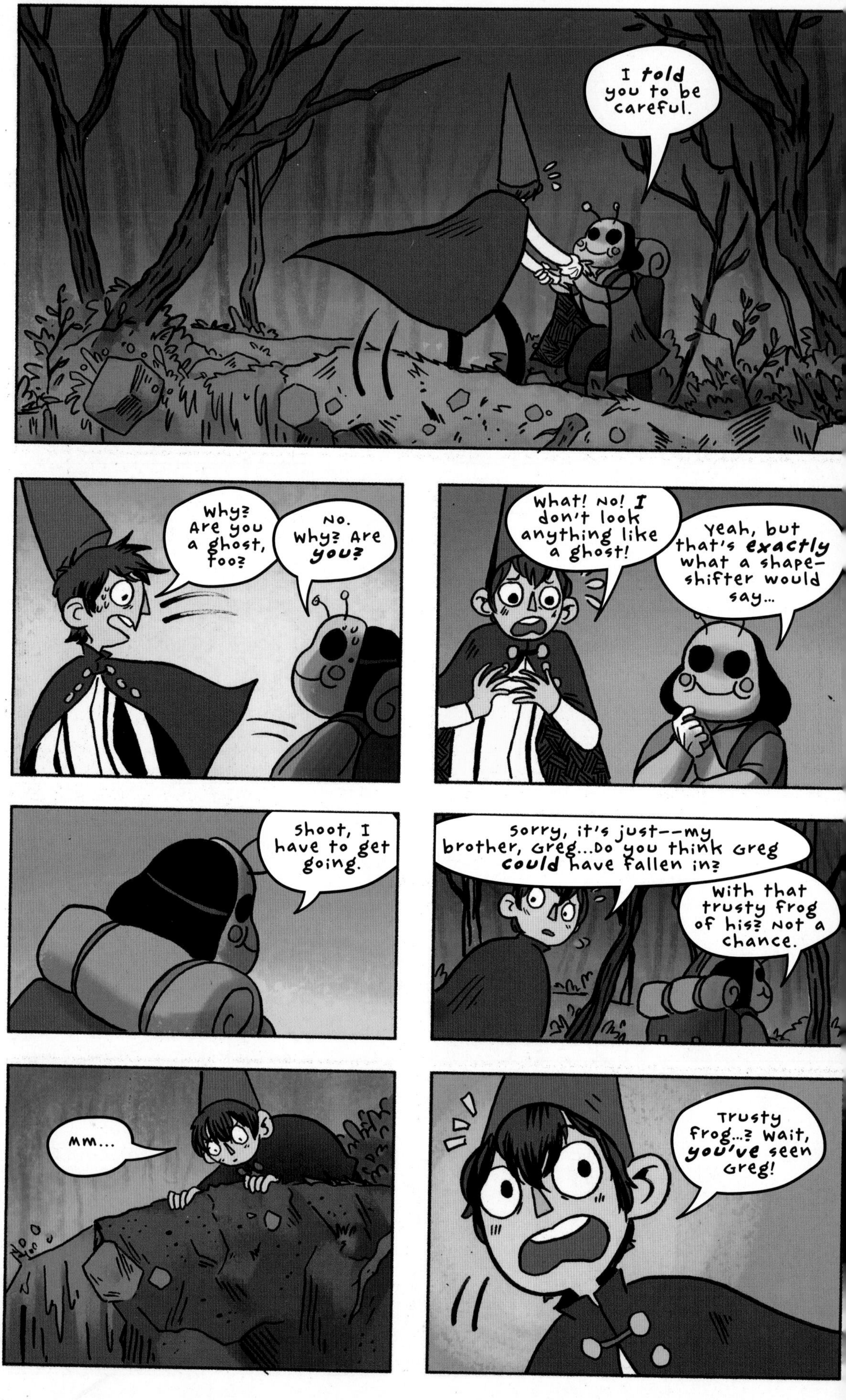
I told you to be careful.
Why? Are you a ghost, too?
No. Why? Are you?
What! No! I don't look anything like a ghost!
Yeah, but that's exactly what a shape-shifter would say...
Shoot, I have to get going.
Sorry, it's just--my brother, Greg...Do you think Greg could have fallen in?
With that trusty frog of his? Not a chance.
Mm...
Trusty frog...? Wait, you've seen Greg!

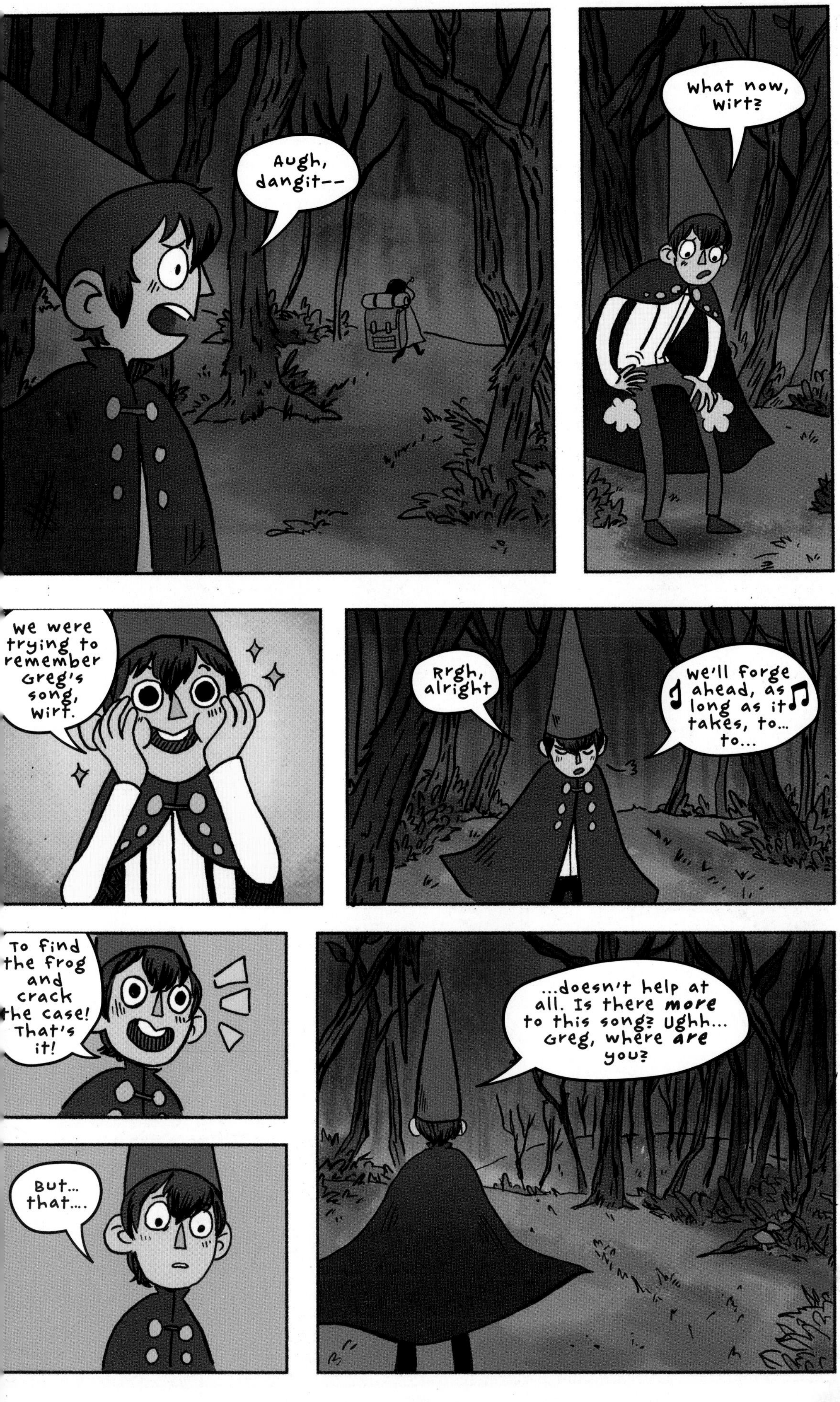

Augh, dangit--
What now, Wirt?
We were trying to remember Greg's song, Wirt.
Rrgh, alright
We'll forge ahead, as long as it takes, to... to...
To find the frog and crack the case! That's it!
But... that....
...doesn't help at all. Is there more to this song? Ughh... Greg, where are you?

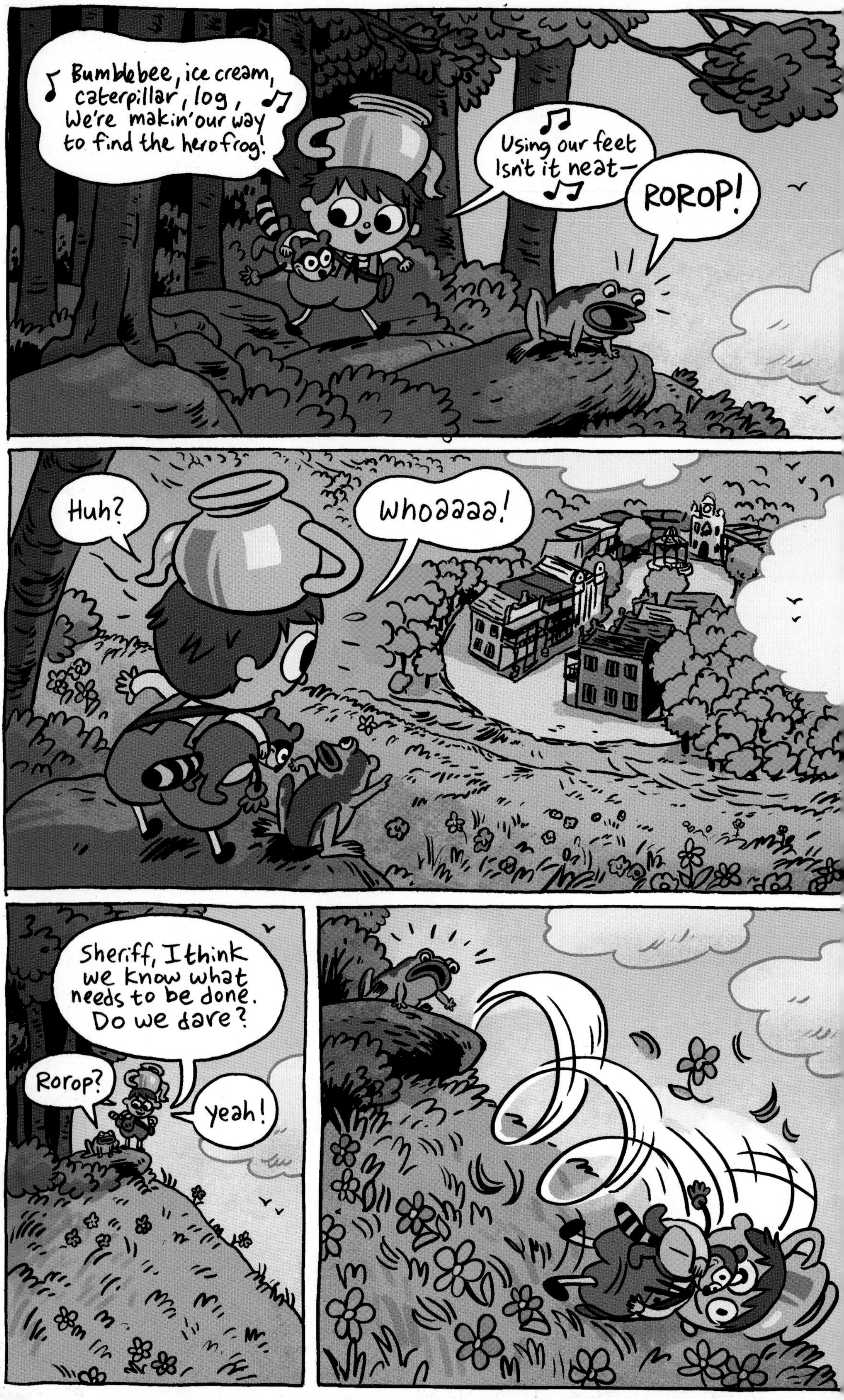

♪ Bumblebee, ice cream, caterpillar, log, We're makin' our way to find the herofrog! ♫
♫ Using our feet Isn't it neat— ♫
ROROP!
Huh?
Whoaaaa!
Sheriff, I think we know what needs to be done. Do we dare?
Rorop?
Yeah!

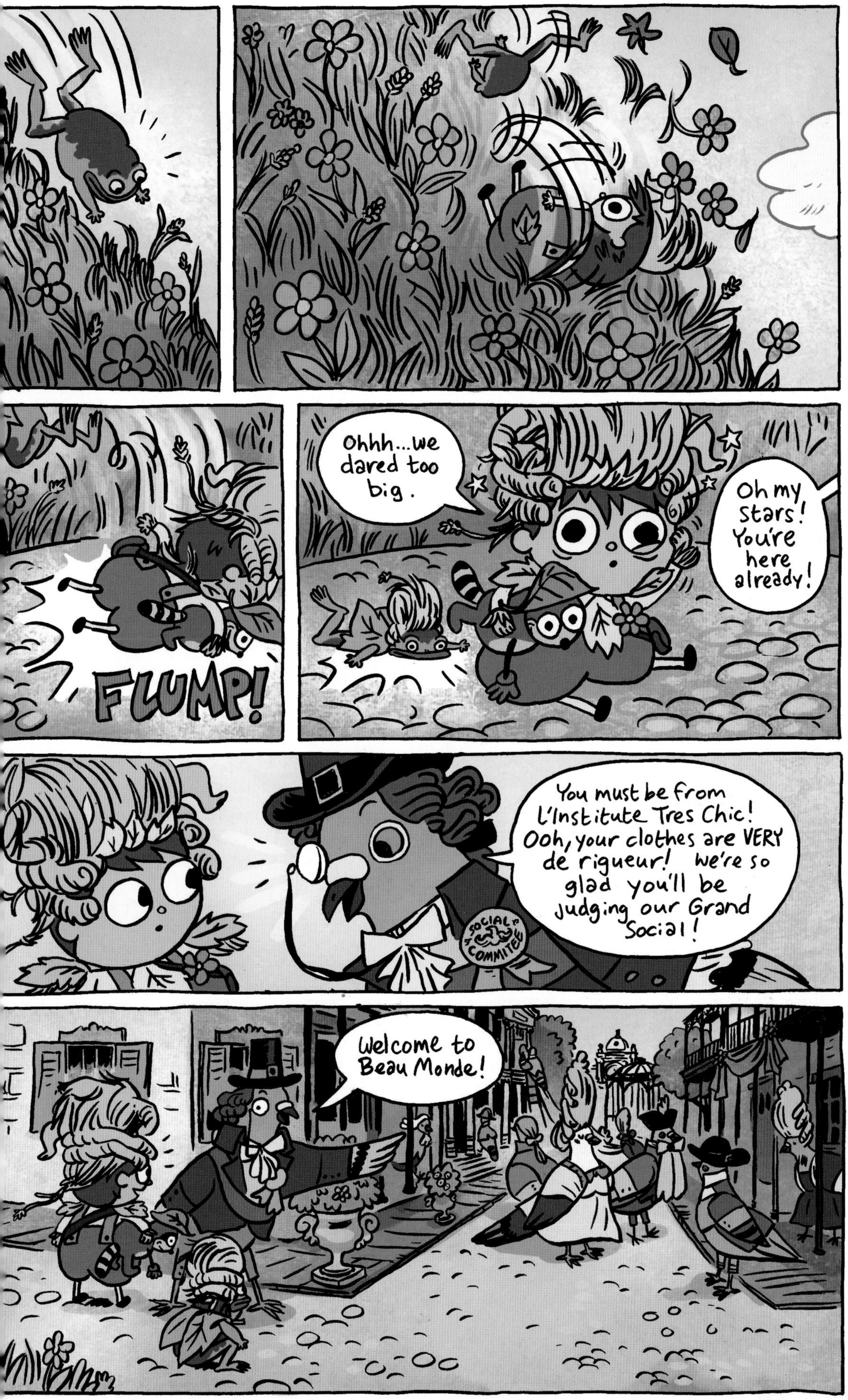
FLUMP!
Ohhh...we dared too big.
Oh my stars! You're here already!
You must be from L'Institute Tres Chic! Ooh, your clothes are VERY de rigueur! We're so glad you'll be judging our Grand Social!
SOCIAL COMMITEE
Welcome to Beau Monde!

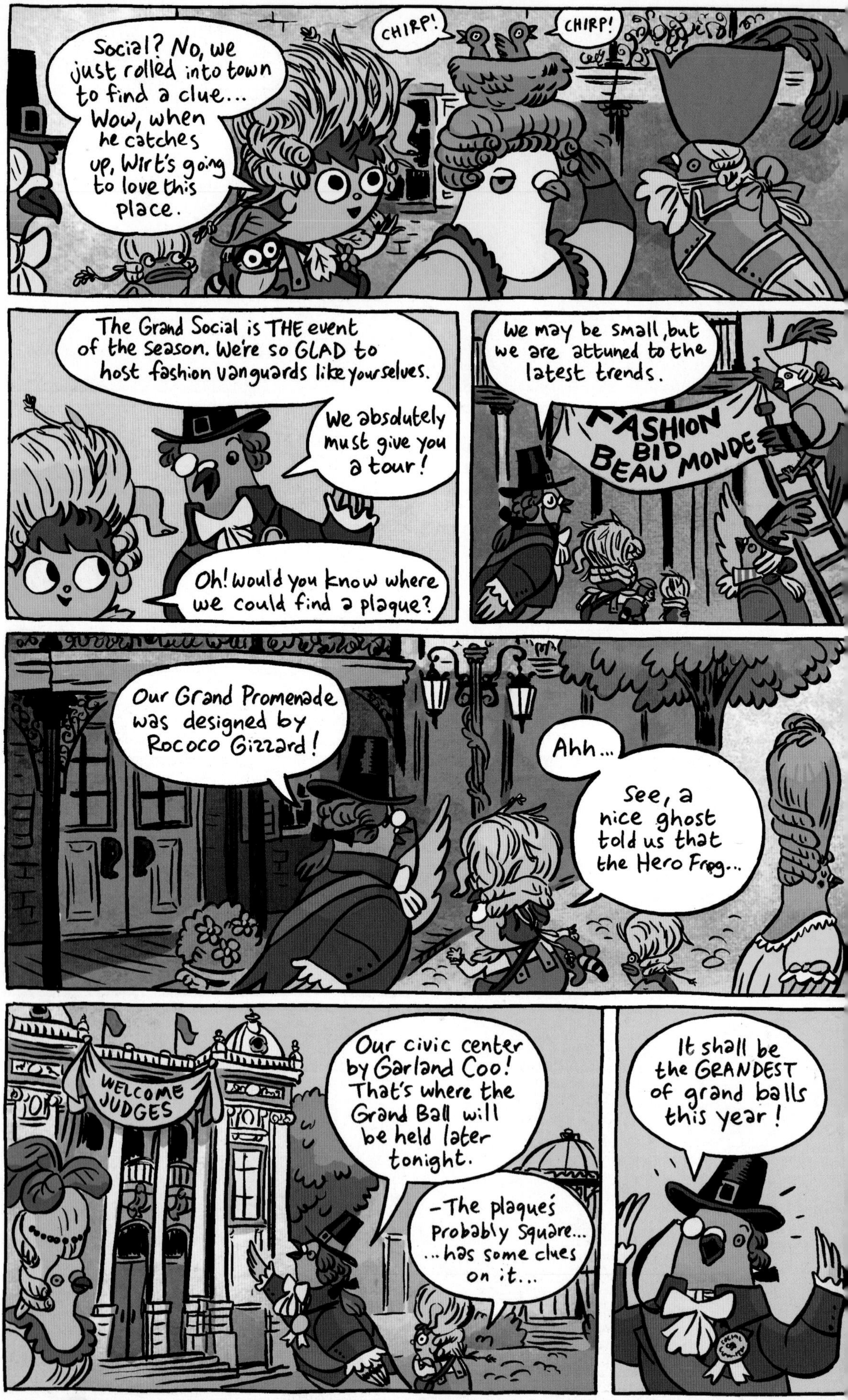

Social? No, we just rolled into town to find a clue... Wow, when he catches up, Wirt's going to love this place.
CHIRP!
CHIRP!
The Grand Social is THE event of the season. We're so GLAD to host fashion vanguards like yourselves.
We absolutely must give you a tour!
Oh! Would you know where we could find a plaque?
We may be small, but we are attuned to the latest trends.
FASHION BID BEAU MONDE
Our Grand Promenade was designed by Rococo Gizzard!
Ahh...
See, a nice ghost told us that the Hero Frog...
WELCOME JUDGES
Our civic center by Garland Coo! That's where the Grand Ball will be held later tonight.
-The plaque's probably Square... ...has some clues on it...
It shall be the GRANDEST of grand balls this year!

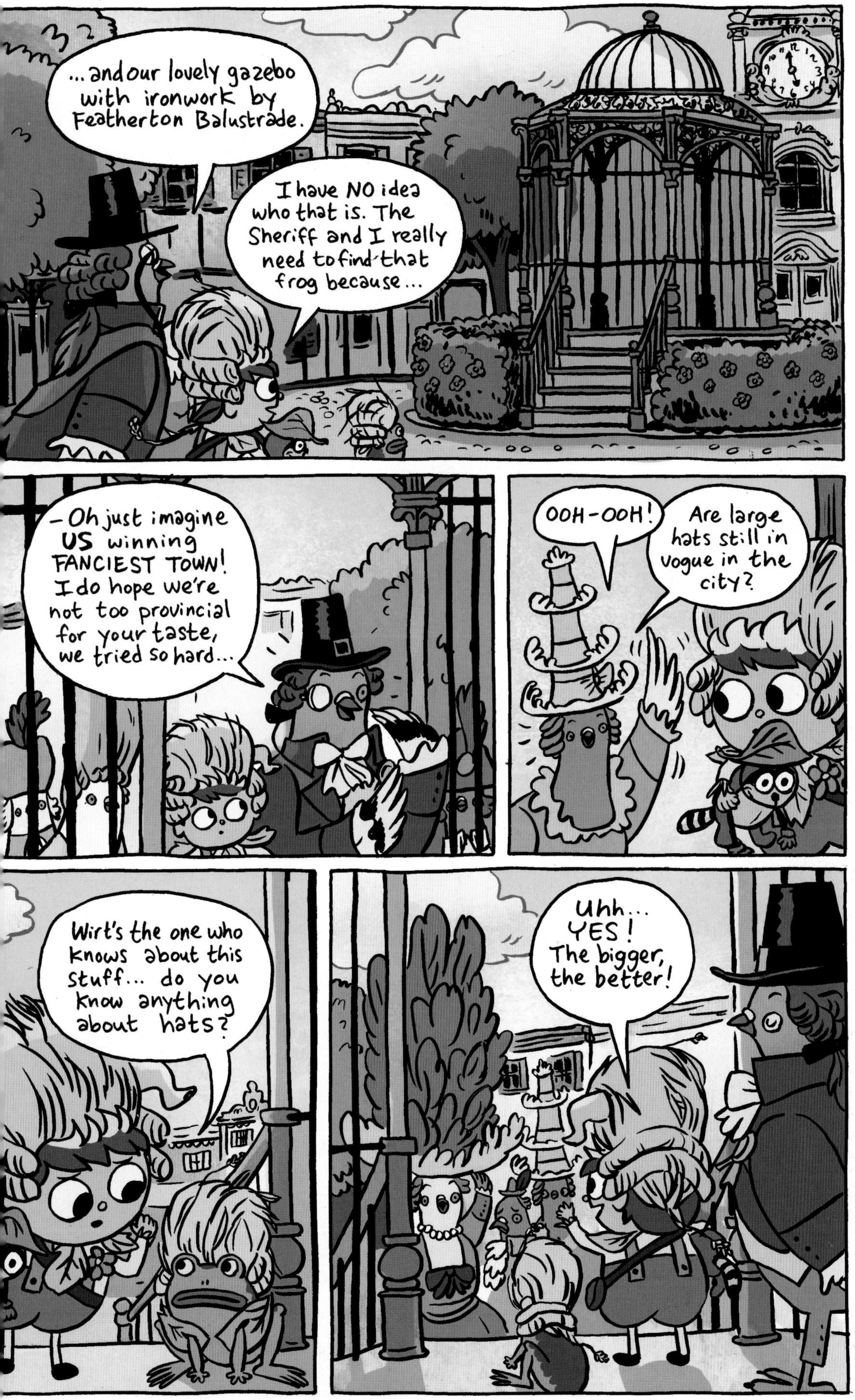

...and our lovely gazebo with ironwork by Featherton Balustrade.
I have NO idea who that is. The Sheriff and I really need to find that frog because...
-Oh just imagine US winning FANCIEST TOWN! I do hope we're not too provincial for your taste, we tried so hard...
OOH-OOH!
Are large hats still in vogue in the city?
Wirt's the one who knows about this stuff... do you know anything about hats?
Uhh... YES! The bigger, the better!

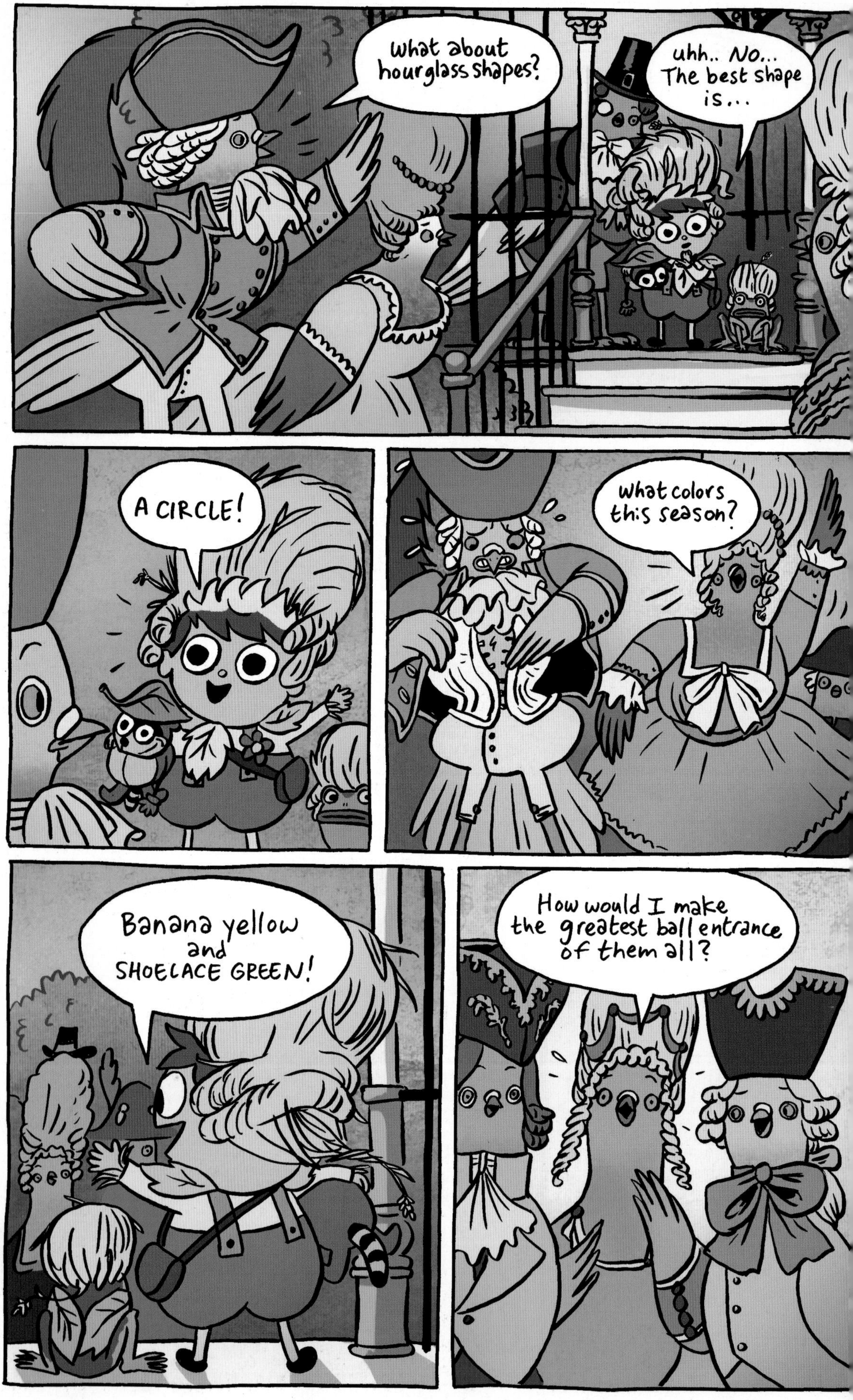
What about hourglass shapes?
uhh.. No... The best shape is...
A CIRCLE!
What colors this season?
Banana yellow and SHOELACE GREEN!
How would I make the greatest ball entrance of them all?

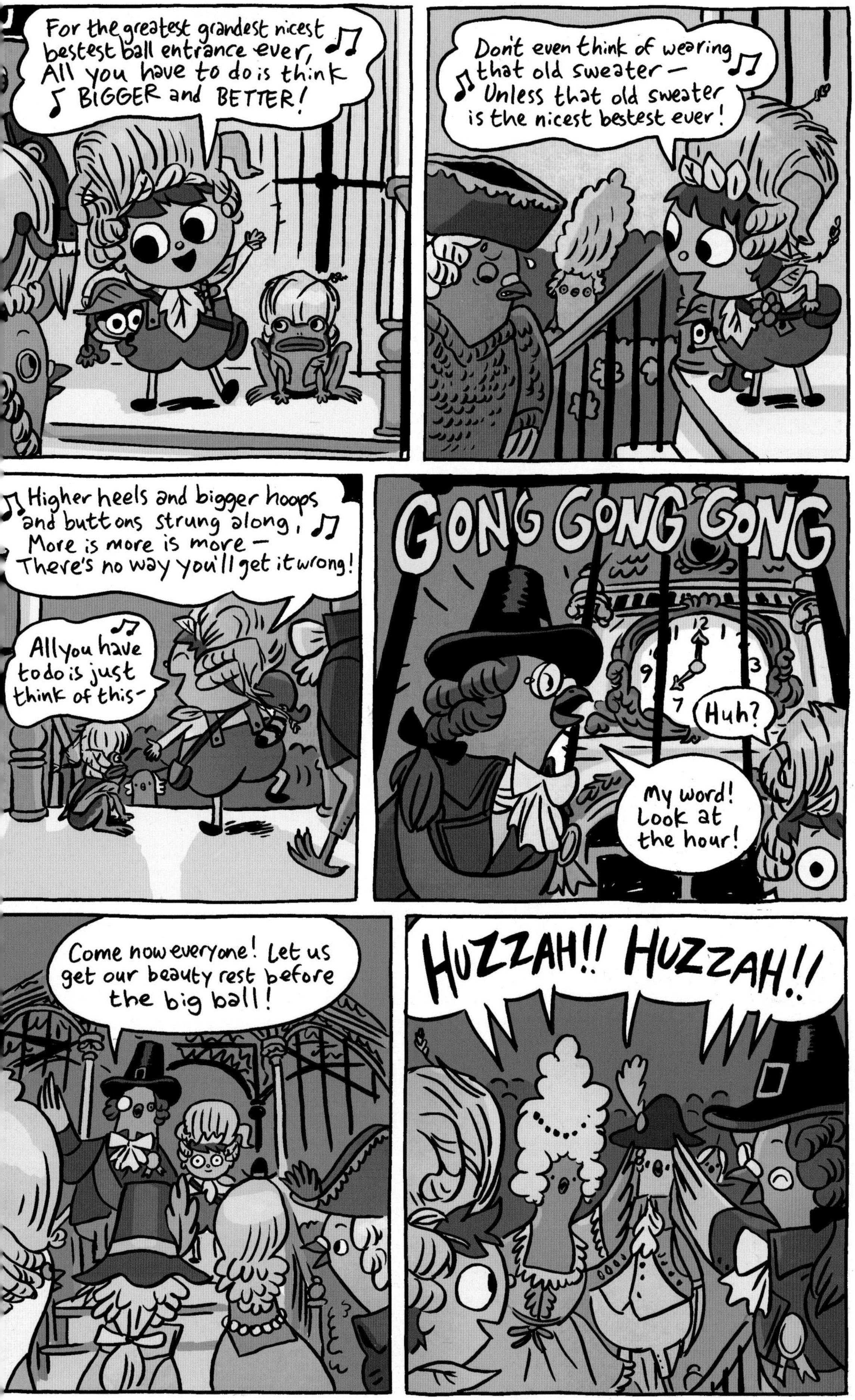
For the greatest grandest nicest bestest ball entrance ever, All you have to do is think BIGGER and BETTER!
Don't even think of wearing that old sweater — Unless that old sweater is the nicest bestest ever!
Higher heels and bigger hoops and buttons strung along, More is more is more — There's no way you'll get it wrong!
All you have to do is just think of this-
GONG GONG GONG
Huh?
My word! Look at the hour!
Come now everyone! Let us get our beauty rest before the big ball!
HUZZAH!! HUZZAH!!

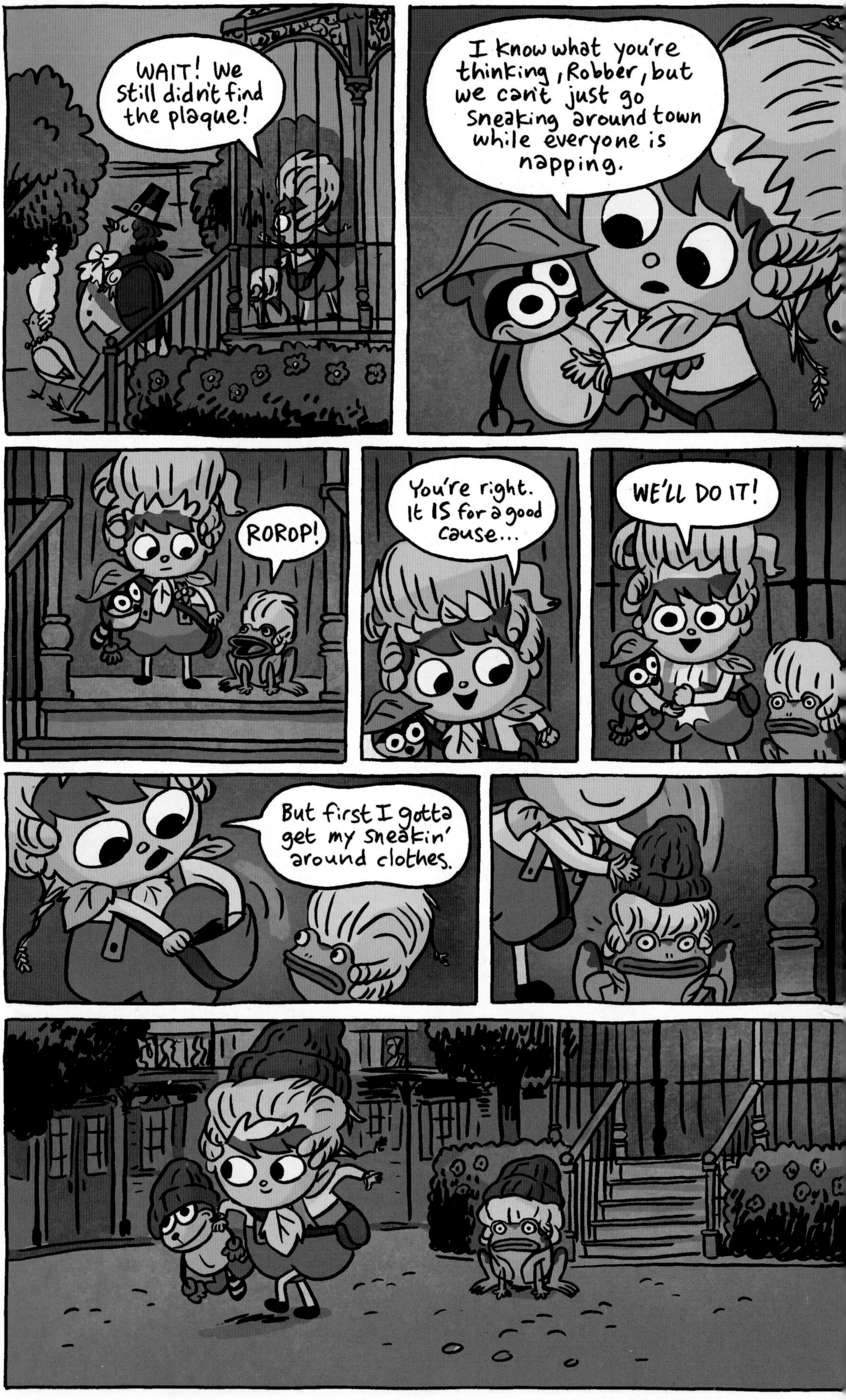
WAIT! We still didn't find the plaque!
I know what you're thinking, Robber, but we can't just go sneaking around town while everyone is napping.
ROROP!
You're right. It IS for a good cause...
WE'LL DO IT!
But first I gotta get my sneakin' around clothes.

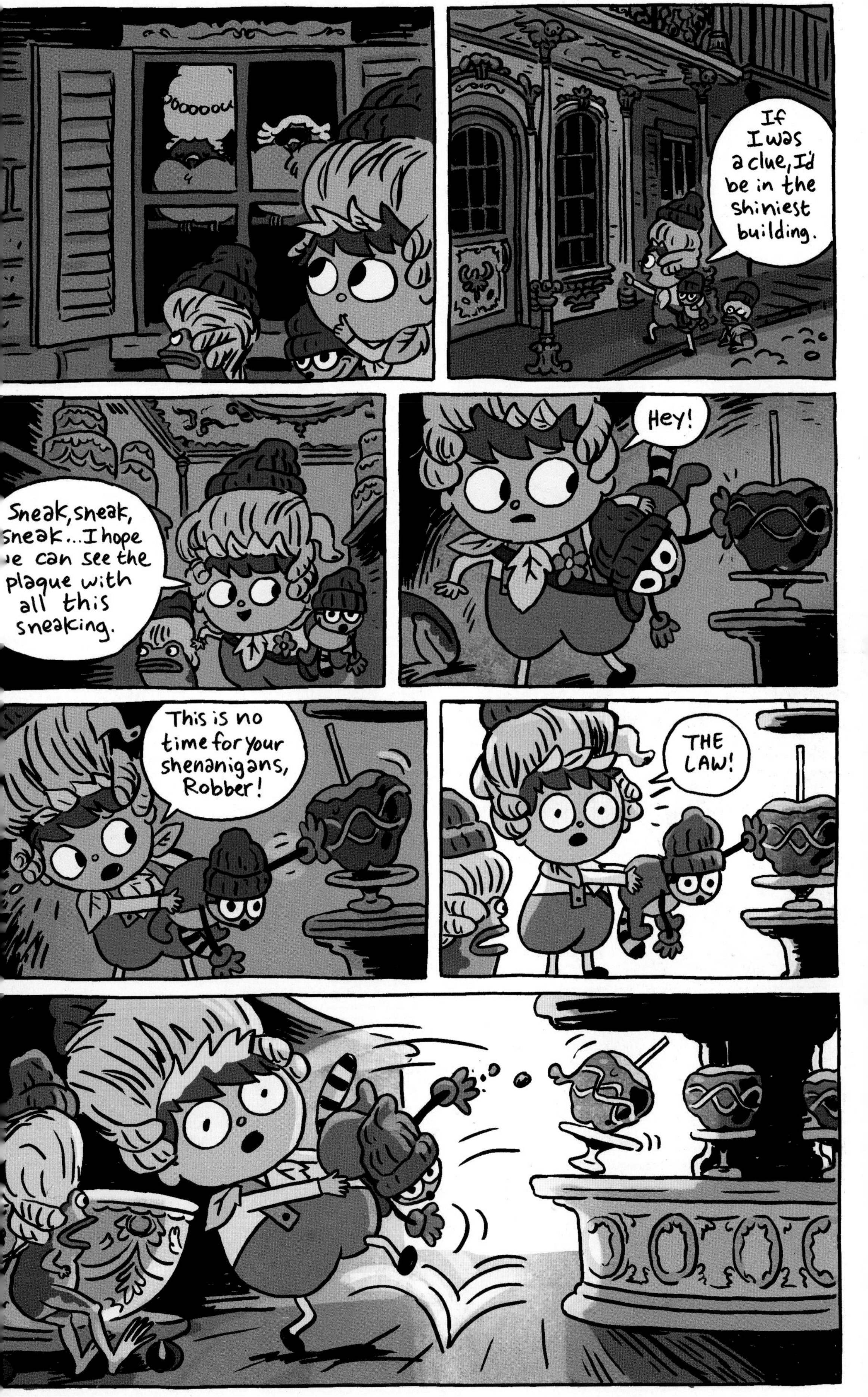

Oooooou
If I was a clue, I'd be in the shiniest building.
Sneak, sneak, sneak...I hope we can see the plaque with all this sneaking.
Hey!
This is no time for your shenanigans, Robber!
THE LAW!

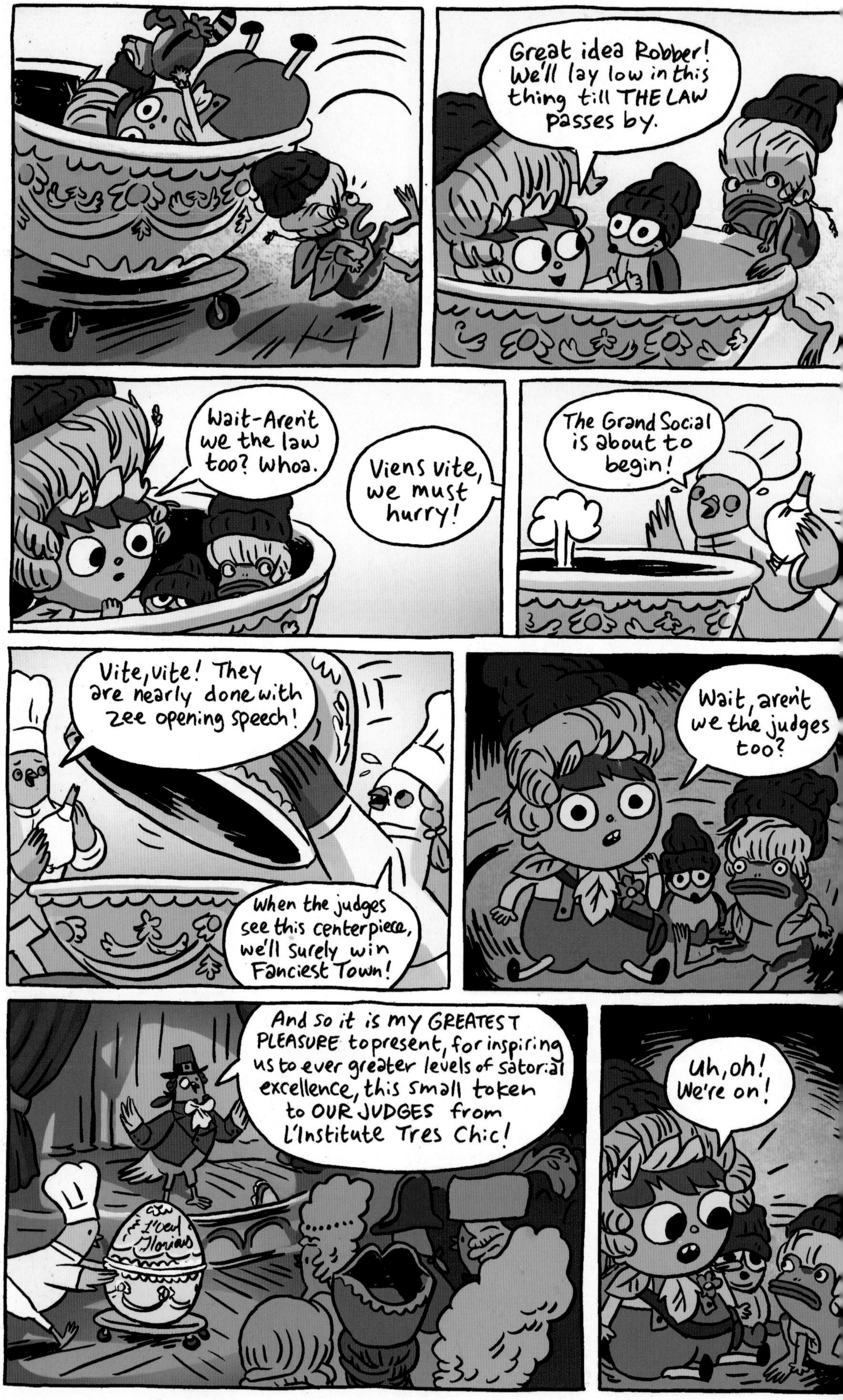
Great idea Robber! We'll lay low in this thing till THE LAW passes by.
Wait-Aren't we the law too? Whoa.
Viens vite, we must hurry!
The Grand Social is about to begin!
Vite, vite! They are nearly done with zee opening speech!
When the judges see this centerpiece, we'll surely win Fanciest Town!
Wait, aren't we the judges too?
And so it is my GREATEST PLEASURE to present, for inspiring us to ever greater levels of satorial excellence, this small token to OUR JUDGES from L'Institute Tres Chic!
L'Oeuf Glorious
Uh, oh! We're on!

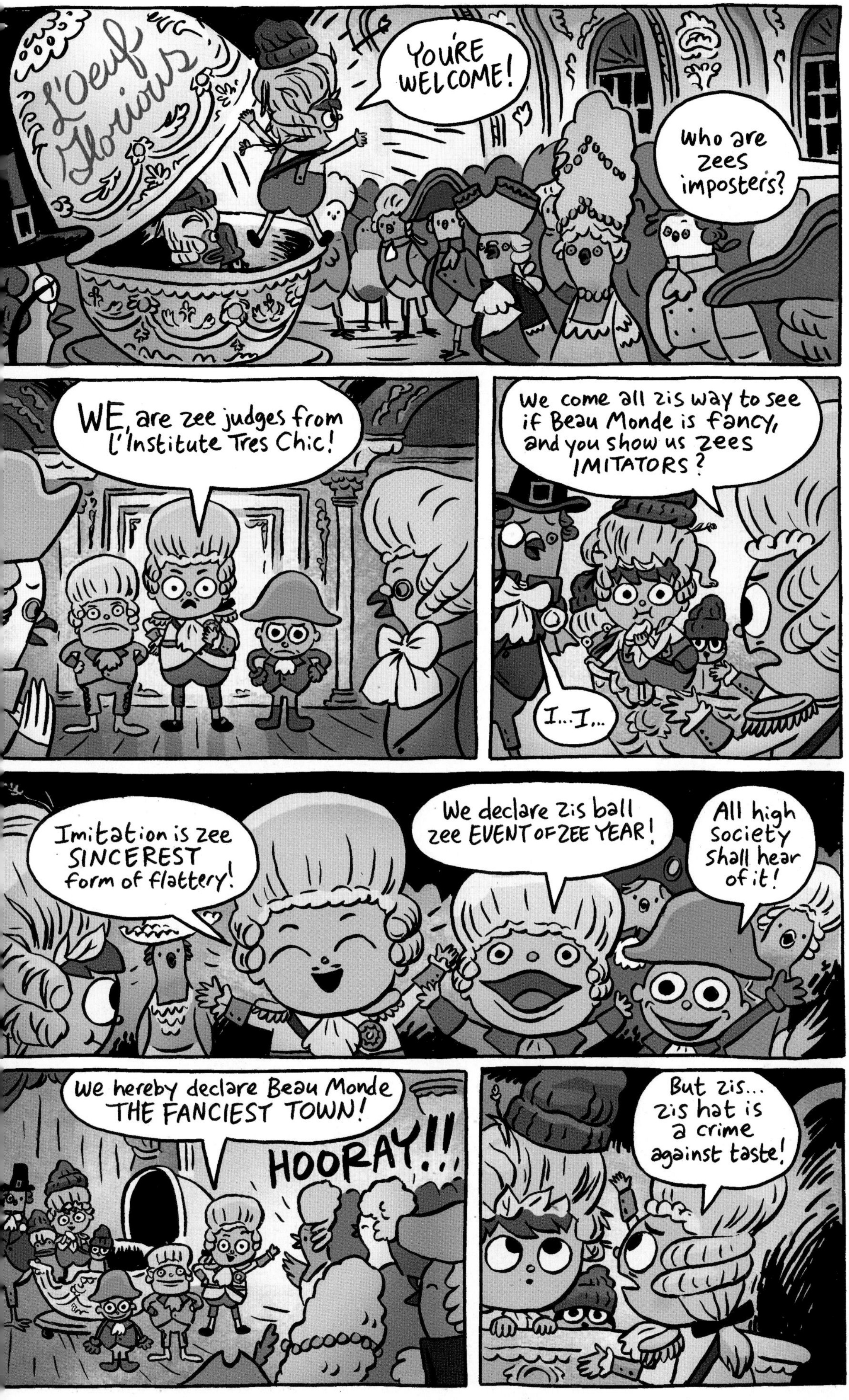
L'Oeuf Glorious
YOU'RE WELCOME!
Who are zees imposters?
WE, are zee judges from l'Institute Tres Chic!
We come all zis way to see if Beau Monde is fancy, and you show us zees IMITATORS?
I...I...
Imitation is zee SINCEREST form of flattery!
We declare zis ball zee EVENT OF ZEE YEAR!
All high society shall hear of it!
We hereby declare Beau Monde THE FANCIEST TOWN!
HOORAY!!!
But zis... zis hat is a crime against taste!

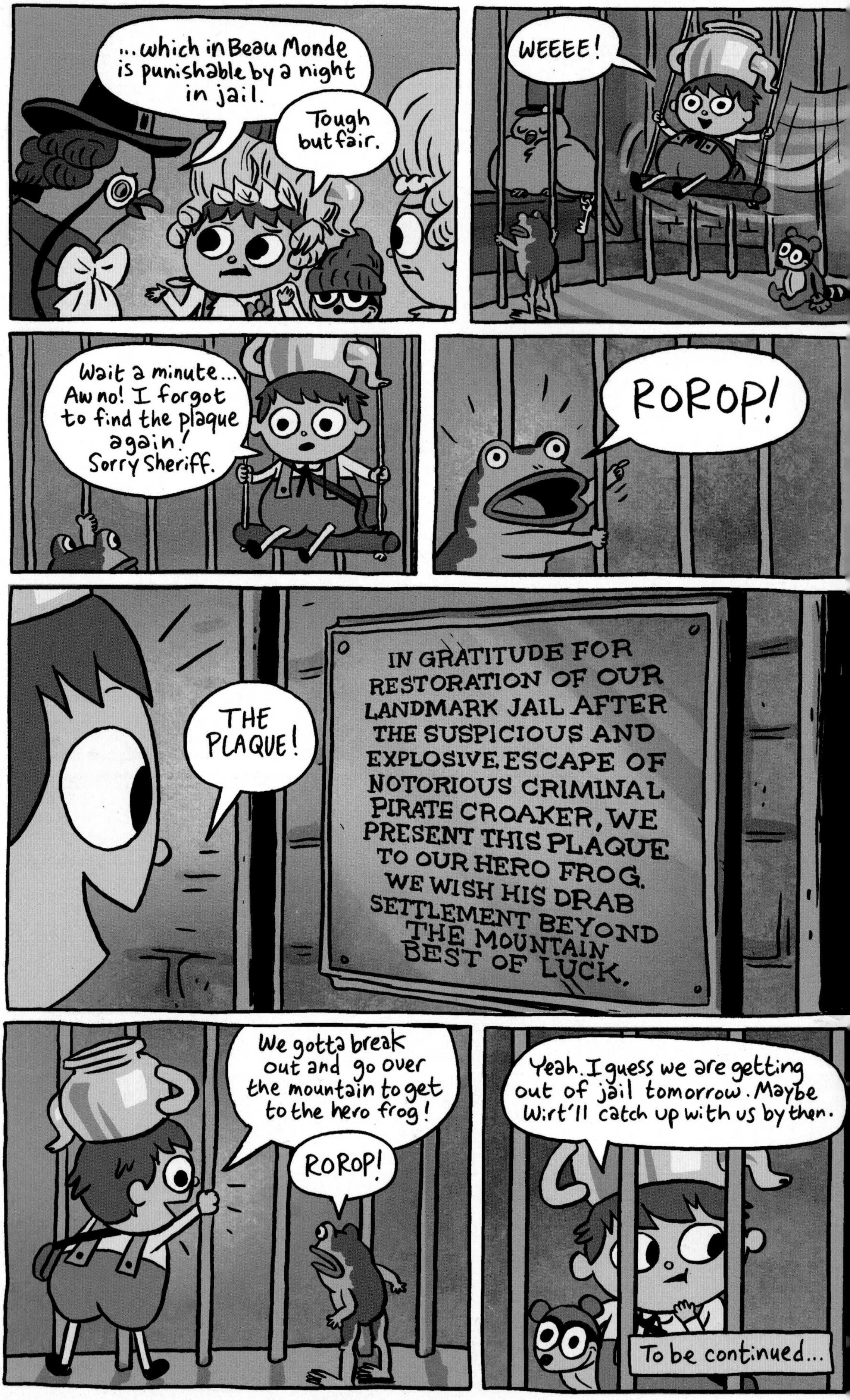
...which in Beau Monde is punishable by a night in jail.
Tough but fair.
WEEEE!
Wait a minute... Aw no! I forgot to find the plaque again! Sorry Sheriff.
ROROP!
THE PLAQUE!
IN GRATITUDE FOR RESTORATION OF OUR LANDMARK JAIL AFTER THE SUSPICIOUS AND EXPLOSIVE ESCAPE OF NOTORIOUS CRIMINAL PIRATE CROAKER, WE PRESENT THIS PLAQUE TO OUR HERO FROG. WE WISH HIS DRAB SETTLEMENT BEYOND THE MOUNTAIN BEST OF LUCK.
We gotta break out and go over the mountain to get to the hero frog!
ROROP!
Yeah. I guess we are getting out of jail tomorrow. Maybe Wirt'll catch up with us by then.
To be continued...

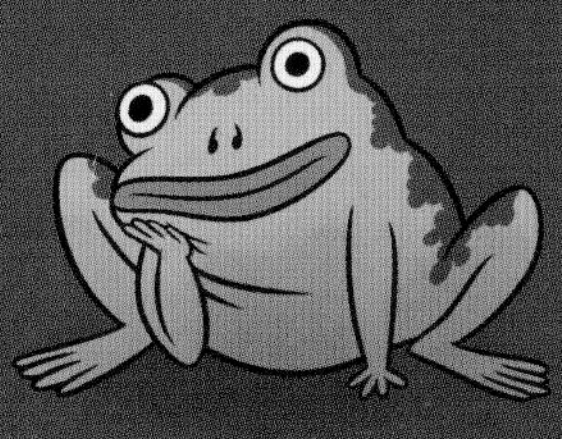

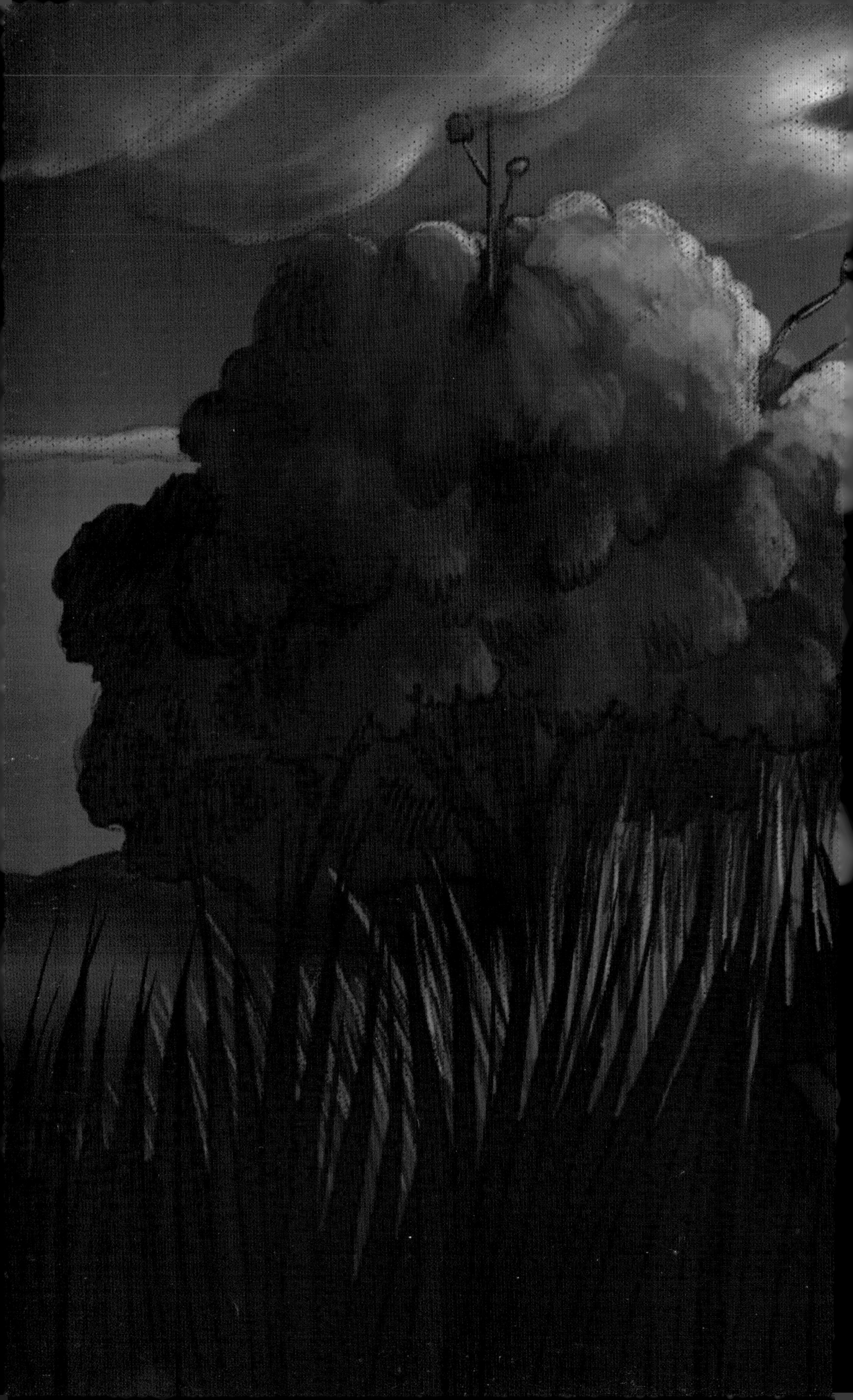

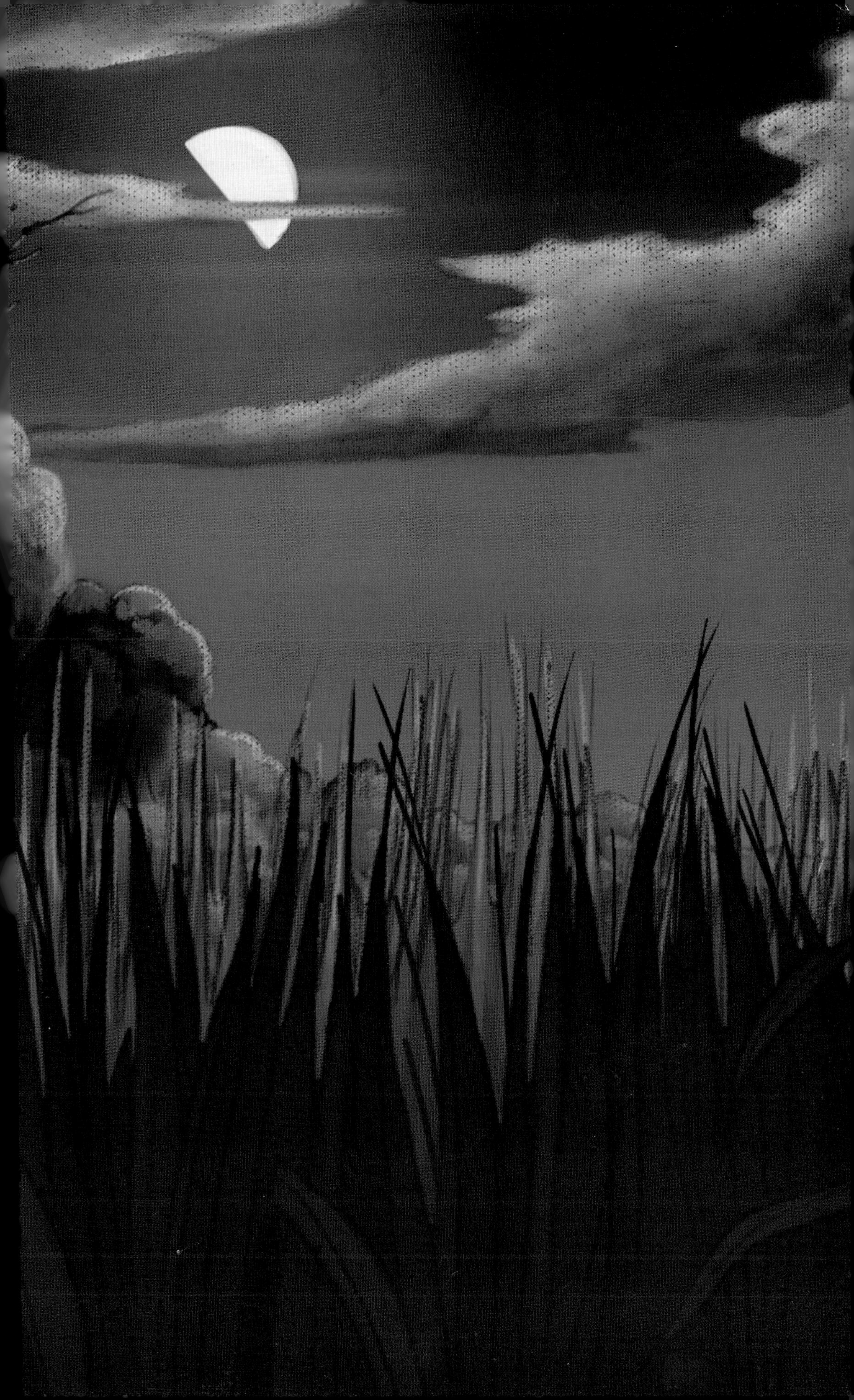

Pooree The Elephant

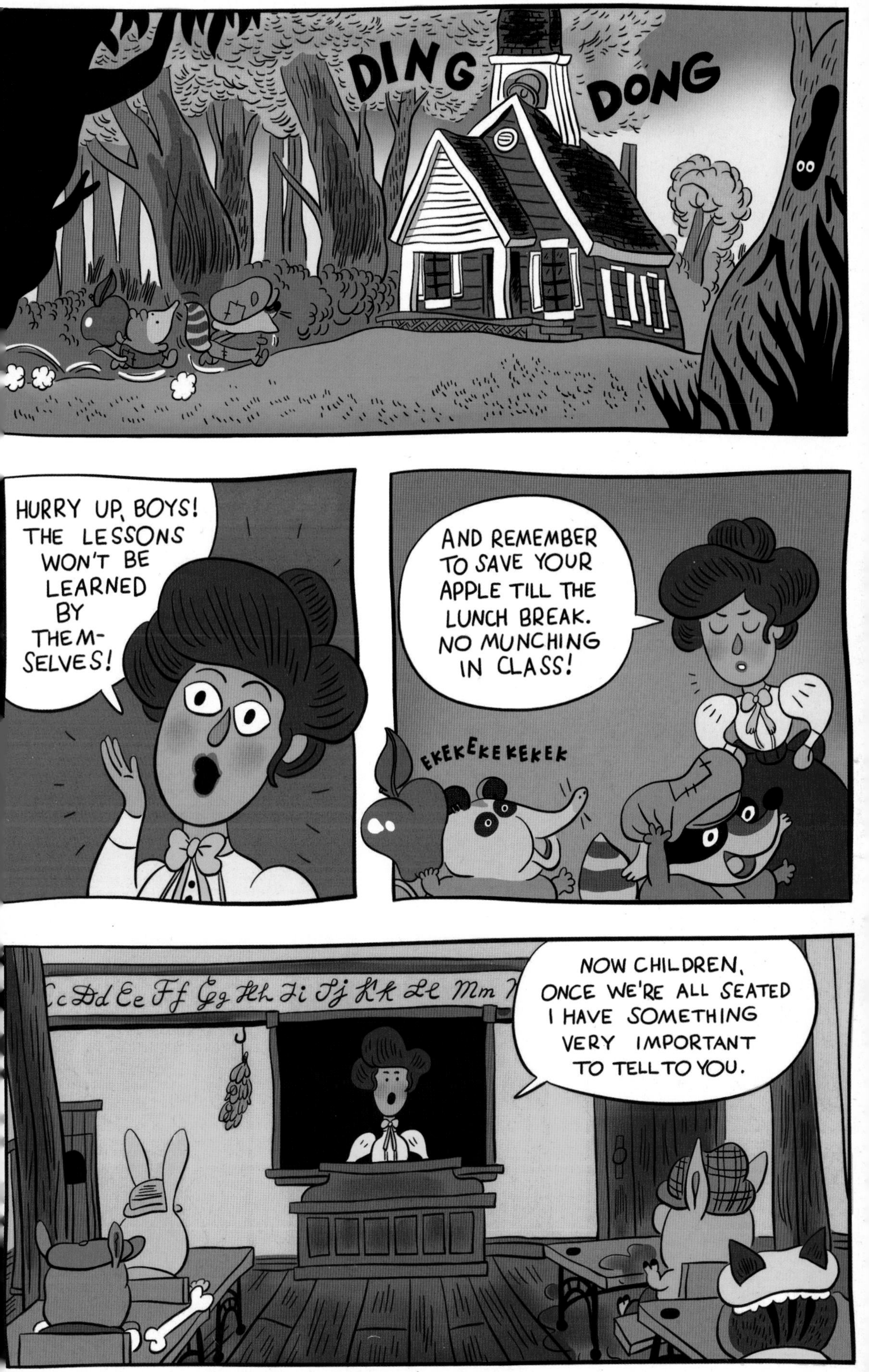
DING
DONG
HURRY UP, BOYS! THE LESSONS WON'T BE LEARNED BY THEMSELVES!
AND REMEMBER TO SAVE YOUR APPLE TILL THE LUNCH BREAK. NO MUNCHING IN CLASS!
EKEKEKEKEKEKEK
NOW CHILDREN, ONCE WE'RE ALL SEATED I HAVE SOMETHING VERY IMPORTANT TO TELL TO YOU.

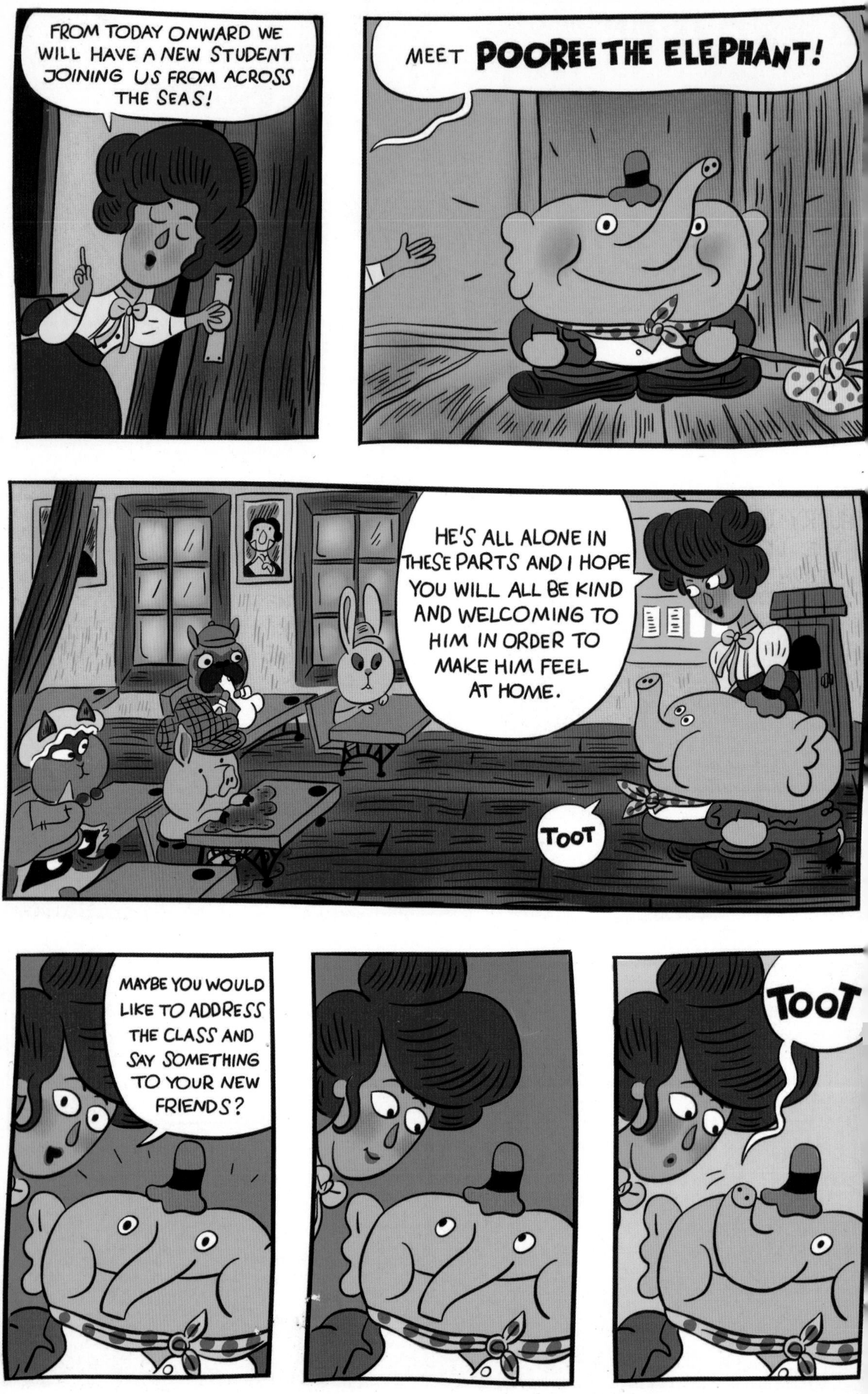
FROM TODAY ONWARD WE WILL HAVE A NEW STUDENT JOINING US FROM ACROSS THE SEAS!
MEET POOREE THE ELEPHANT!
HE'S ALL ALONE IN THESE PARTS AND I HOPE YOU WILL ALL BE KIND AND WELCOMING TO HIM IN ORDER TO MAKE HIM FEEL AT HOME.
TOOT
MAYBE YOU WOULD LIKE TO ADDRESS THE CLASS AND SAY SOMETHING TO YOUR NEW FRIENDS?
TOOT

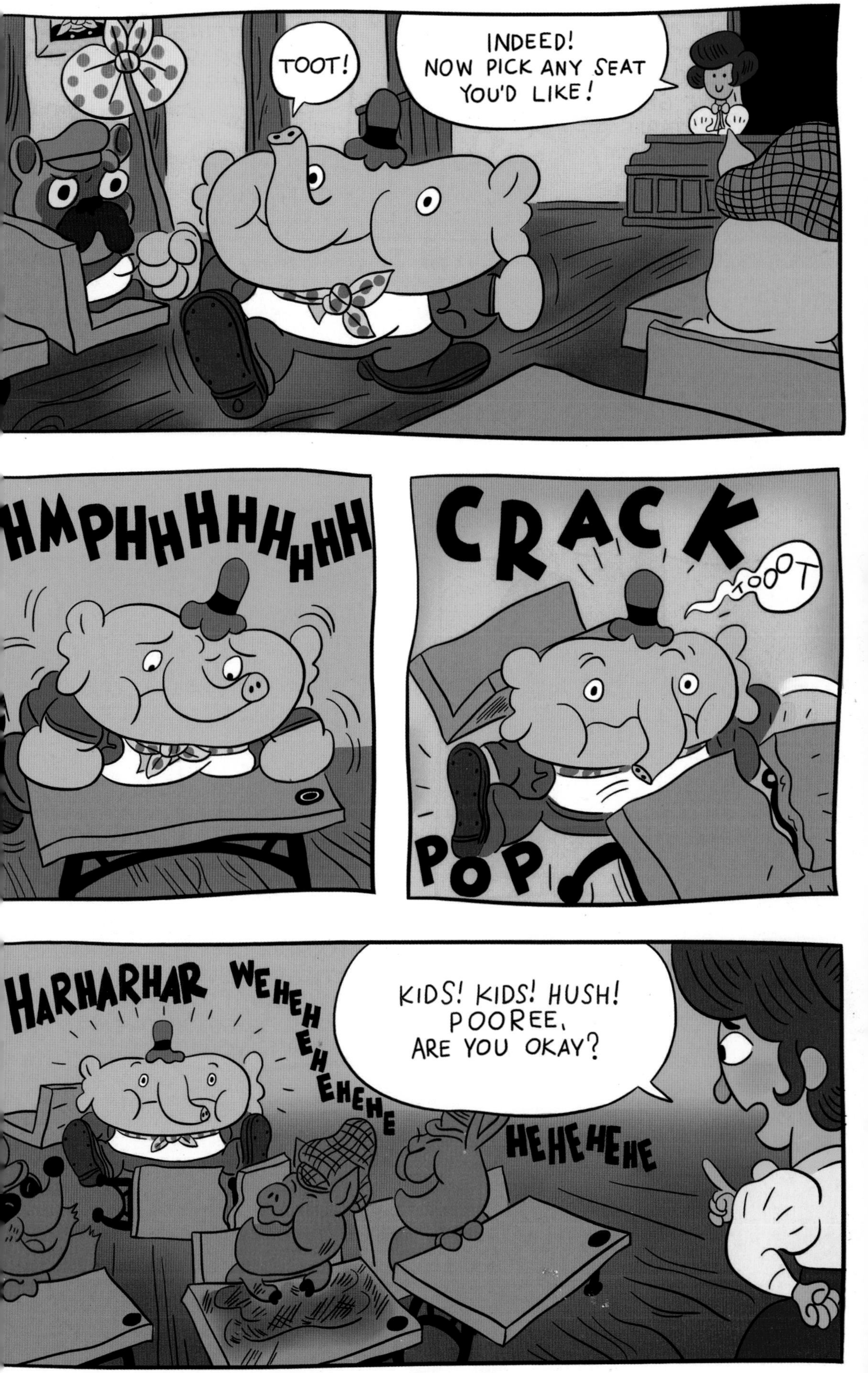
TOOT!
INDEED! NOW PICK ANY SEAT YOU'D LIKE!
HMPHHHHHHHHH
CRACK
TOOOT
POP
HARHARHAR
WEHEHEHEHEHEHE
KIDS! KIDS! HUSH! POOREE, ARE YOU OKAY?
HEHEHEHEHE

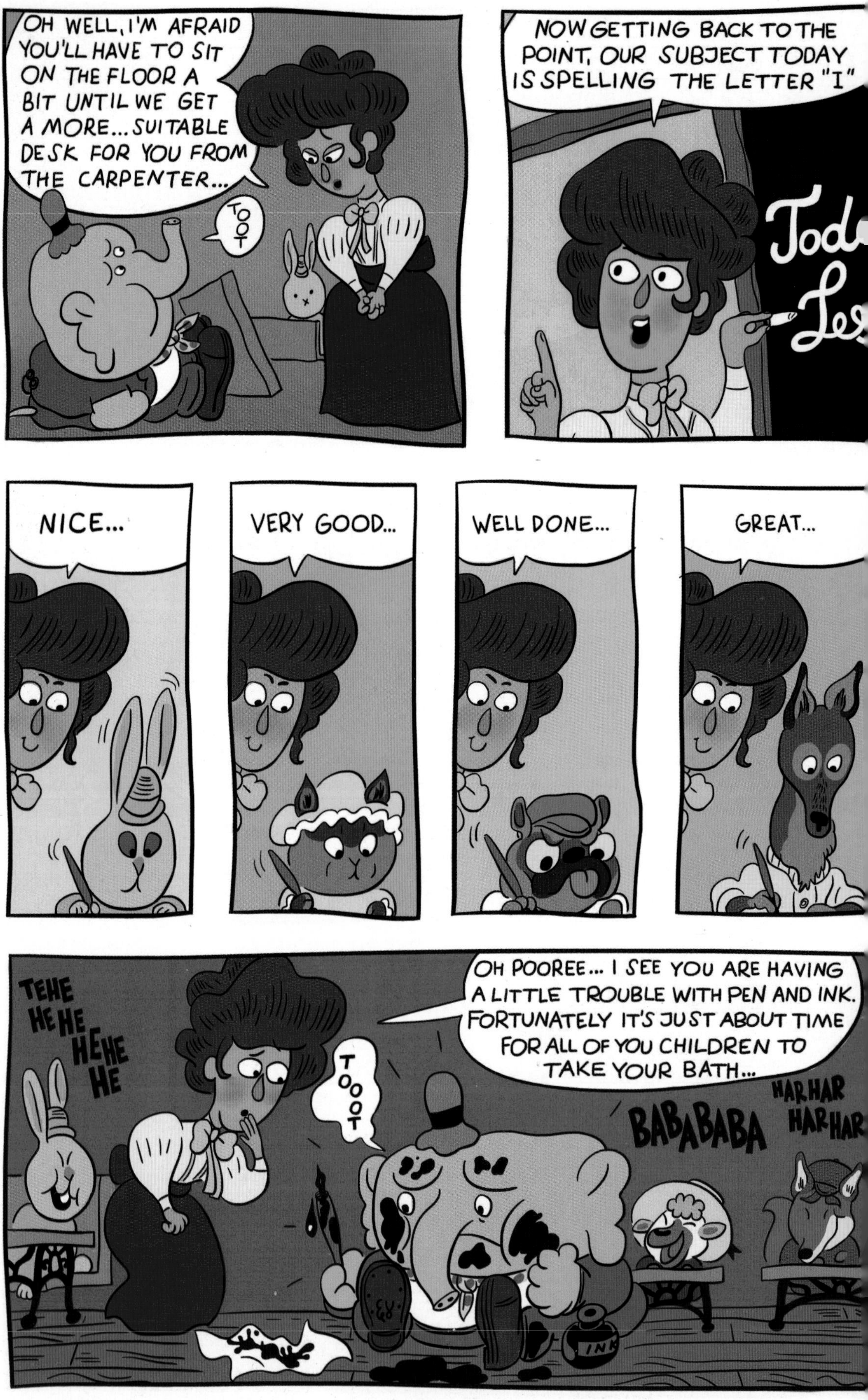
OH WELL, I'M AFRAID YOU'LL HAVE TO SIT ON THE FLOOR A BIT UNTIL WE GET A MORE... SUITABLE DESK FOR YOU FROM THE CARPENTER...
TOOT
NOW GETTING BACK TO THE POINT, OUR SUBJECT TODAY IS SPELLING THE LETTER "I"
NICE...
VERY GOOD...
WELL DONE...
GREAT...
TEHE HE HE HEHE HE
TOOOT
OH POOREE... I SEE YOU ARE HAVING A LITTLE TROUBLE WITH PEN AND INK. FORTUNATELY IT'S JUST ABOUT TIME FOR ALL OF YOU CHILDREN TO TAKE YOUR BATH...
BABABABA
HARHAR HARHAR
INK

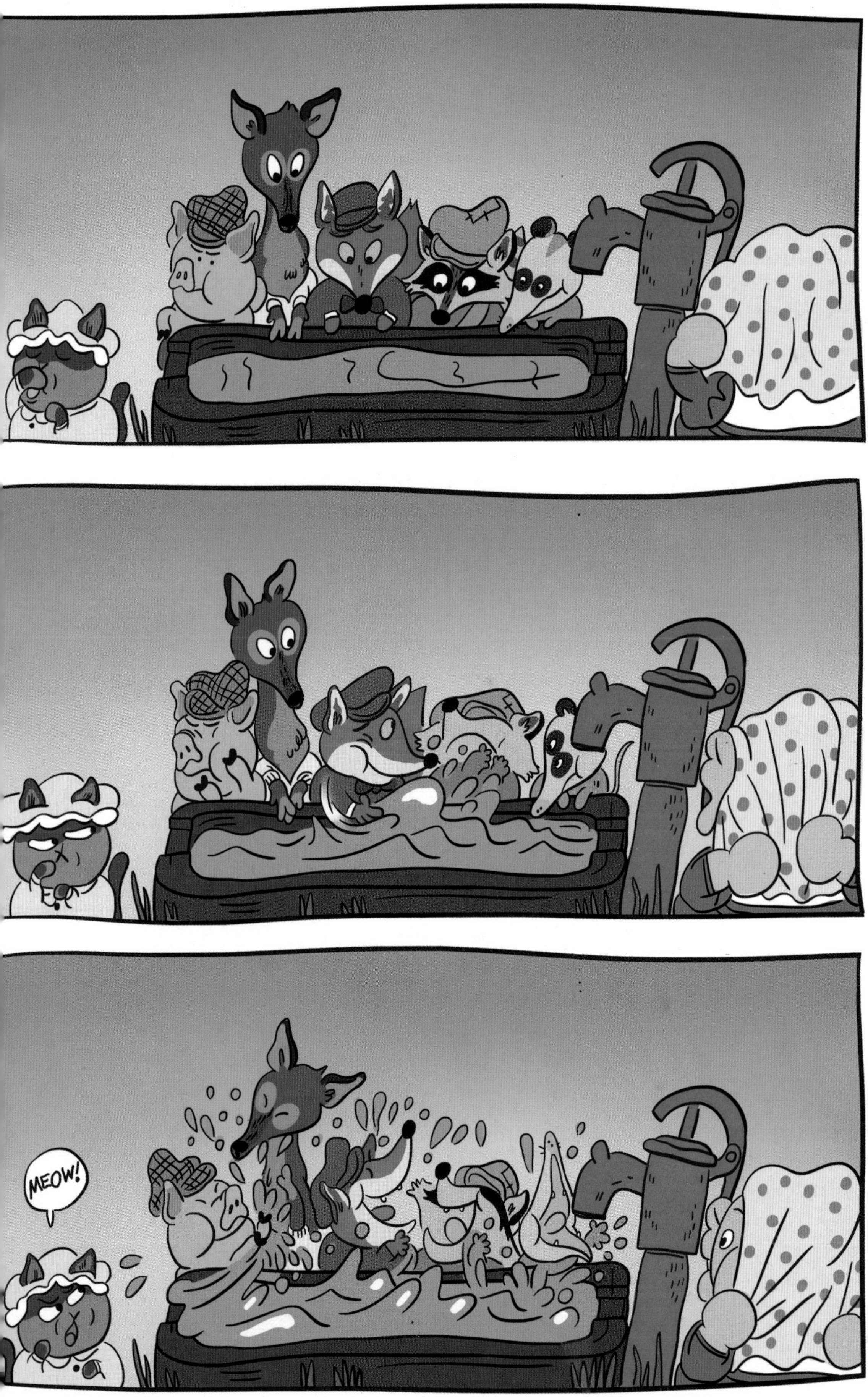
MEOW!

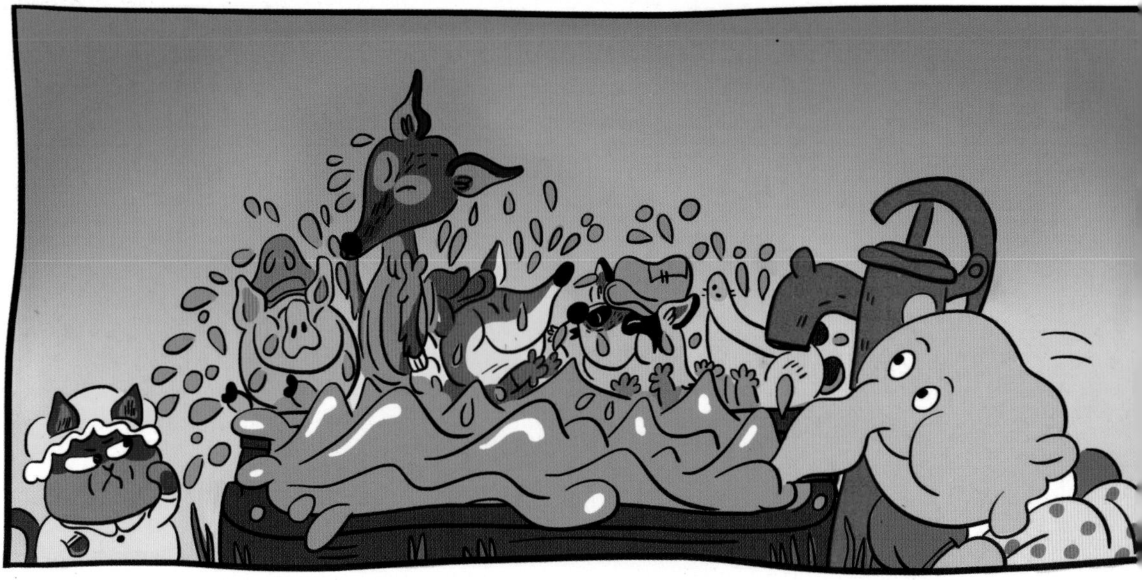
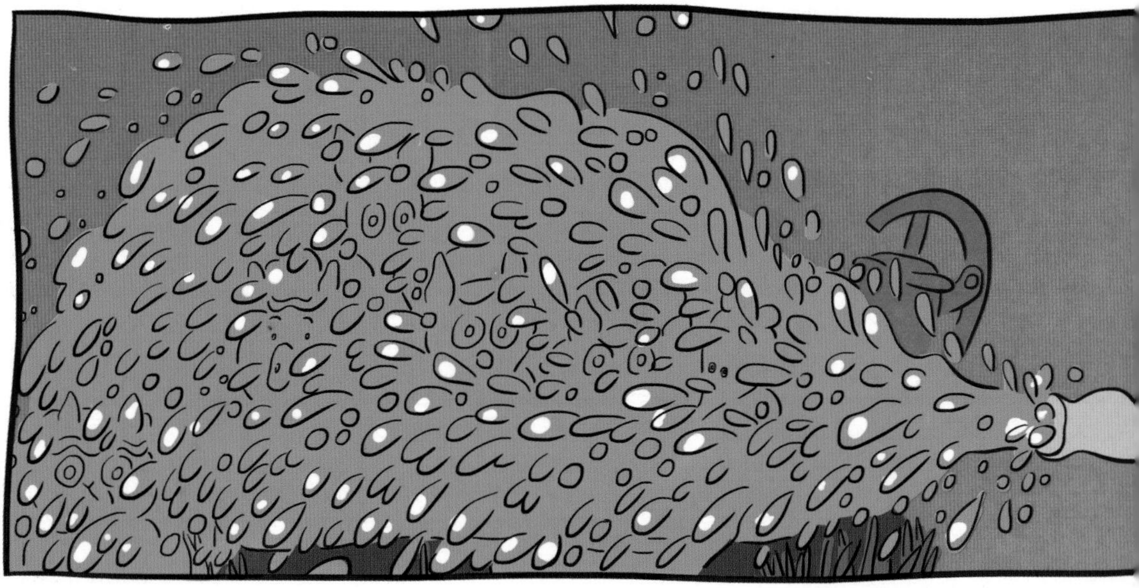
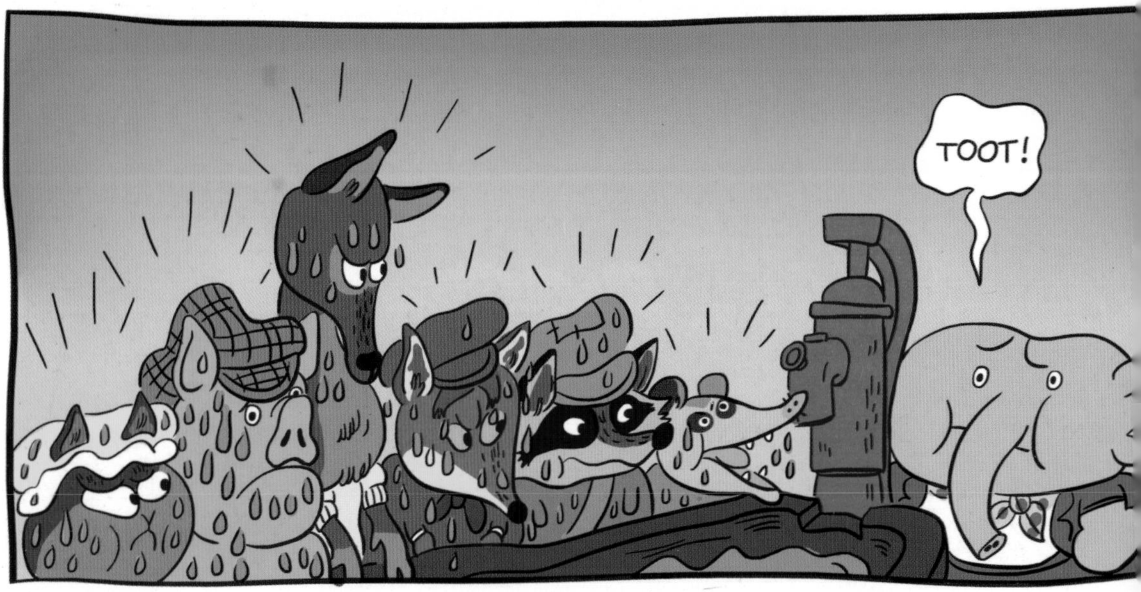
TOOT!

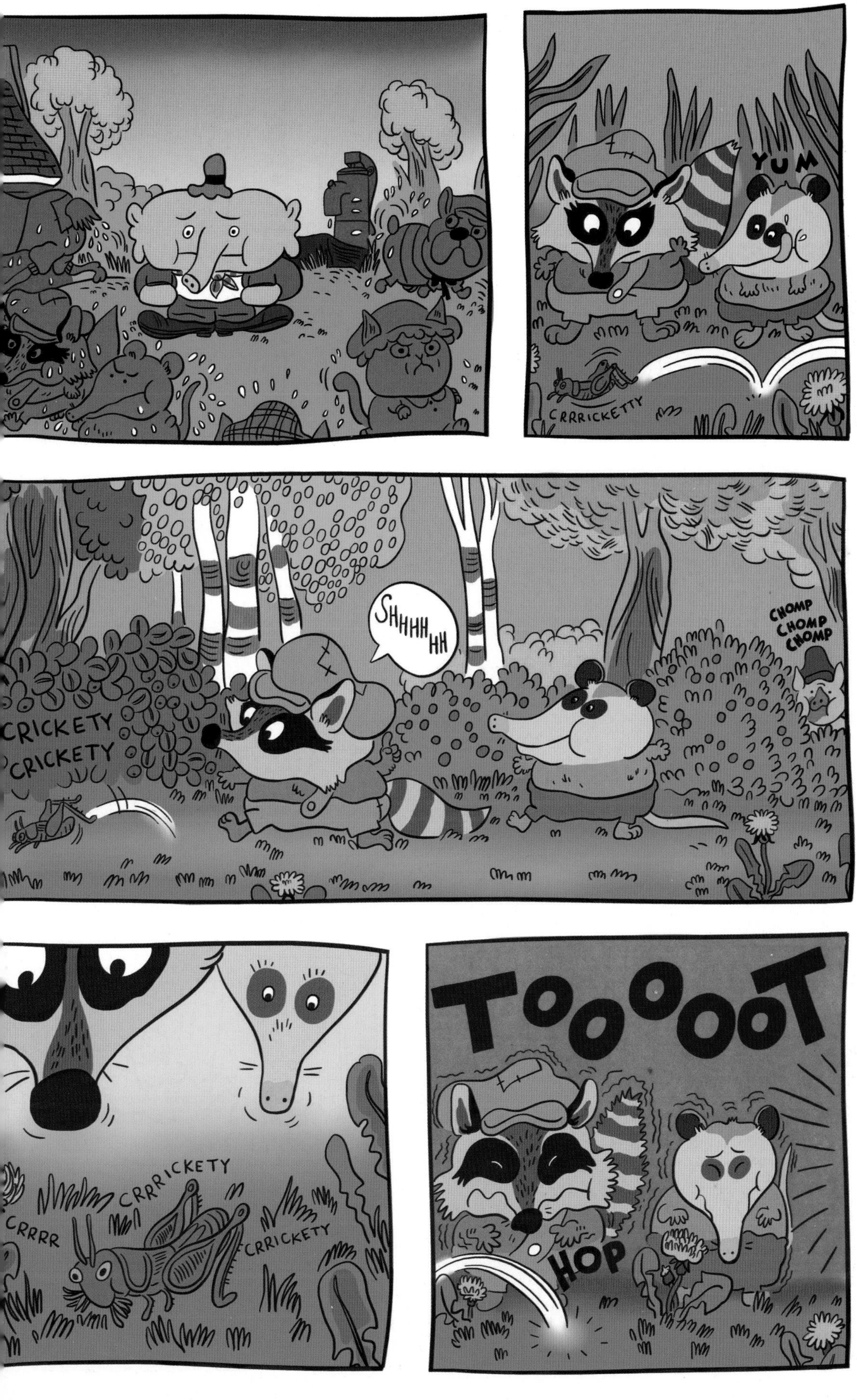
YUM
CRRRICKETTY
SHHHHHH
CHOMP CHOMP CHOMP
CRICKETY CRICKETY
CRRRICKETY
CRRRR
CRRICKETY
TOOOOOT
HOP

TOOOT

EKEKEKEK

POOPEE

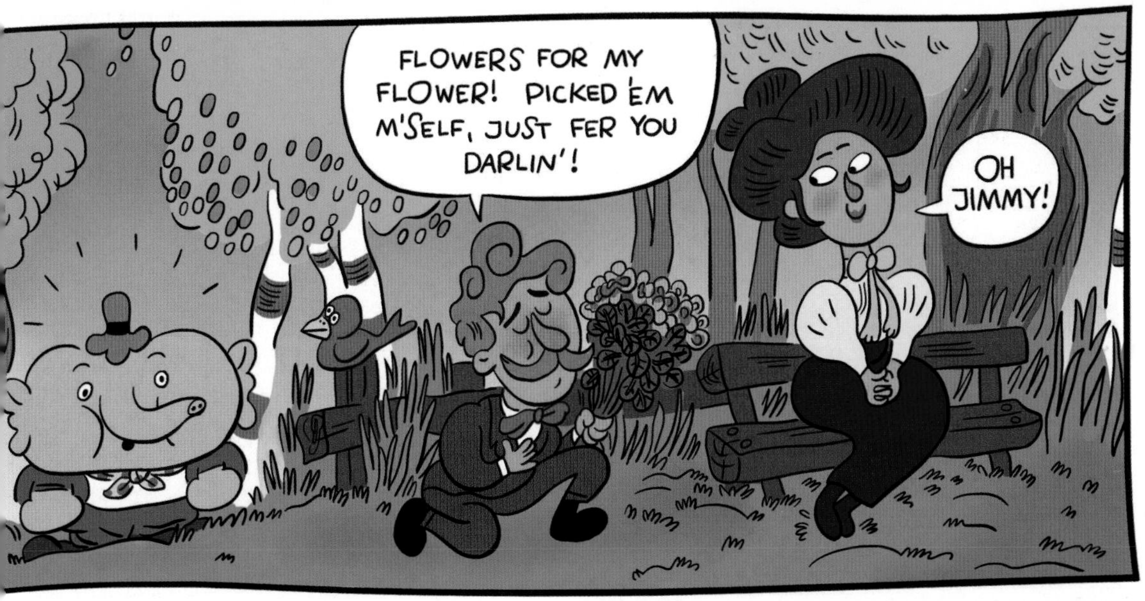
FLOWERS FOR MY FLOWER! PICKED 'EM M'SELF, JUST FER YOU DARLIN'!
OH JIMMY!

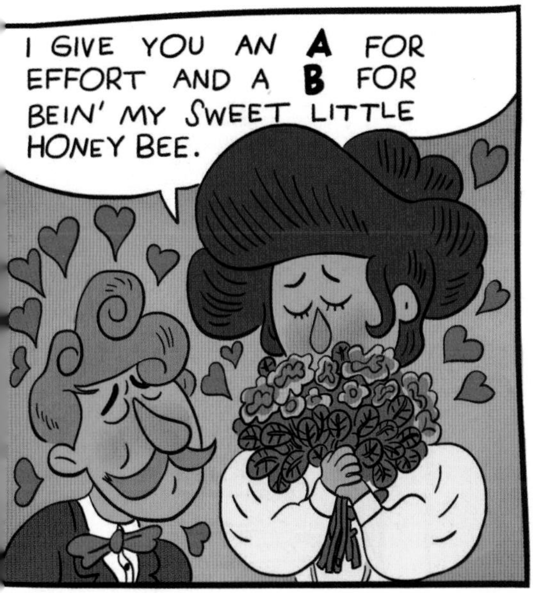
I GIVE YOU AN A FOR EFFORT AND A B FOR BEIN' MY SWEET LITTLE HONEY BEE.

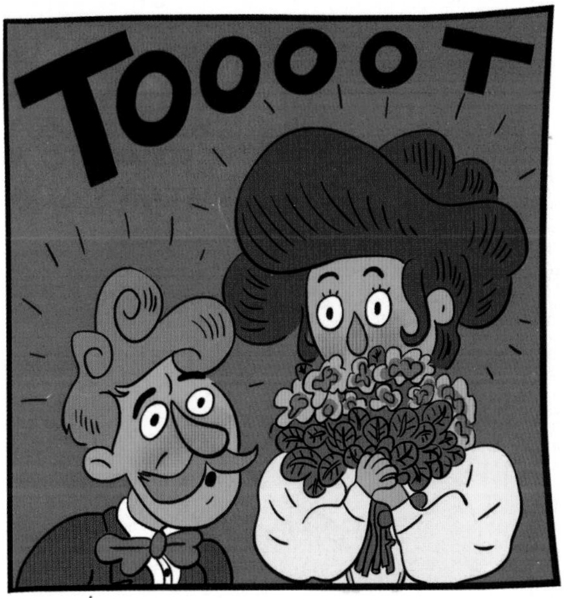
TOOOOT

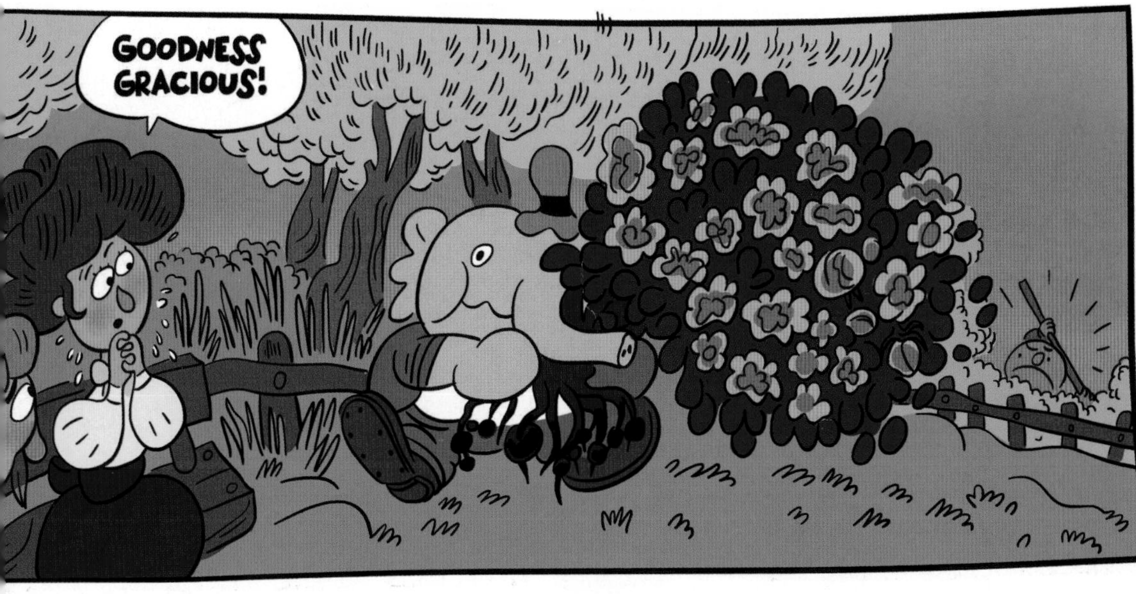
GOODNESS GRACIOUS!

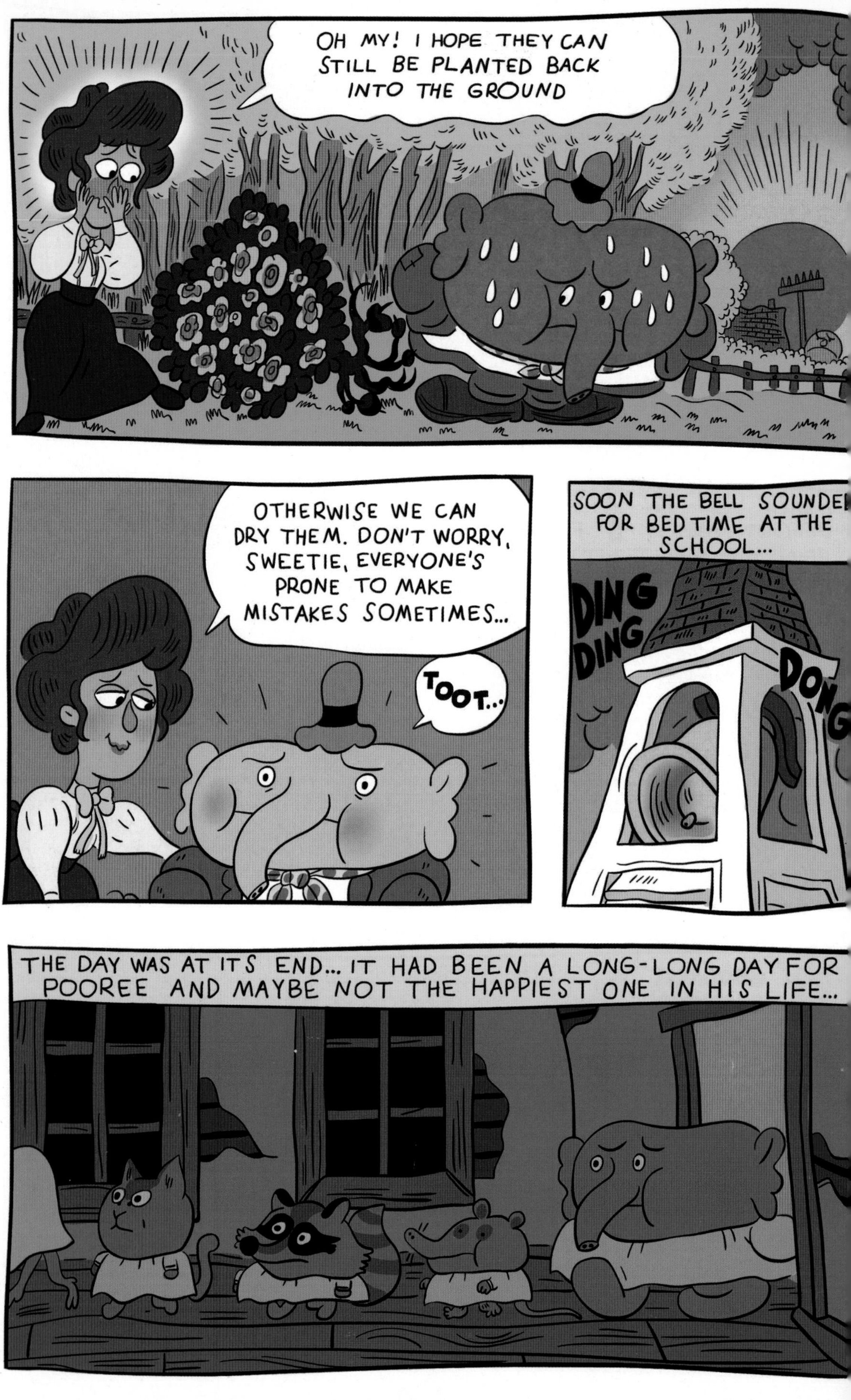
OH MY! I HOPE THEY CAN STILL BE PLANTED BACK INTO THE GROUND
OTHERWISE WE CAN DRY THEM. DON'T WORRY, SWEETIE, EVERYONE'S PRONE TO MAKE MISTAKES SOMETIMES...
TOOT...
SOON THE BELL SOUNDE FOR BEDTIME AT THE SCHOOL...
DING DING
DING
DONG
THE DAY WAS AT ITS END... IT HAD BEEN A LONG-LONG DAY FOR POOREE AND MAYBE NOT THE HAPPIEST ONE IN HIS LIFE...

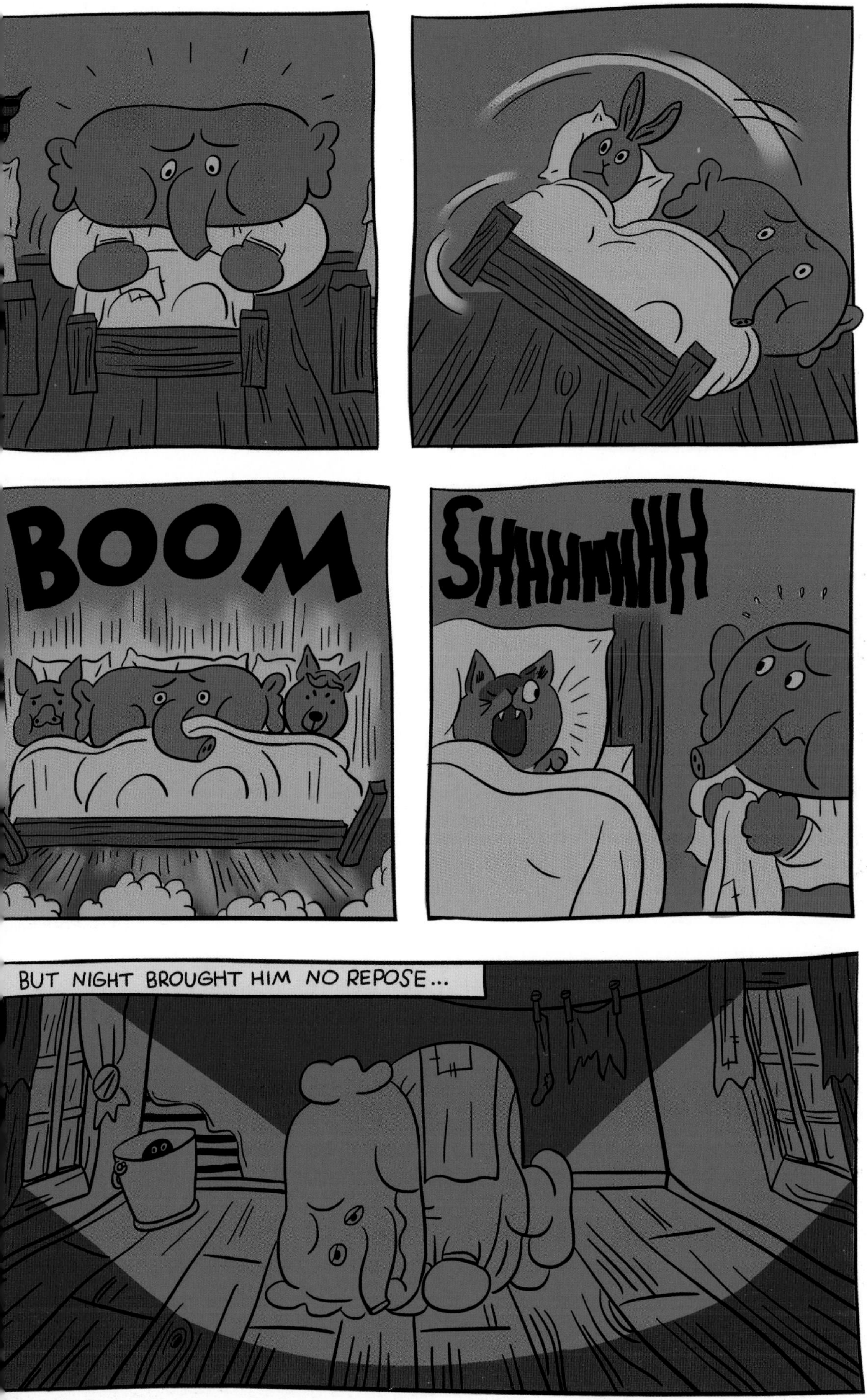
BOOM
SHHHHHHH
BUT NIGHT BROUGHT HIM NO REPOSE...

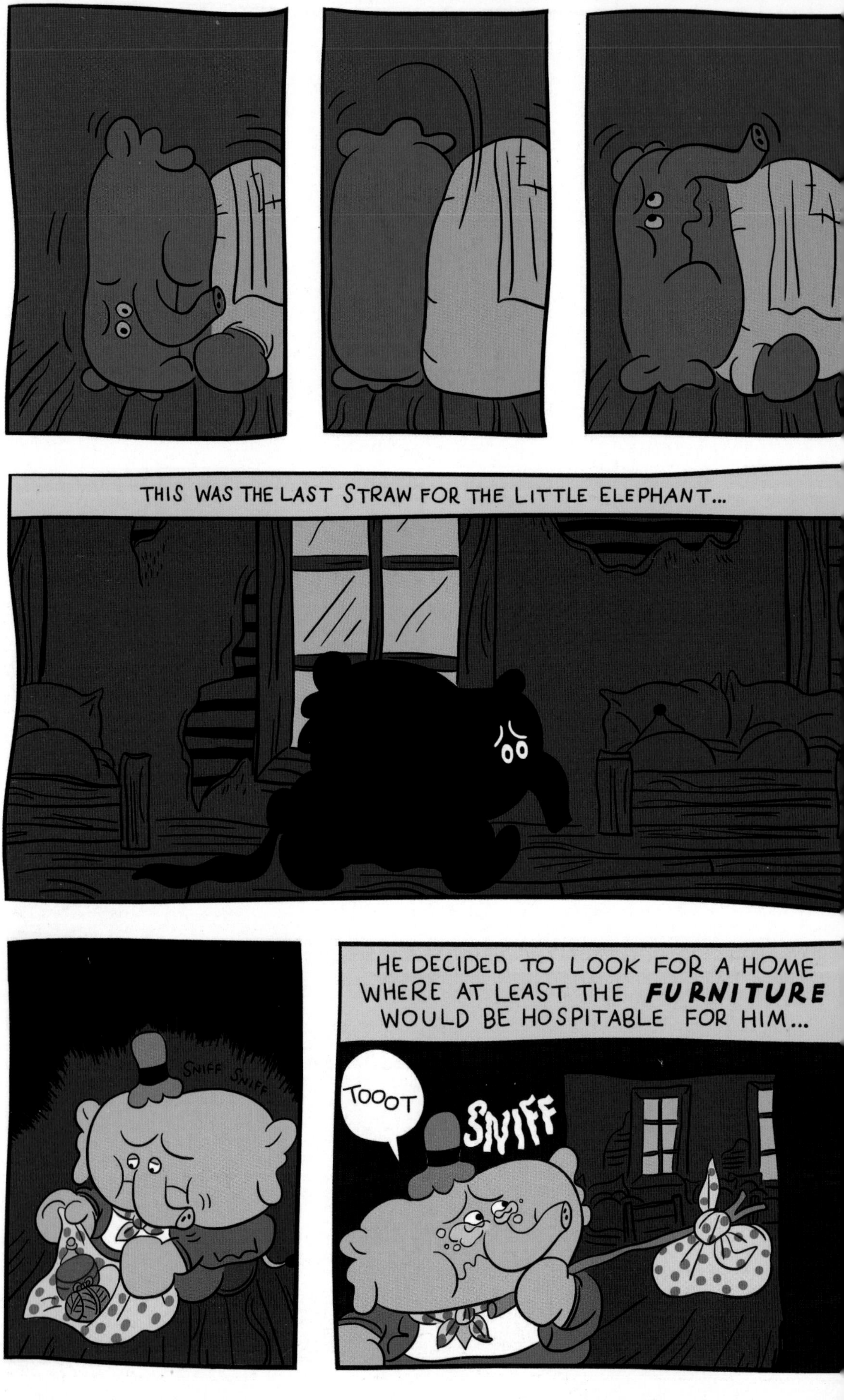
THIS WAS THE LAST STRAW FOR THE LITTLE ELEPHANT...
SNIFF SNIFF
HE DECIDED TO LOOK FOR A HOME WHERE AT LEAST THE FURNITURE WOULD BE HOSPITABLE FOR HIM...
TOOOT
SNIFF

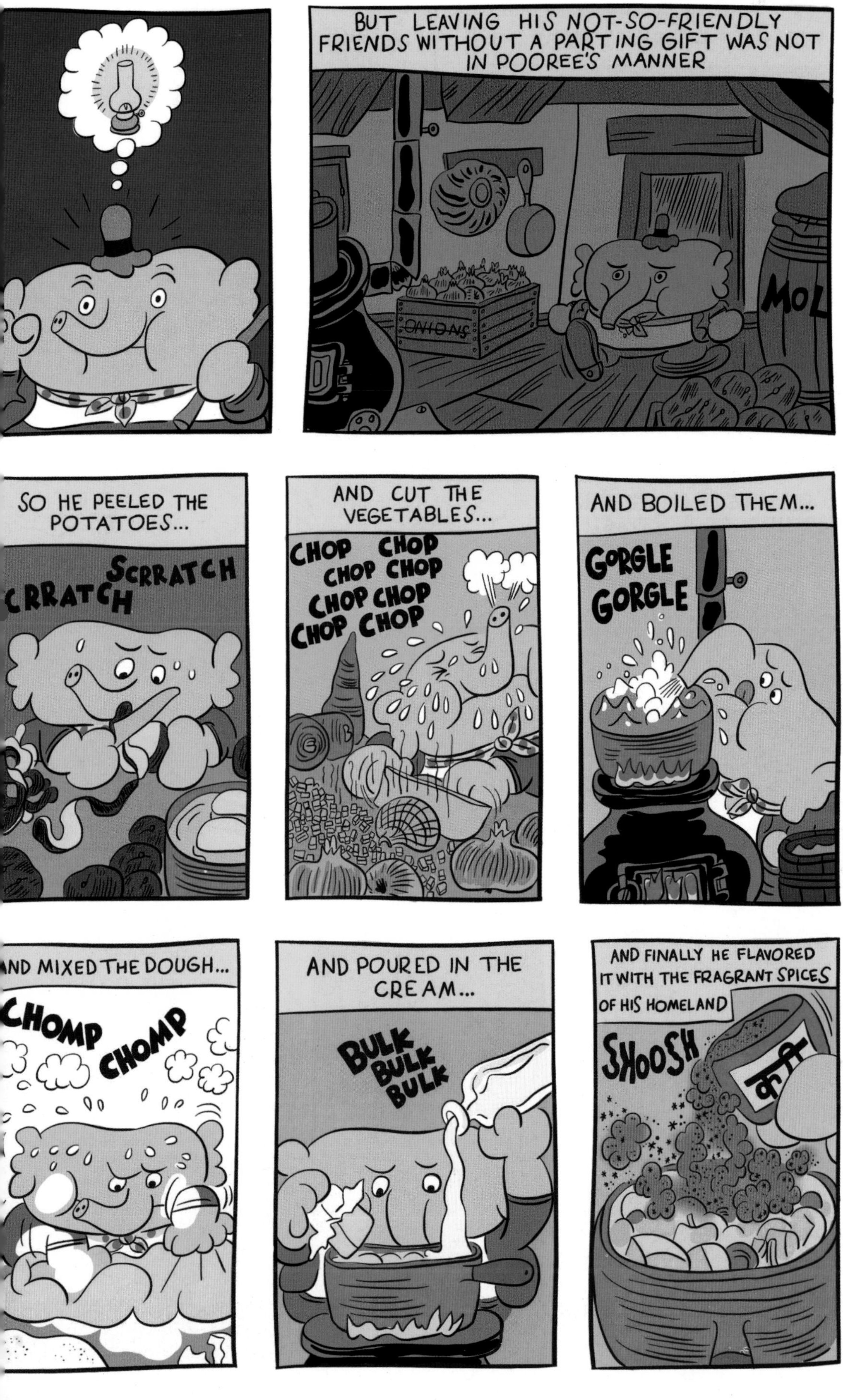
BUT LEAVING HIS NOT-SO-FRIENDLY FRIENDS WITHOUT A PARTING GIFT WAS NOT IN POOREE'S MANNER
ONIONS
MOL
SO HE PEELED THE POTATOES...
CRRATCH
SCRRATCH
AND CUT THE VEGETABLES...
CHOP CHOP CHOP CHOP CHOP CHOP CHOP CHOP
AND BOILED THEM...
GORGLE GORGLE
AND MIXED THE DOUGH...
CHOMP CHOMP
AND POURED IN THE CREAM...
BULK BULK BULK
AND FINALLY HE FLAVORED IT WITH THE FRAGRANT SPICES OF HIS HOMELAND
SHOOSH

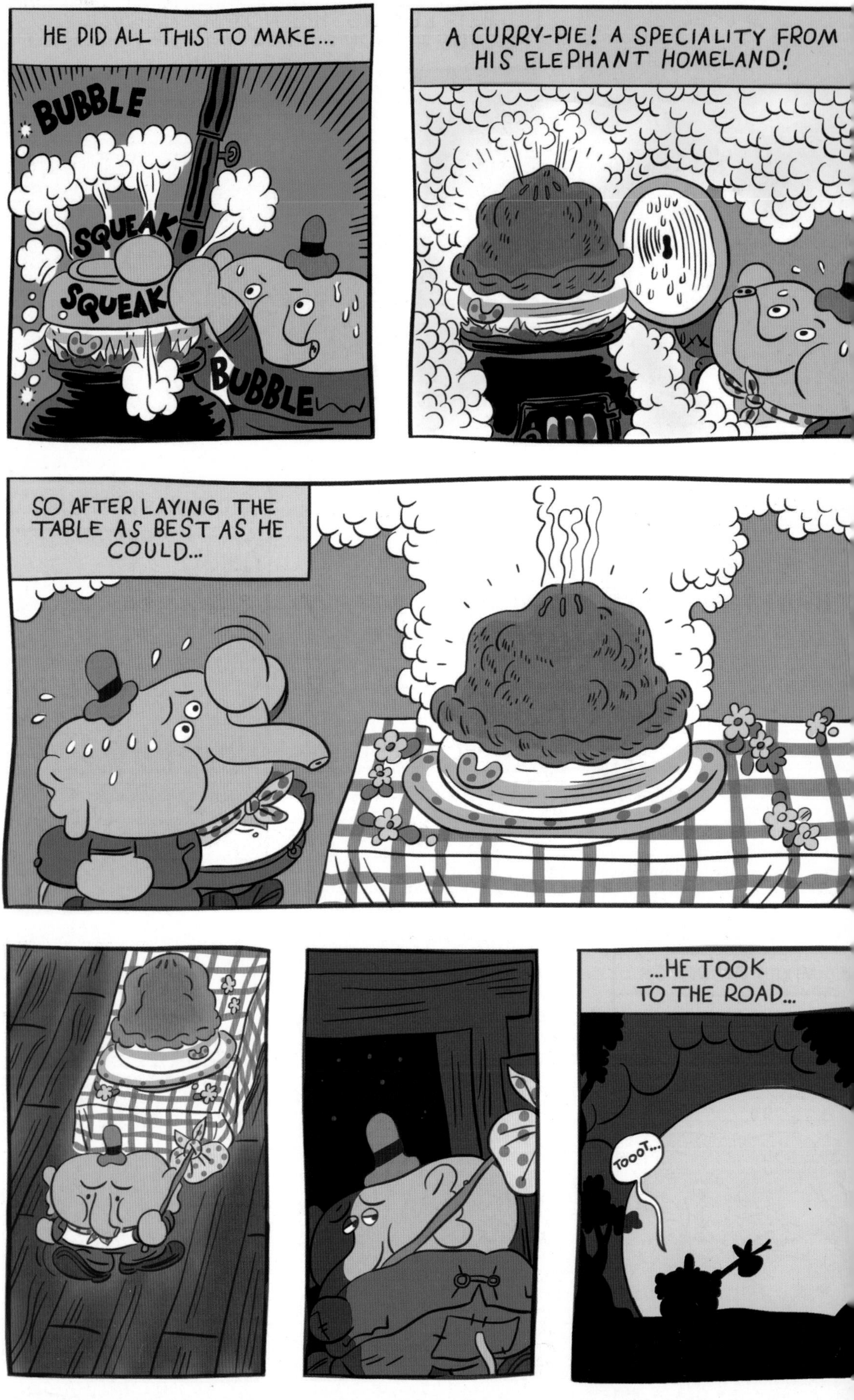
HE DID ALL THIS TO MAKE...
BUBBLE
SQUEAK
SQUEAK
BUBBLE
A CURRY-PIE! A SPECIALITY FROM HIS ELEPHANT HOMELAND!
SO AFTER LAYING THE TABLE AS BEST AS HE COULD...
...HE TOOK TO THE ROAD...
TOOOT...

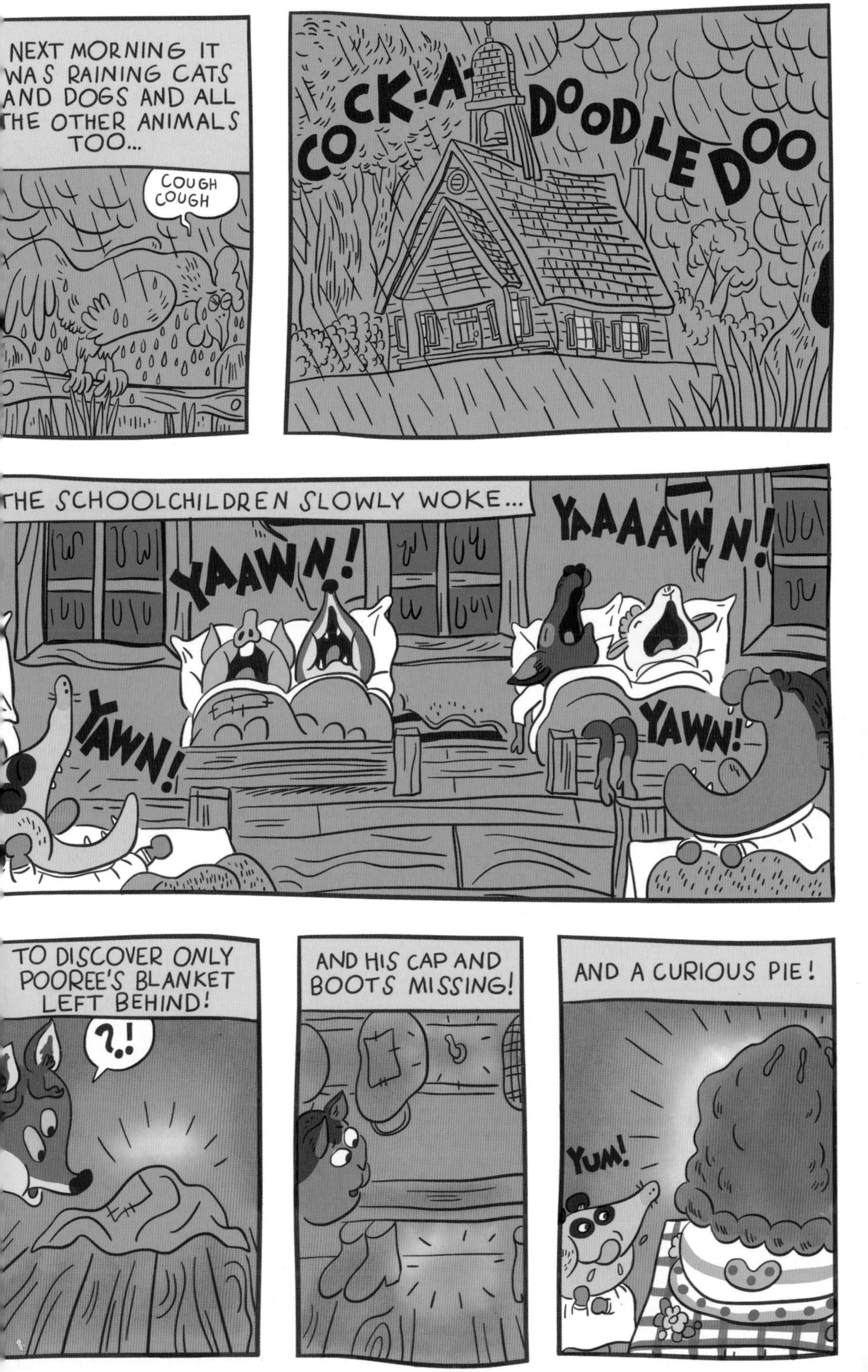
NEXT MORNING IT WAS RAINING CATS AND DOGS AND ALL THE OTHER ANIMALS TOO...
COUGH COUGH
COCK-A-DOODLEDOO
THE SCHOOLCHILDREN SLOWLY WOKE...
YAAWN!
YAAAAWN!
YAWN!
YAWN!
TO DISCOVER ONLY POOREE'S BLANKET LEFT BEHIND!
?.!
AND HIS CAP AND BOOTS MISSING!
AND A CURIOUS PIE!
YUM!

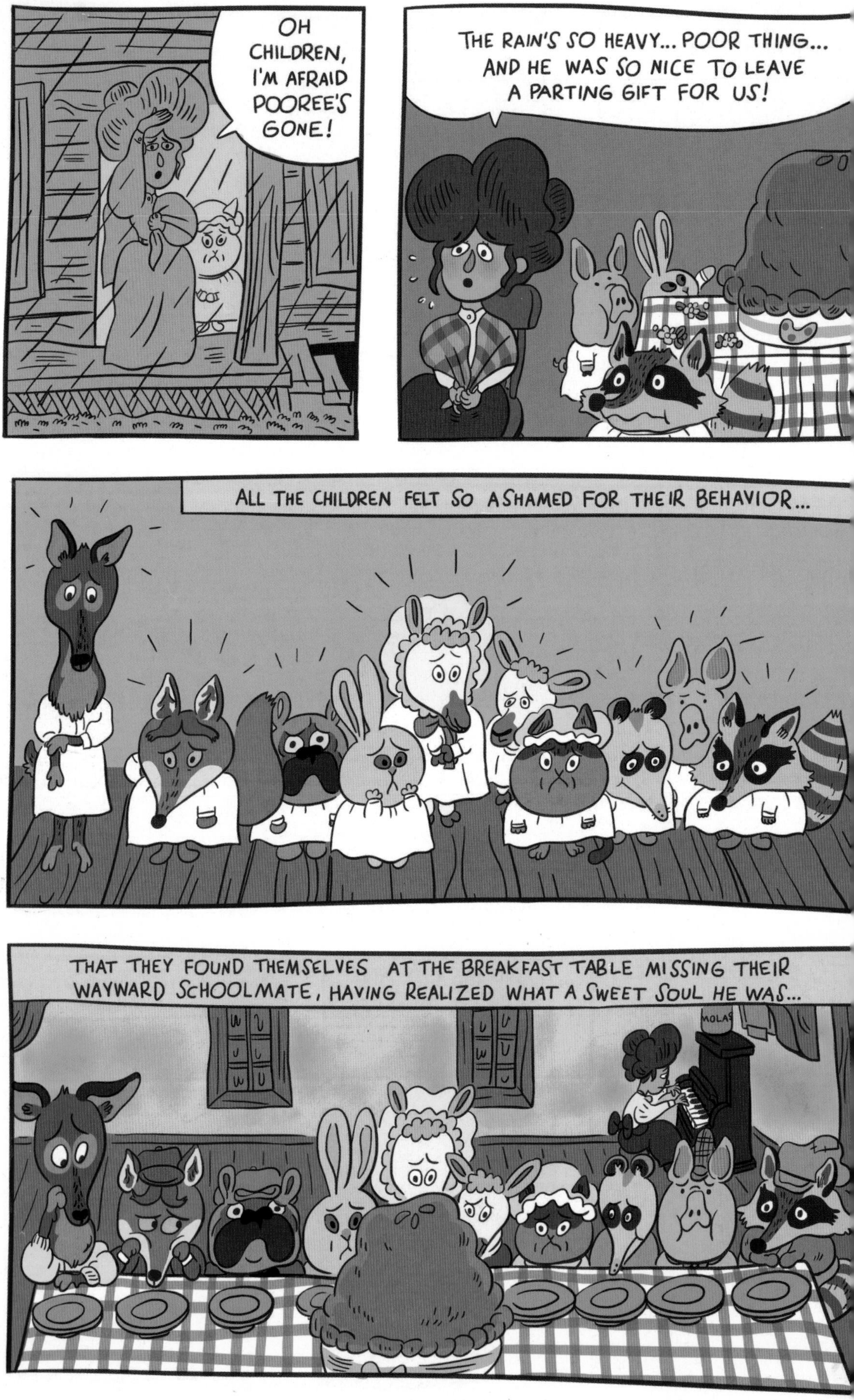
OH CHILDREN, I'M AFRAID POOREE'S GONE!
THE RAIN'S SO HEAVY... POOR THING... AND HE WAS SO NICE TO LEAVE A PARTING GIFT FOR US!
ALL THE CHILDREN FELT SO ASHAMED FOR THEIR BEHAVIOR...
THAT THEY FOUND THEMSELVES AT THE BREAKFAST TABLE MISSING THEIR WAYWARD SCHOOLMATE, HAVING REALIZED WHAT A SWEET SOUL HE WAS...

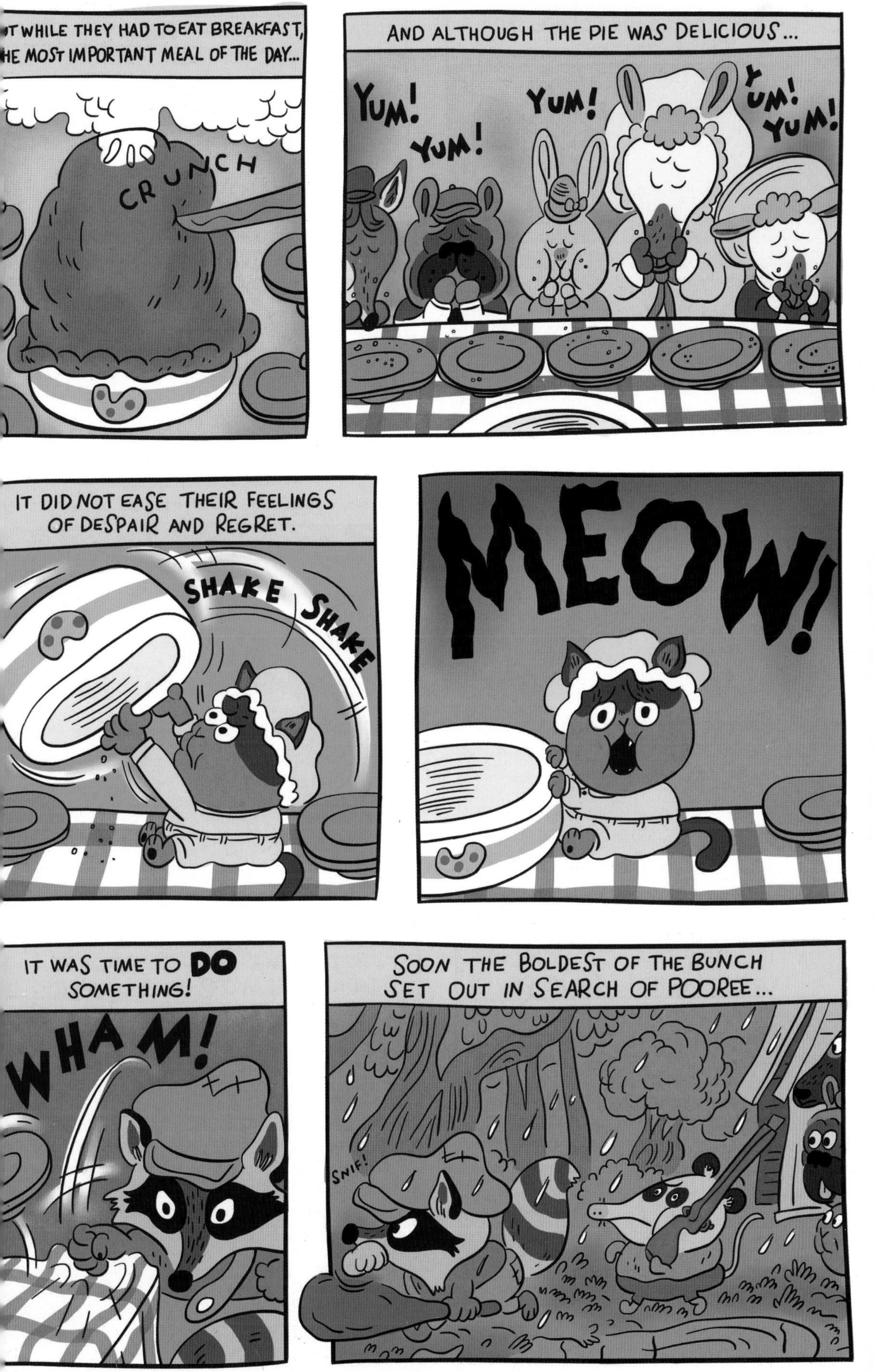

T WHILE THEY HAD TO EAT BREAKFAST,
HE MOST IMPORTANT MEAL OF THE DAY...
CRUNCH
AND ALTHOUGH THE PIE WAS DELICIOUS...
YUM!
YUM!
YUM!
YUM!
YUM!
IT DID NOT EASE THEIR FEELINGS OF DESPAIR AND REGRET.
SHAKE
SHAKE
MEOW!
IT WAS TIME TO DO SOMETHING!
WHAM!
SOON THE BOLDEST OF THE BUNCH SET OUT IN SEARCH OF POOREE...
SNIF!

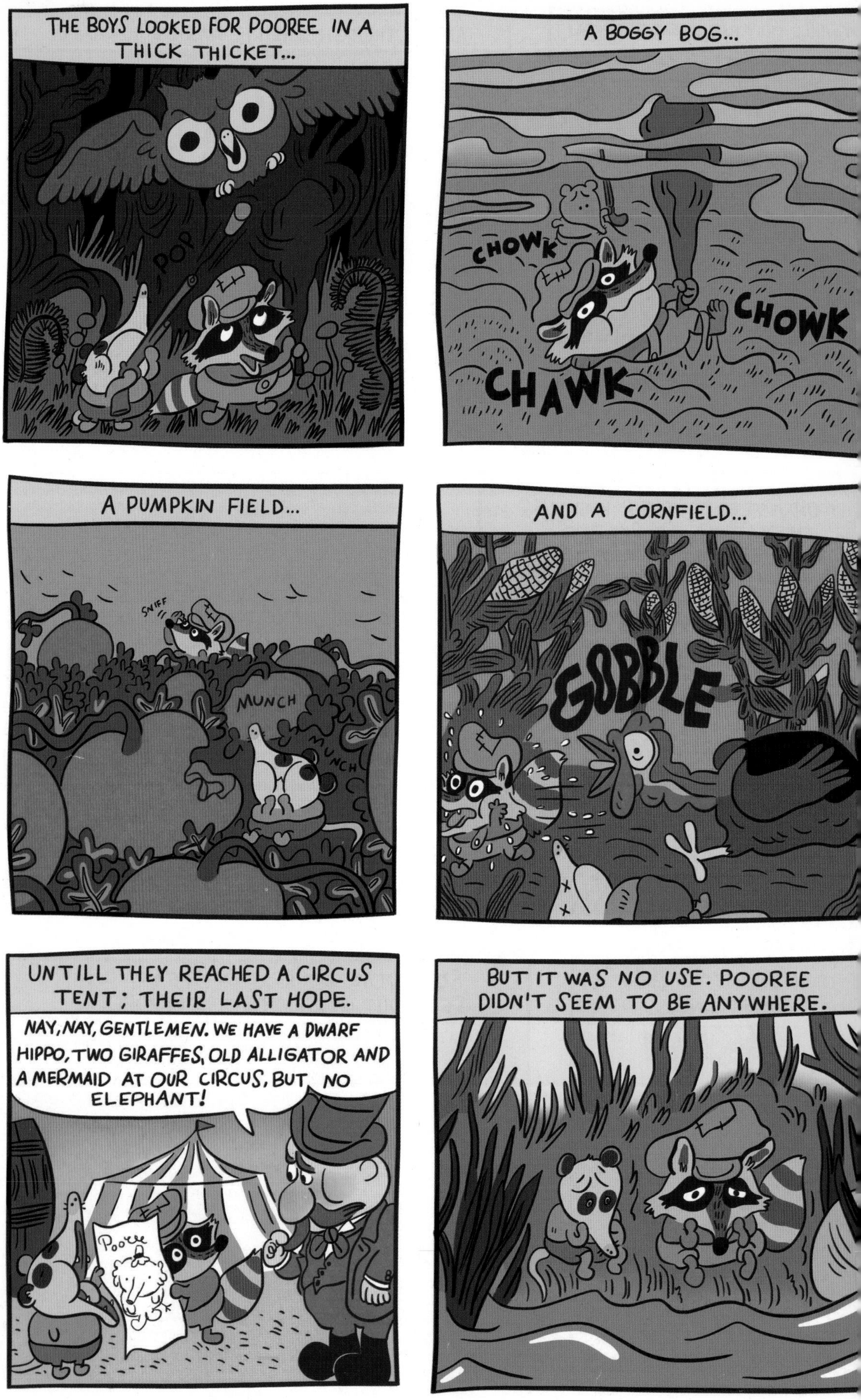
THE BOYS LOOKED FOR POOREE IN A THICK THICKET...
POP
A BOGGY BOG...
CHOWK
CHOWK
CHAWK
A PUMPKIN FIELD...
SNIFF
MUNCH
MUNCH
AND A CORNFIELD...
GOBBLE
UNTILL THEY REACHED A CIRCUS TENT; THEIR LAST HOPE.
NAY, NAY, GENTLEMEN. WE HAVE A DWARF HIPPO, TWO GIRAFFES, OLD ALLIGATOR AND A MERMAID AT OUR CIRCUS, BUT NO ELEPHANT!
Pooree
BUT IT WAS NO USE. POOREE DIDN'T SEEM TO BE ANYWHERE.

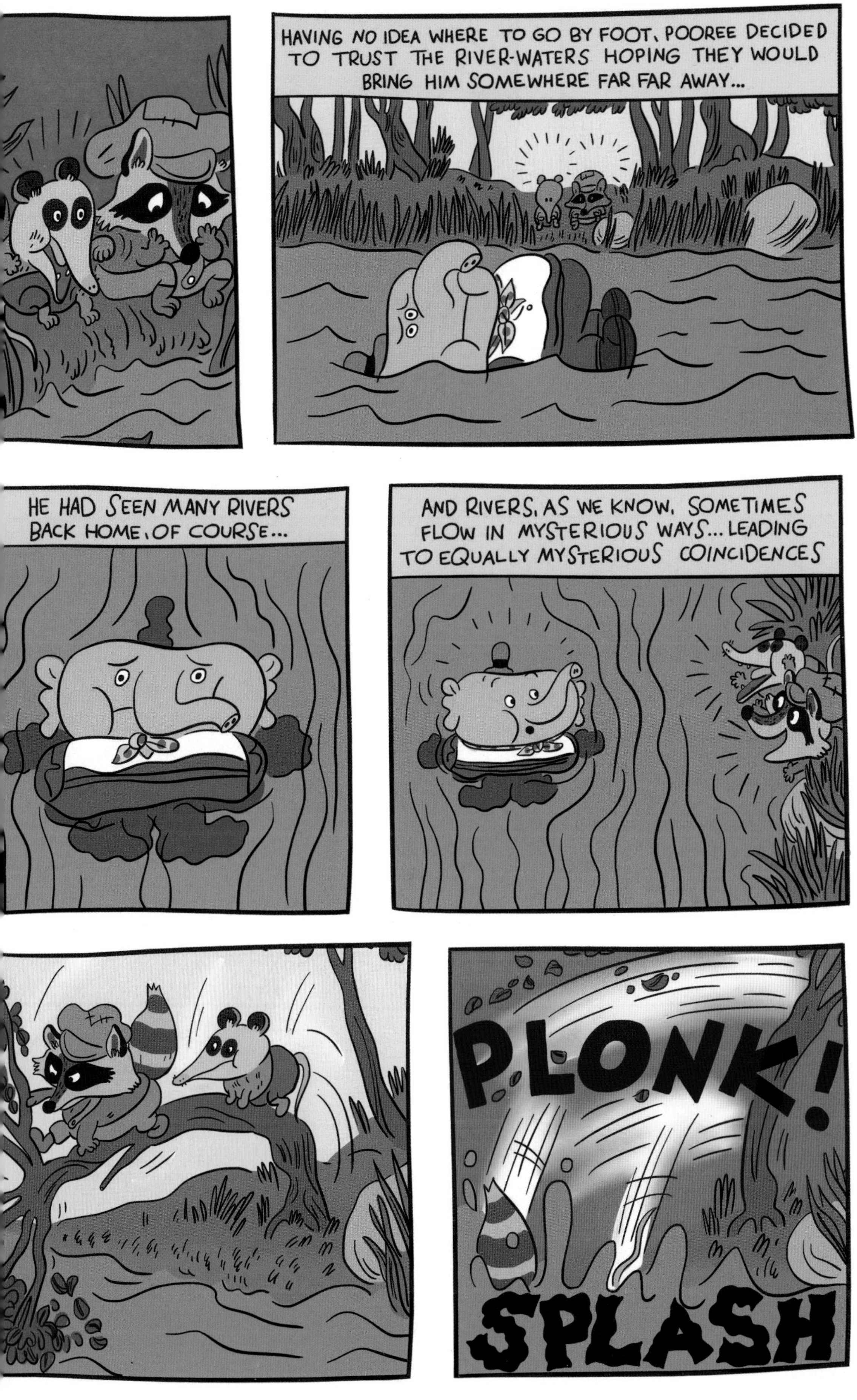
HAVING NO IDEA WHERE TO GO BY FOOT, POOREE DECIDED TO TRUST THE RIVER-WATERS HOPING THEY WOULD BRING HIM SOMEWHERE FAR FAR AWAY...
HE HAD SEEN MANY RIVERS BACK HOME, OF COURSE...
AND RIVERS, AS WE KNOW, SOMETIMES FLOW IN MYSTERIOUS WAYS... LEADING TO EQUALLY MYSTERIOUS COINCIDENCES
PLONK!
SPLASH

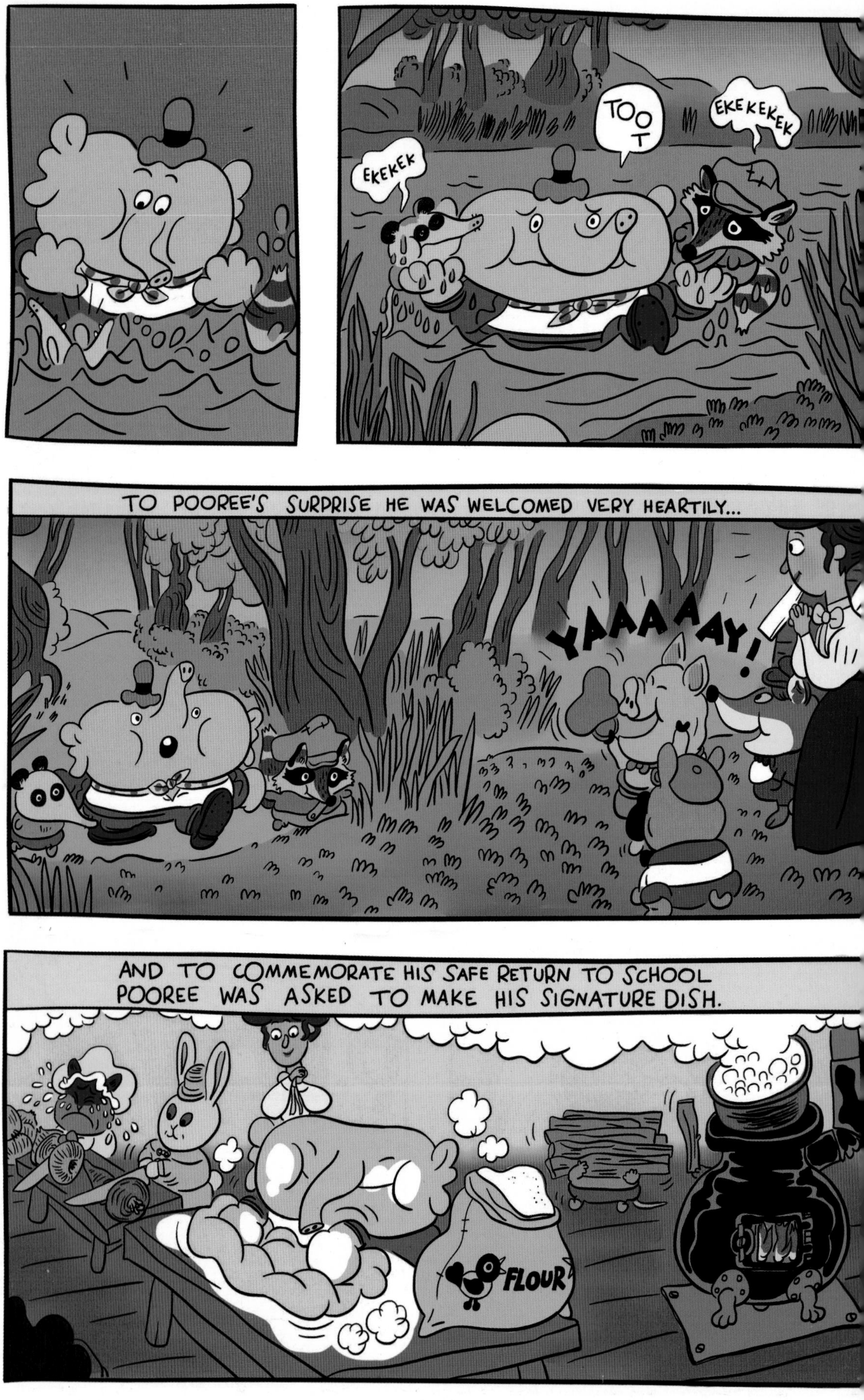
TOOT
EKEKEKEKEK
EKEKEK
TO POOREE'S SURPRISE HE WAS WELCOMED VERY HEARTILY...
YAAAAAY!
AND TO COMMEMORATE HIS SAFE RETURN TO SCHOOL POOREE WAS ASKED TO MAKE HIS SIGNATURE DISH.
FLOUR

AND **THAT** CURRY-PIE WAS EVEN BIGGER AND TASTIER THAN THE FIRST BECAUSE IT WASN'T BITTERED BY SHAME AND REGRETS... BUT INSTEAD SAVORED WITH FORGIVENESS AND FRIENDSHIP

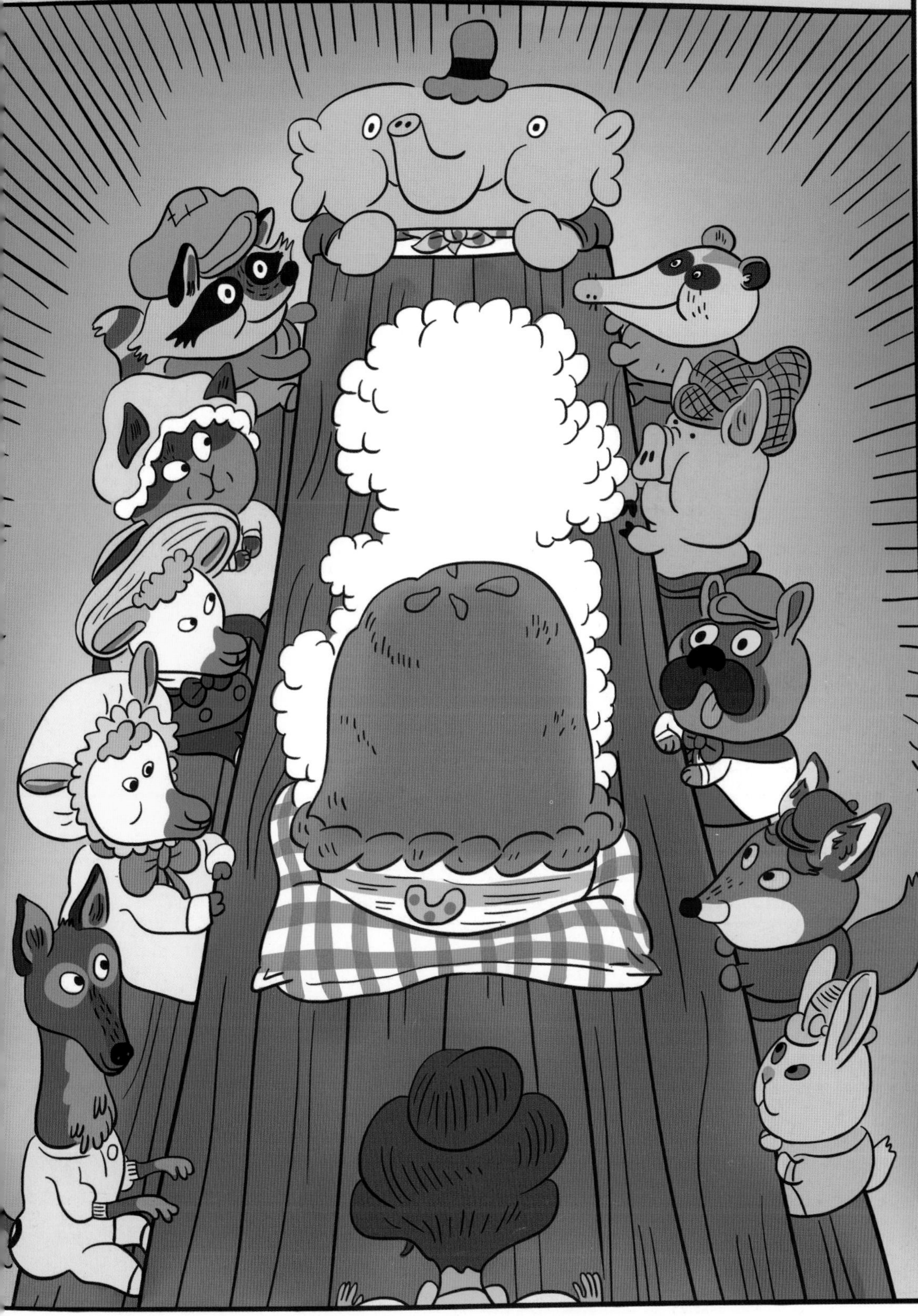

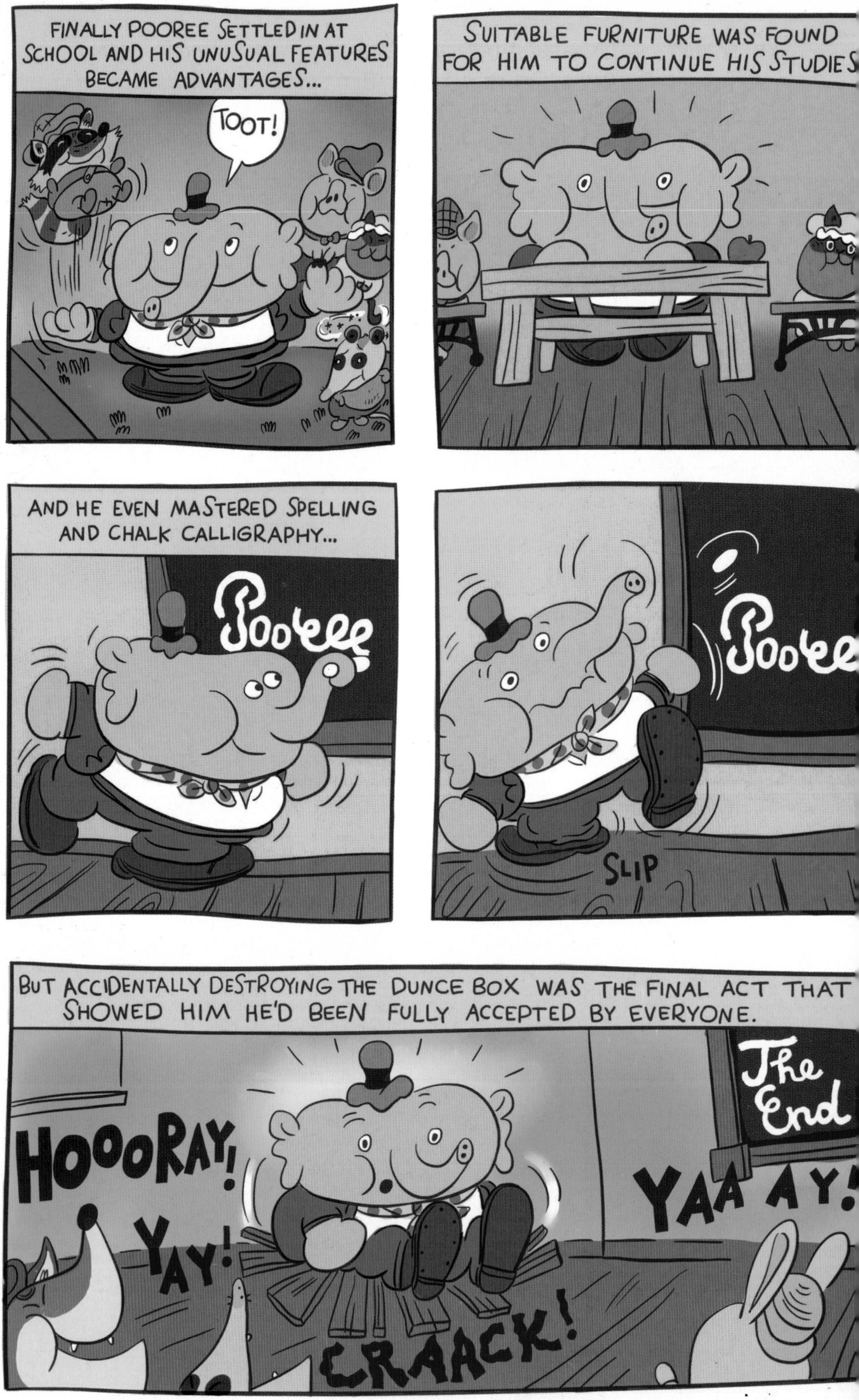
FINALLY POOREE SETTLED IN AT SCHOOL AND HIS UNUSUAL FEATURES BECAME ADVANTAGES...
TOOT!
SUITABLE FURNITURE WAS FOUND FOR HIM TO CONTINUE HIS STUDIES
AND HE EVEN MASTERED SPELLING AND CHALK CALLIGRAPHY...
Pooree
Pooree
SLIP
BUT ACCIDENTALLY DESTROYING THE DUNCE BOX WAS THE FINAL ACT THAT SHOWED HIM HE'D BEEN FULLY ACCEPTED BY EVERYONE.
HOOORAY!
YAY!
The End
YAA AY!
CRAACK!

THE RAFT

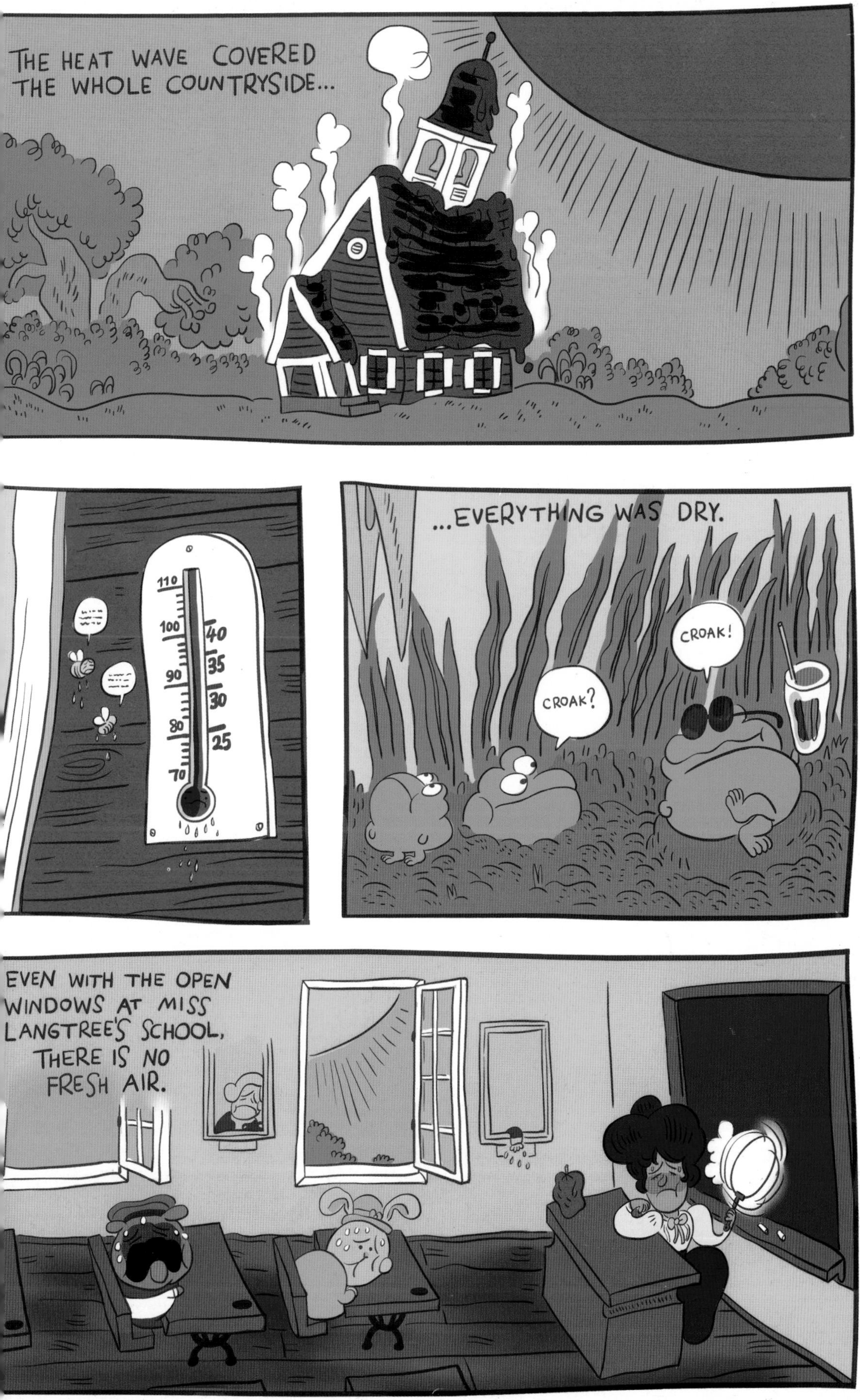
THE HEAT WAVE COVERED THE WHOLE COUNTRYSIDE...
110
100
40
35
90
30
80
25
70
...EVERYTHING WAS DRY.
CROAK!
CROAK?
EVEN WITH THE OPEN WINDOWS AT MISS LANGTREE'S SCHOOL, THERE IS NO FRESH AIR.

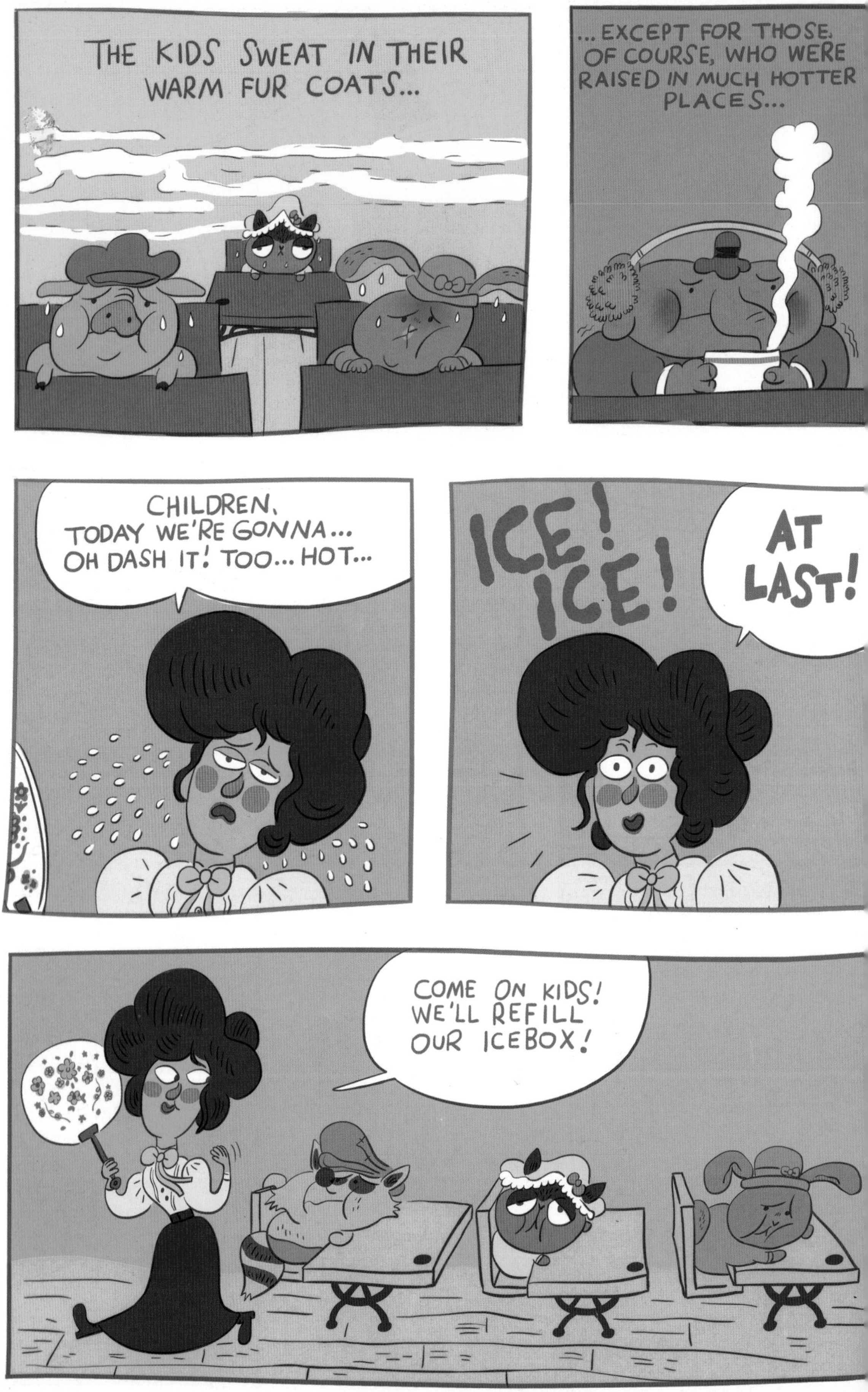
THE KIDS SWEAT IN THEIR WARM FUR COATS...
...EXCEPT FOR THOSE, OF COURSE, WHO WERE RAISED IN MUCH HOTTER PLACES...
CHILDREN, TODAY WE'RE GONNA... OH DASH IT! TOO... HOT...
ICE! ICE!
AT LAST!
COME ON KIDS! WE'LL REFILL OUR ICEBOX!

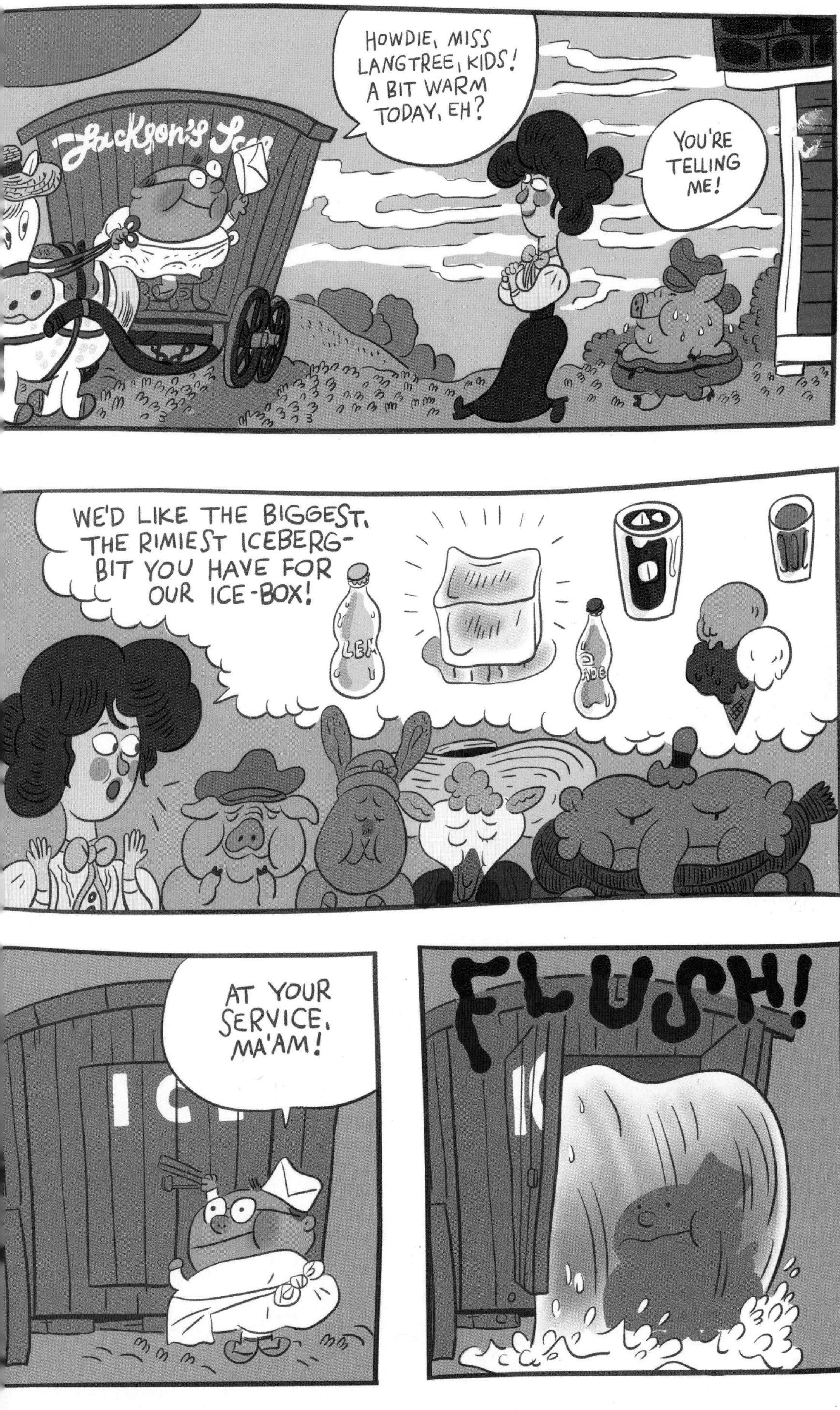
HOWDIE, MISS LANGTREE, KIDS! A BIT WARM TODAY, EH?
YOU'RE TELLING ME!
WE'D LIKE THE BIGGEST, THE RIMIEST ICEBERG-BIT YOU HAVE FOR OUR ICE-BOX!
AT YOUR SERVICE, MA'AM!
FLUSH!

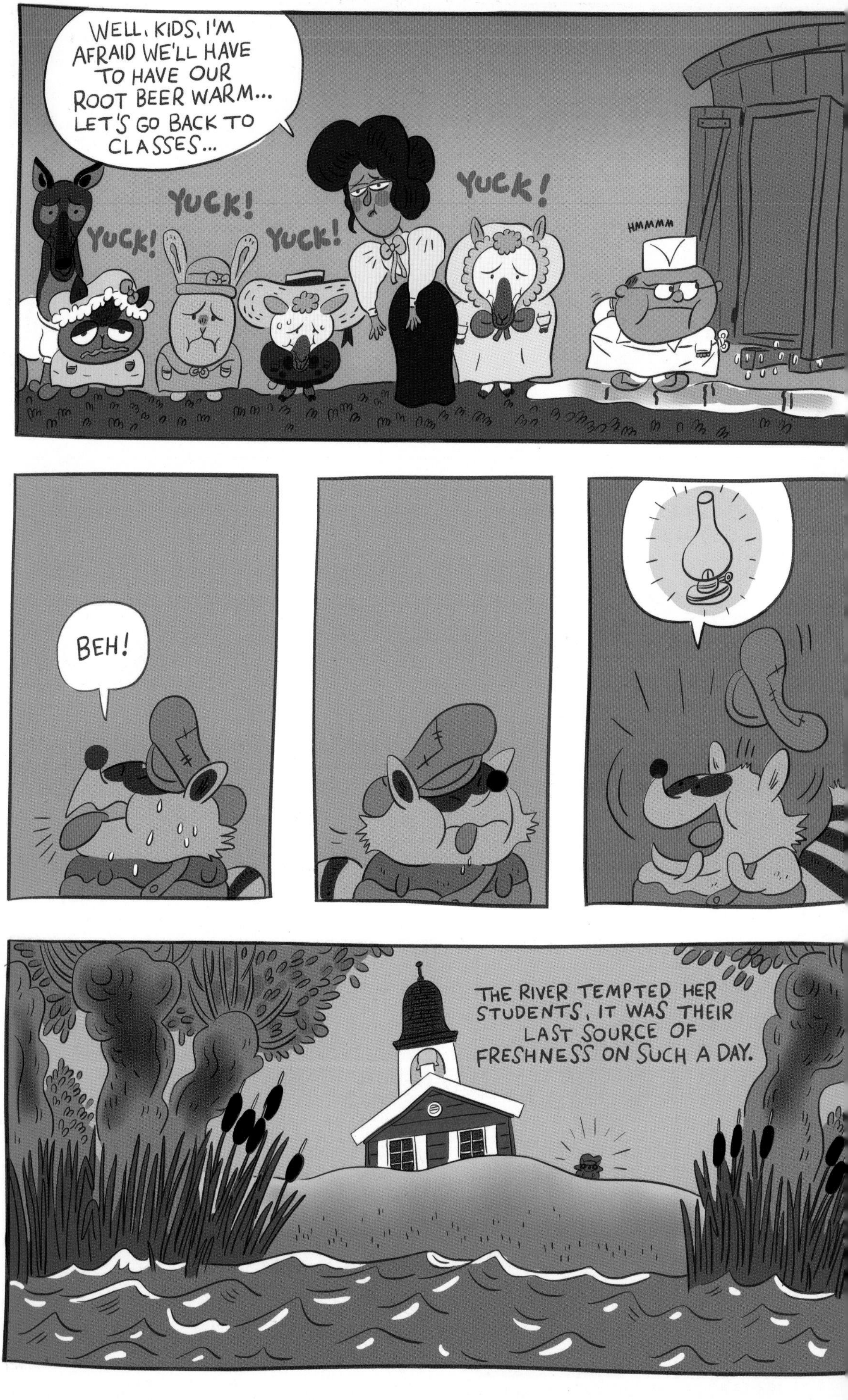
WELL, KIDS, I'M AFRAID WE'LL HAVE TO HAVE OUR ROOT BEER WARM... LET'S GO BACK TO CLASSES...
YUCK!
YUCK!
YUCK!
YUCK!
HMMMM
BEH!
THE RIVER TEMPTED HER STUDENTS, IT WAS THEIR LAST SOURCE OF FRESHNESS ON SUCH A DAY.

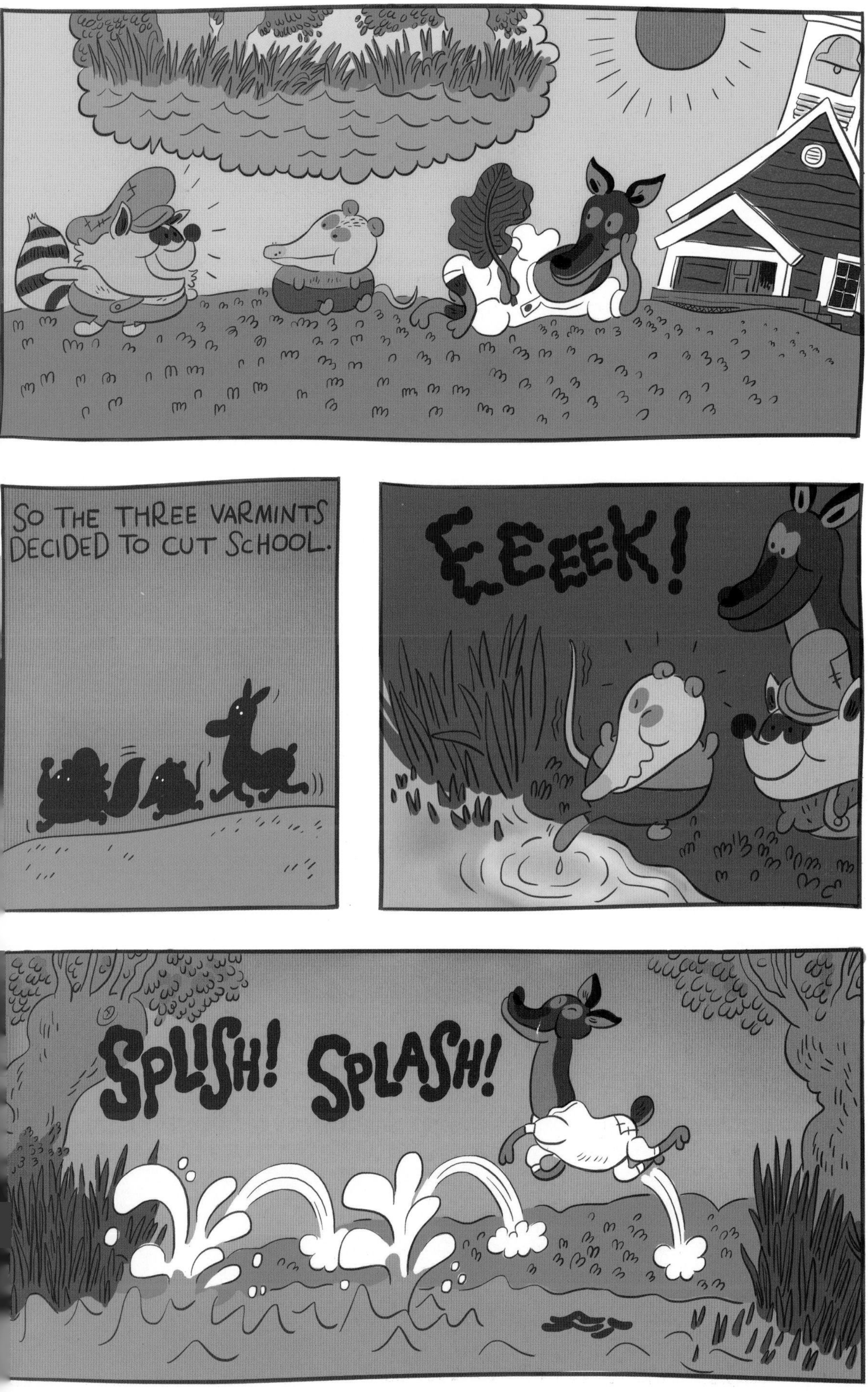
SO THE THREE VARMINTS DECIDED TO CUT SCHOOL.
EEEEK!
SPLISH! SPLASH!

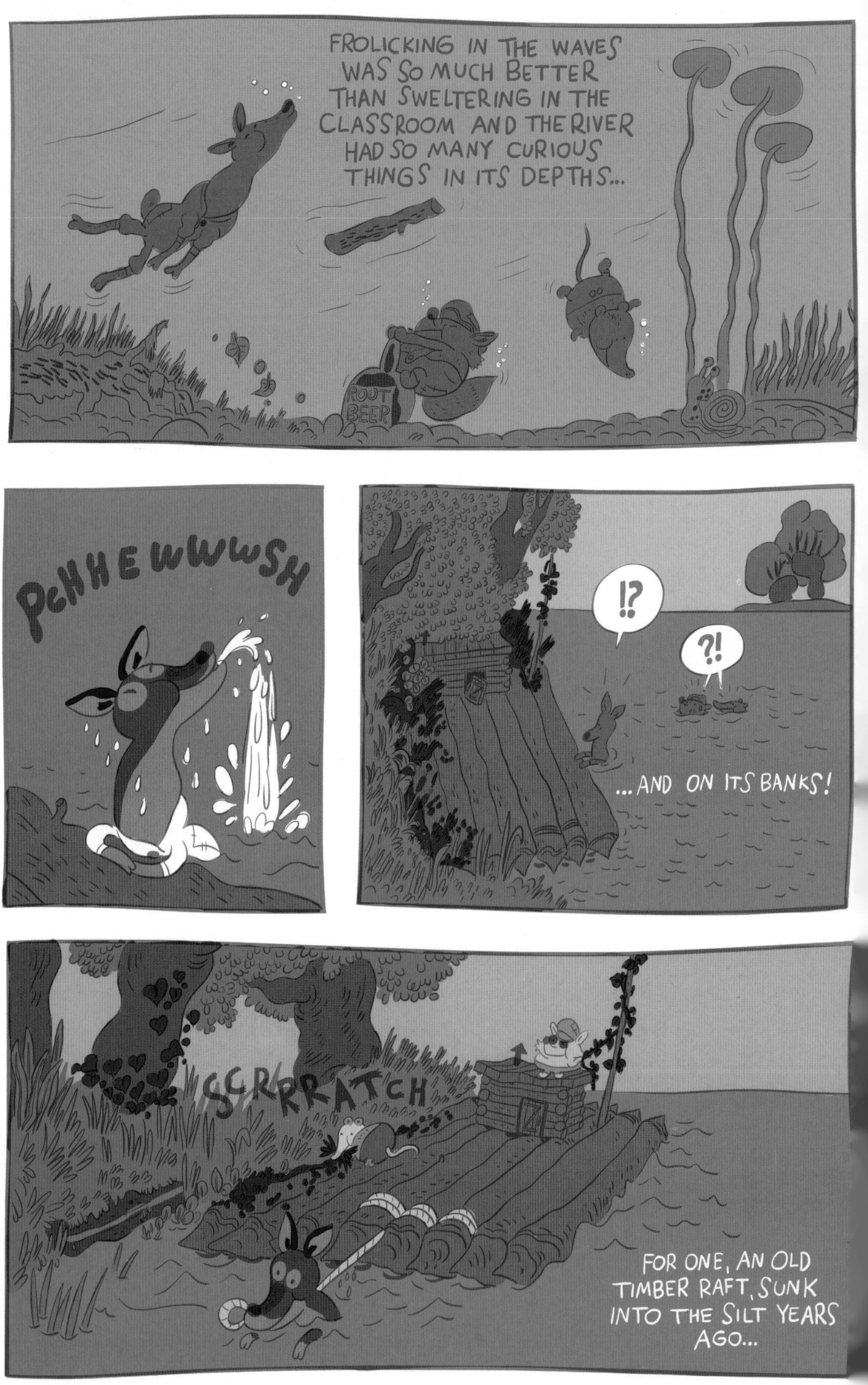
FROLICKING IN THE WAVES WAS SO MUCH BETTER THAN SWELTERING IN THE CLASSROOM AND THE RIVER HAD SO MANY CURIOUS THINGS IN ITS DEPTHS...
ROOT BEER
PcHHEWWWSH
!?
?!
...AND ON ITS BANKS!
SCRRRATCH
FOR ONE, AN OLD TIMBER RAFT, SUNK INTO THE SILT YEARS AGO...

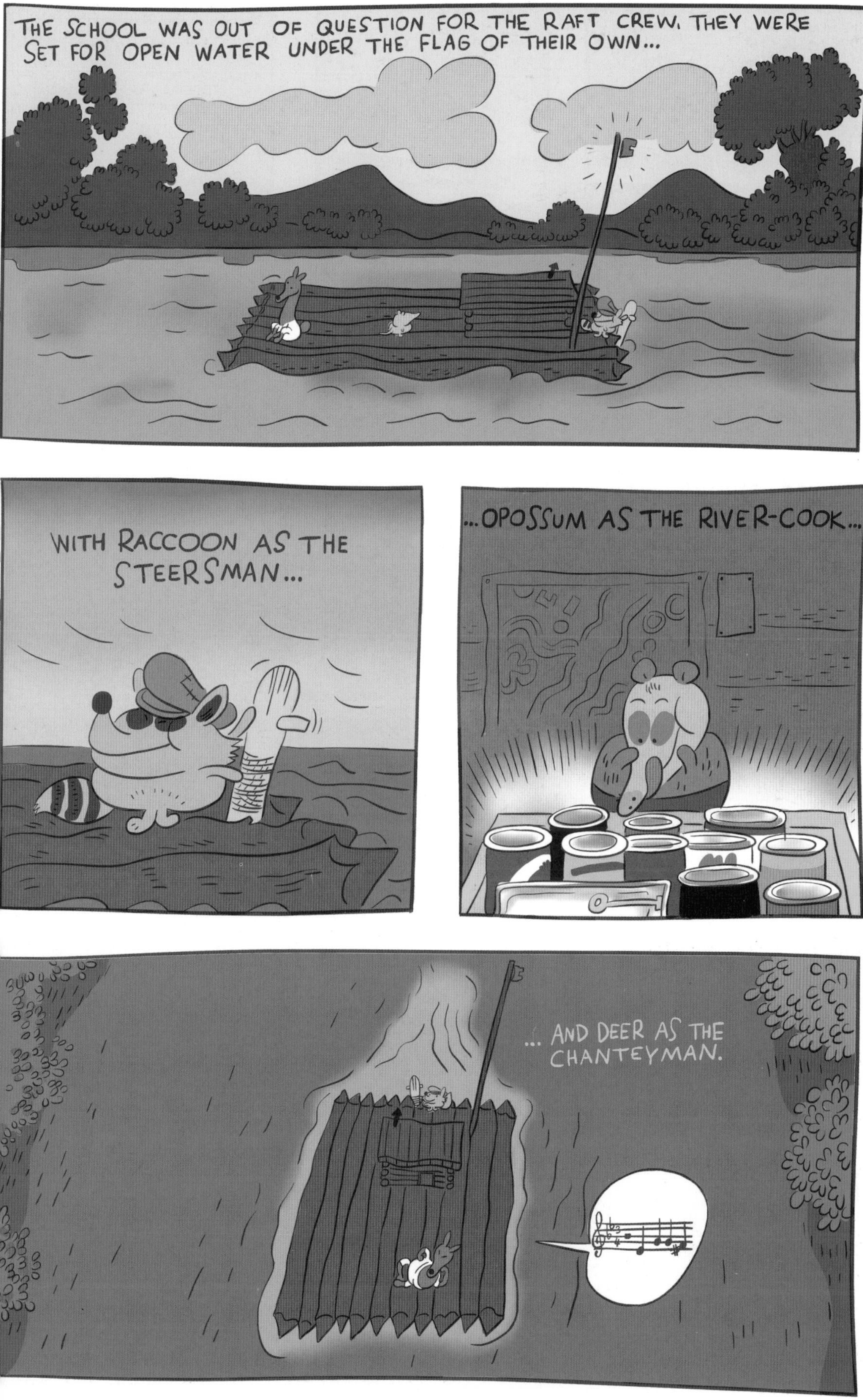
THE SCHOOL WAS OUT OF QUESTION FOR THE RAFT CREW. THEY WERE SET FOR OPEN WATER UNDER THE FLAG OF THEIR OWN...
WITH RACCOON AS THE STEERSMAN...
...OPOSSUM AS THE RIVER-COOK...
... AND DEER AS THE CHANTEYMAN.

THE FOG IS VERY THICK BY THE WATER.

IT FALLS VERY QUICK...

... COVERING EVERYTHING...

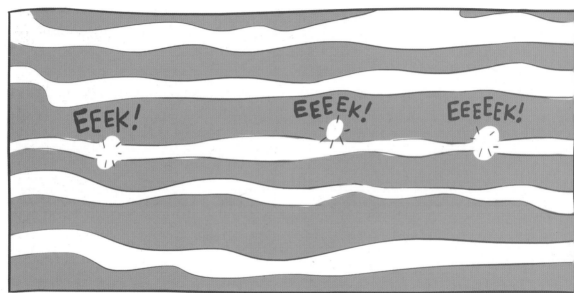

EEEK!

EEEEK!

EEEEEK!

THE MAIN THING NOW IS NOT TO FALL OVERBOARD.

HOOONK

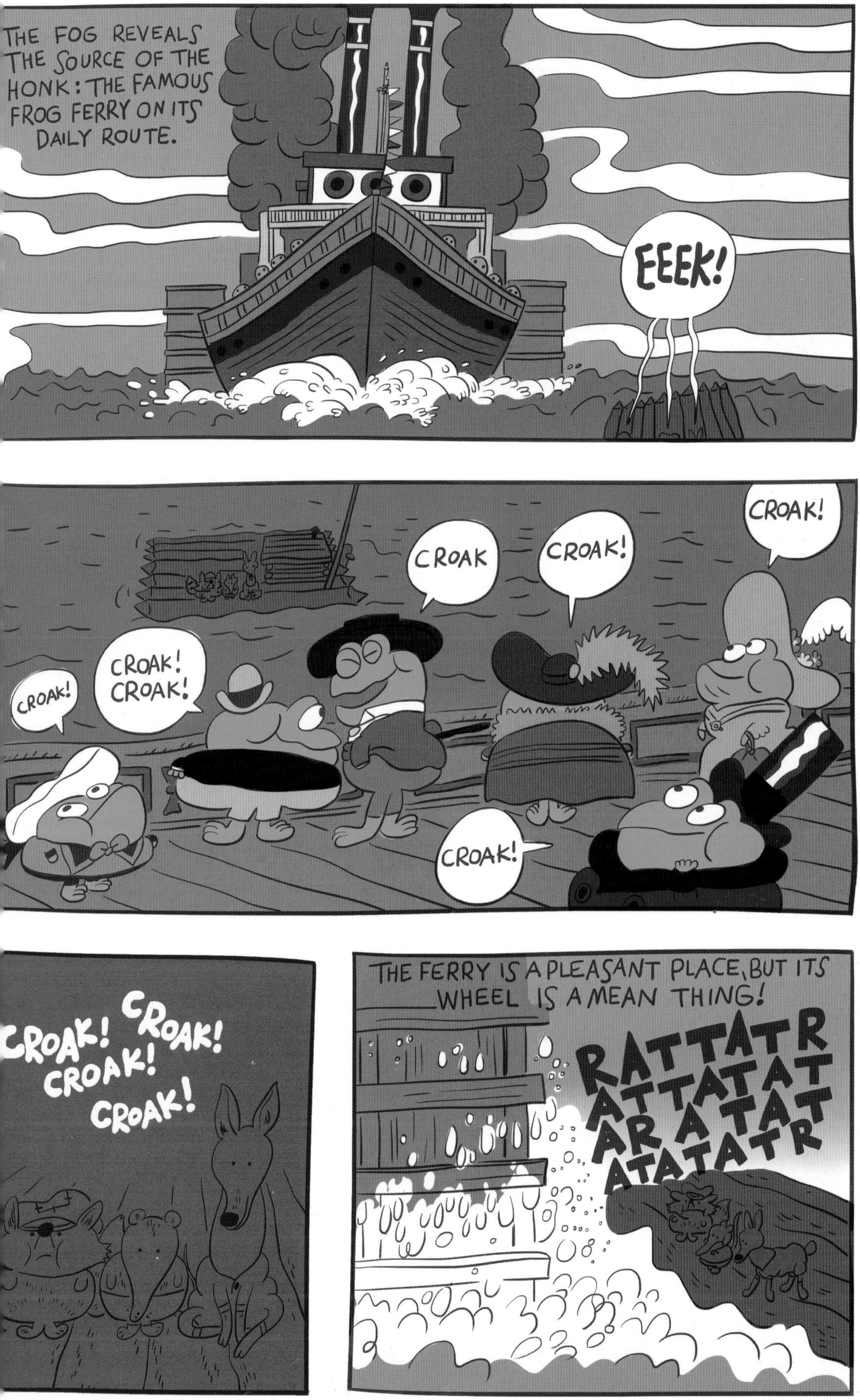
THE FOG REVEALS THE SOURCE OF THE HONK: THE FAMOUS FROG FERRY ON ITS DAILY ROUTE.
EEEK!
CROAK!
CROAK! CROAK!
CROAK
CROAK!
CROAK!
CROAK!
CROAK! CROAK! CROAK! CROAK!
THE FERRY IS A PLEASANT PLACE, BUT ITS WHEEL IS A MEAN THING!
RATTATR ATTATAT ARATAT ATATATR

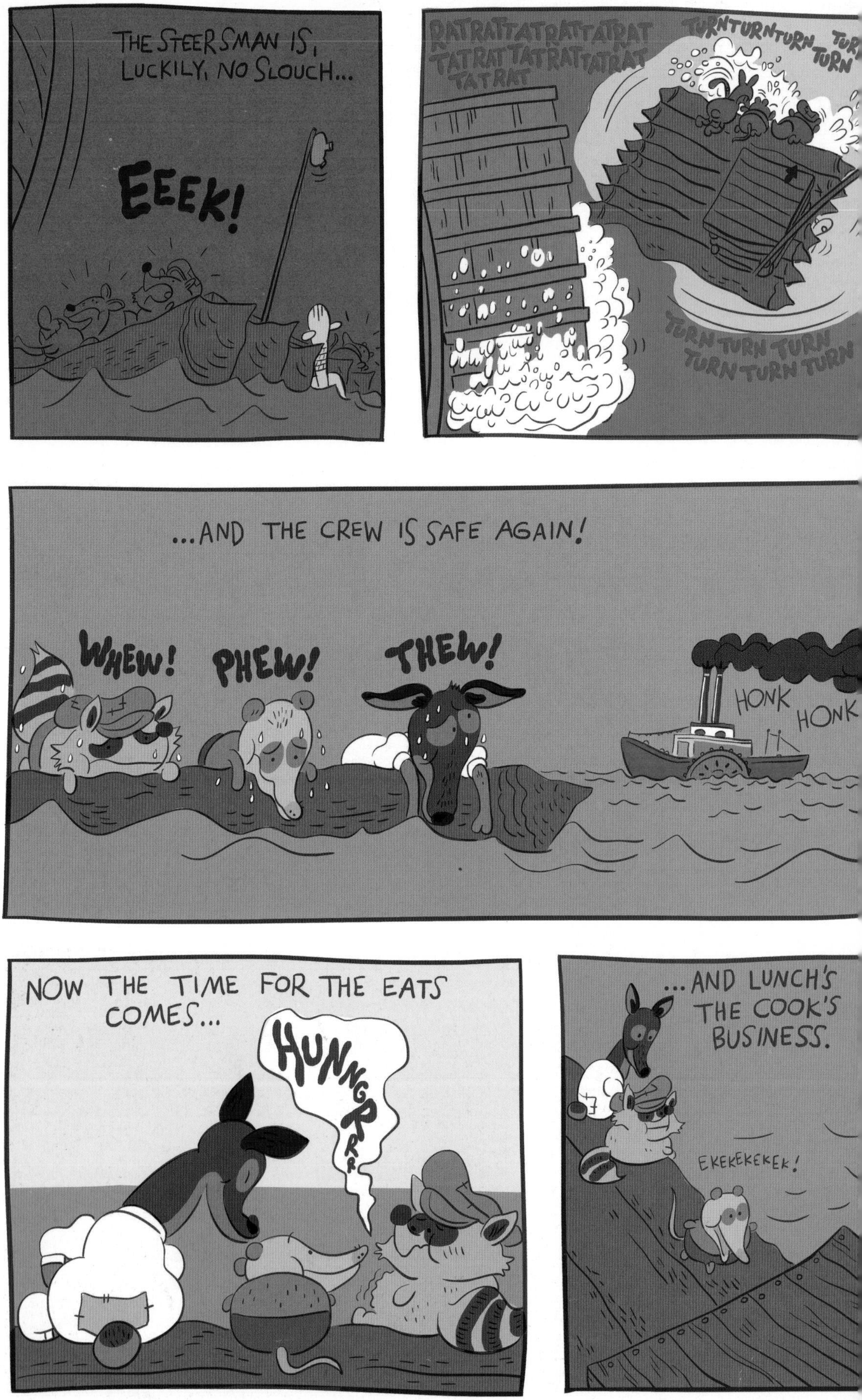
THE STEERSMAN IS, LUCKILY, NO SLOUCH...
EEEK!
RATRATTATRATTATRAT TATRATTATRATTATRAT TATRAT
TURNTURNTURNTURN TURN
TURN TURN TURN TURN TURN TURN
...AND THE CREW IS SAFE AGAIN!
WHEW!
PHEW!
THEW!
HONK HONK
NOW THE TIME FOR THE EATS COMES...
HUNNGRRR
...AND LUNCH'S THE COOK'S BUSINESS.
EKEKEKEKEK!

LUNCH ABOARD IS FRESH FISH RIGHT OUT OF THE WATER.

CAUGHT WITH A CAN OF SPAM.

CHPOCK

SWOOOOOOOOSH

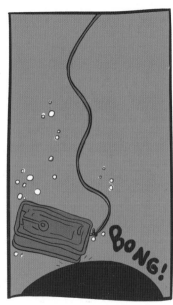

BONG!

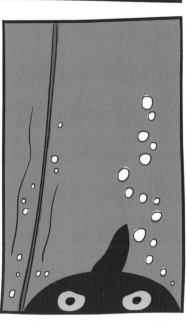

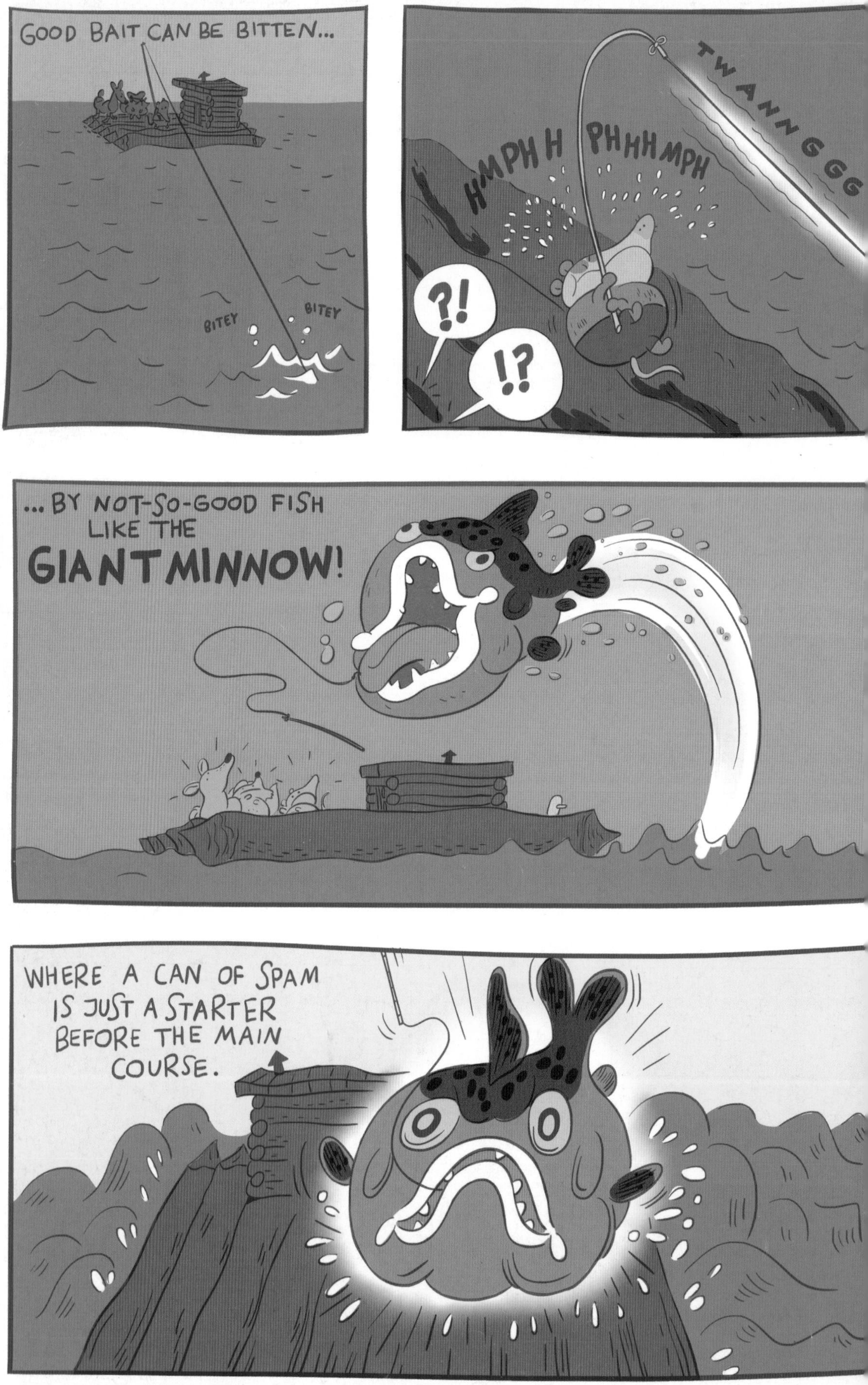
GOOD BAIT CAN BE BITTEN...
BITEY
BITEY
TWANNGGG
H'MPH H
PHHHMPH
?!
!?
... BY NOT-SO-GOOD FISH LIKE THE
GIANT MINNOW!
WHERE A CAN OF SPAM IS JUST A STARTER BEFORE THE MAIN COURSE.

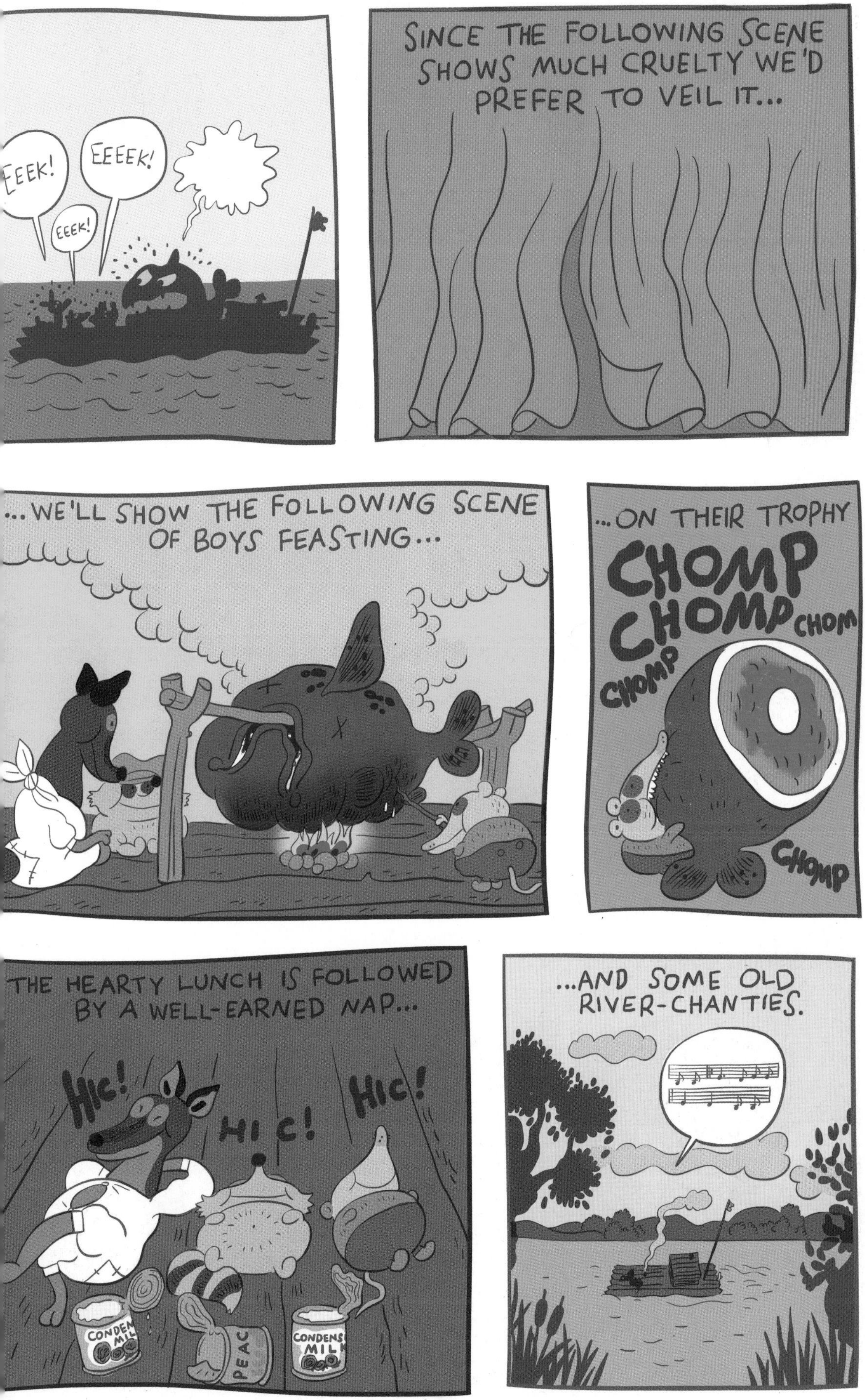
EEEK!
EEEK!
EEEEK!
SINCE THE FOLLOWING SCENE SHOWS MUCH CRUELTY WE'D PREFER TO VEIL IT...
...WE'LL SHOW THE FOLLOWING SCENE OF BOYS FEASTING...
...ON THEIR TROPHY
CHOMP
CHOMP
CHOM
CHOMP
CHOMP
THE HEARTY LUNCH IS FOLLOWED BY A WELL-EARNED NAP...
HIC!
HI C!
HIC!
CONDEN MIL
PEAC
CONDENS MILK
...AND SOME OLD RIVER-CHANTIES.

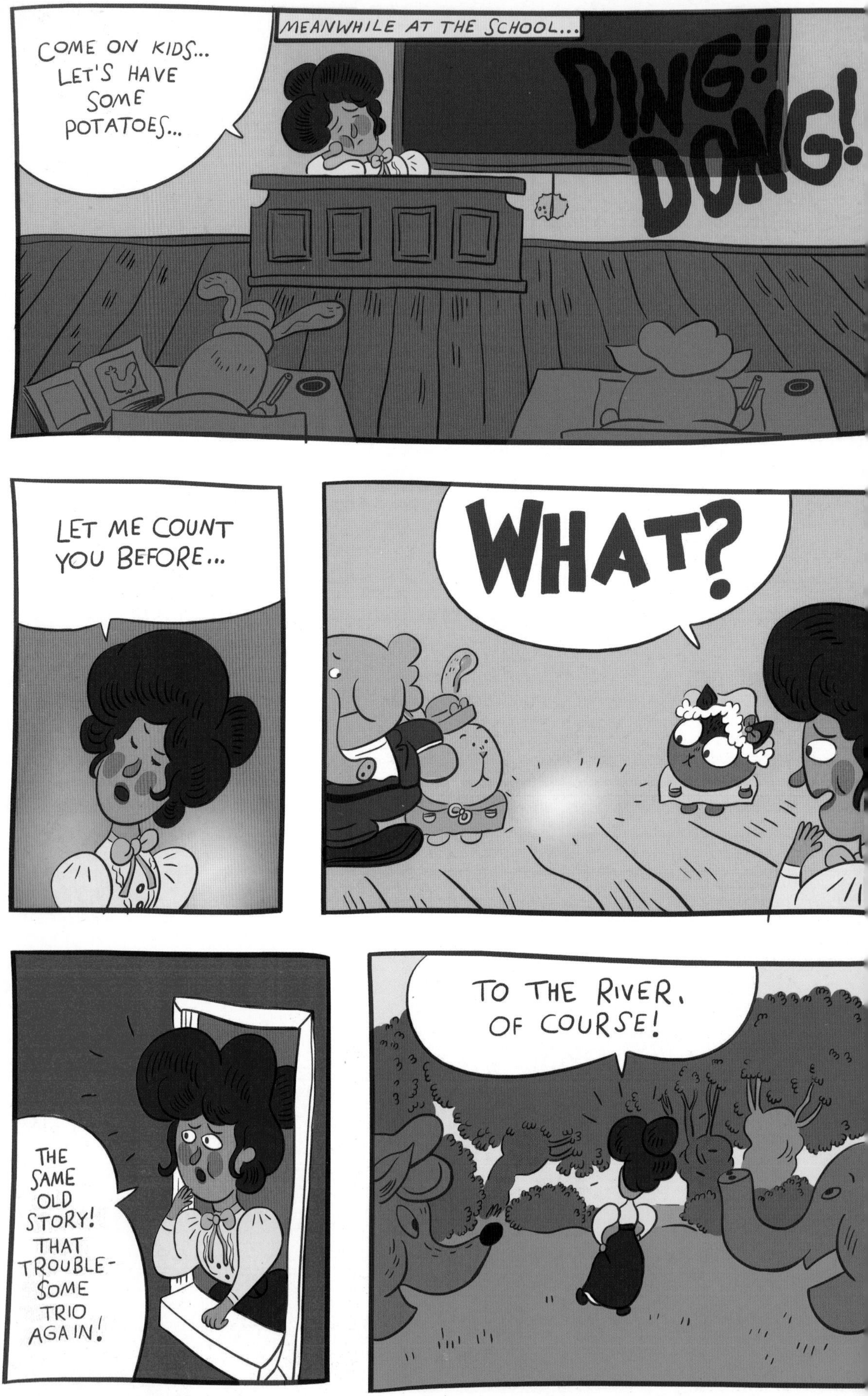
MEANWHILE AT THE SCHOOL...
COME ON KIDS... LET'S HAVE SOME POTATOES...
DING! DONG!
LET ME COUNT YOU BEFORE...
WHAT?
THE SAME OLD STORY! THAT TROUBLESOME TRIO AGAIN!
TO THE RIVER, OF COURSE!

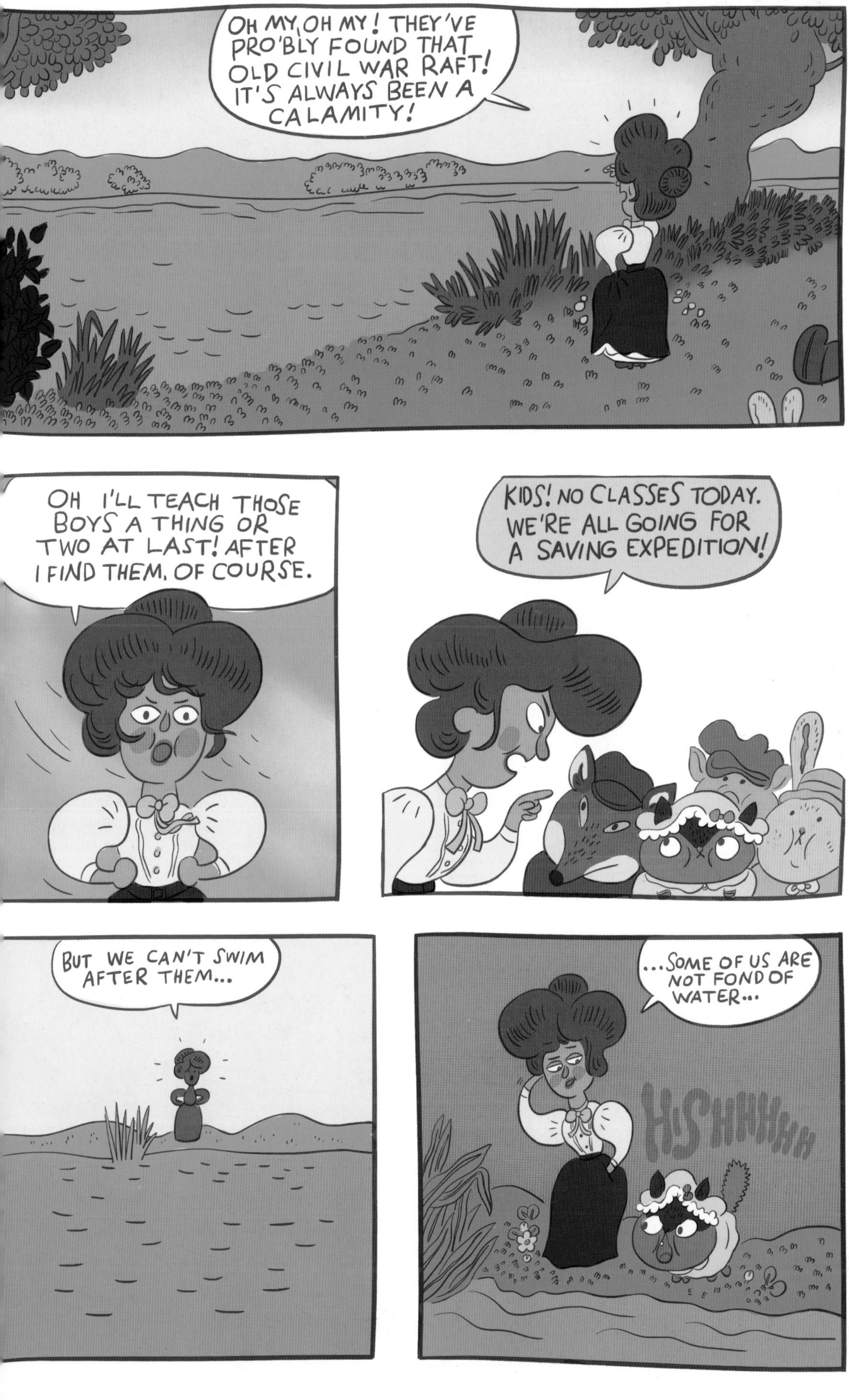
OH MY, OH MY! THEY'VE PRO'BLY FOUND THAT OLD CIVIL WAR RAFT! IT'S ALWAYS BEEN A CALAMITY!
OH I'LL TEACH THOSE BOYS A THING OR TWO AT LAST! AFTER I FIND THEM, OF COURSE.
KIDS! NO CLASSES TODAY. WE'RE ALL GOING FOR A SAVING EXPEDITION!
BUT WE CAN'T SWIM AFTER THEM...
...SOME OF US ARE NOT FOND OF WATER...
HSHHHHH

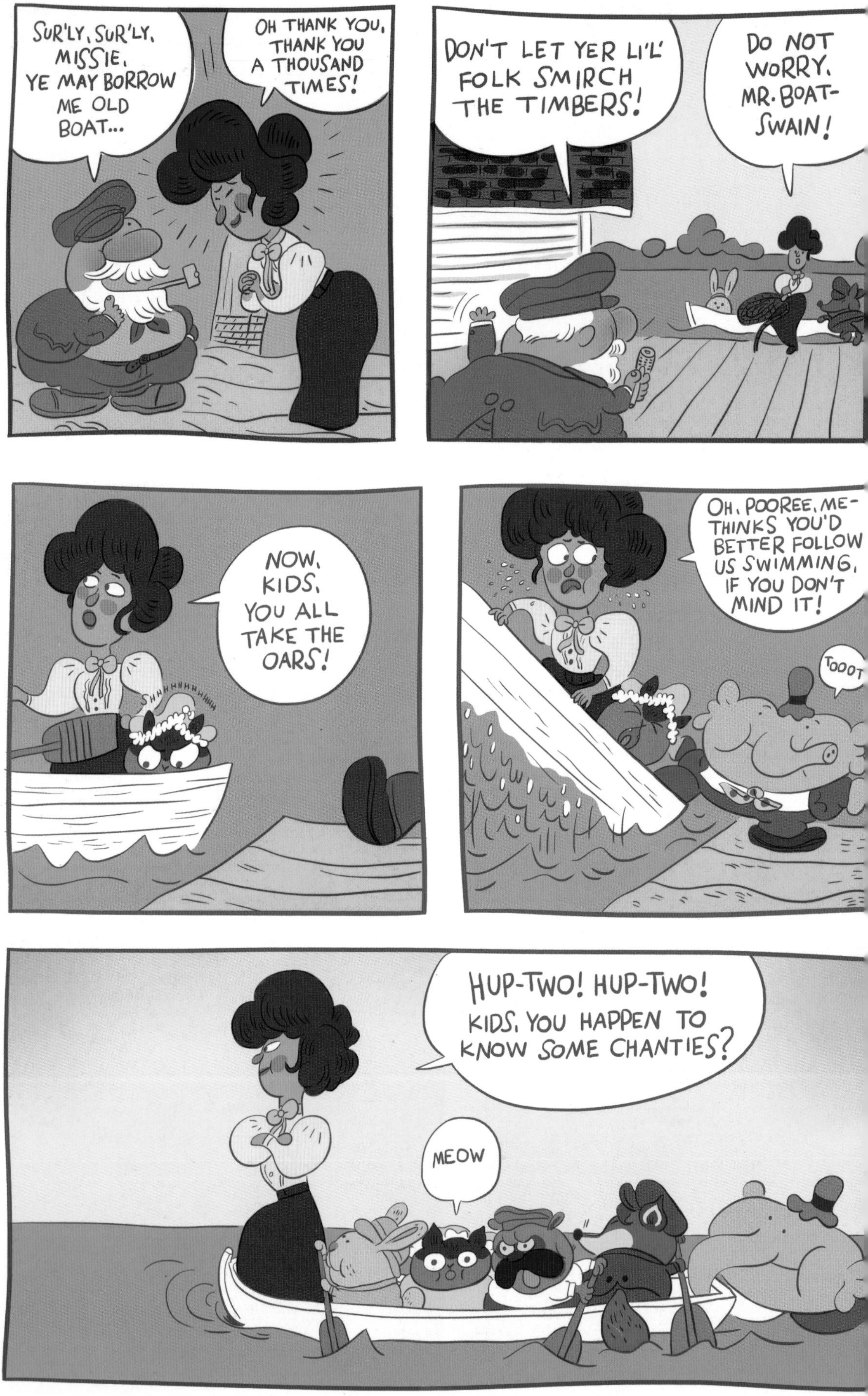
SUR'LY, SUR'LY, MISSIE, YE MAY BORROW ME OLD BOAT...
OH THANK YOU, THANK YOU A THOUSAND TIMES!
DON'T LET YER LI'L' FOLK SMIRCH THE TIMBERS!
DO NOT WORRY, MR. BOAT-SWAIN!
NOW, KIDS, YOU ALL TAKE THE OARS!
SHHHHHHHHHHH
OH, POOREE, ME-THINKS YOU'D BETTER FOLLOW US SWIMMING, IF YOU DON'T MIND IT!
TOOOT
HUP-TWO! HUP-TWO! KIDS, YOU HAPPEN TO KNOW SOME CHANTIES?
MEOW

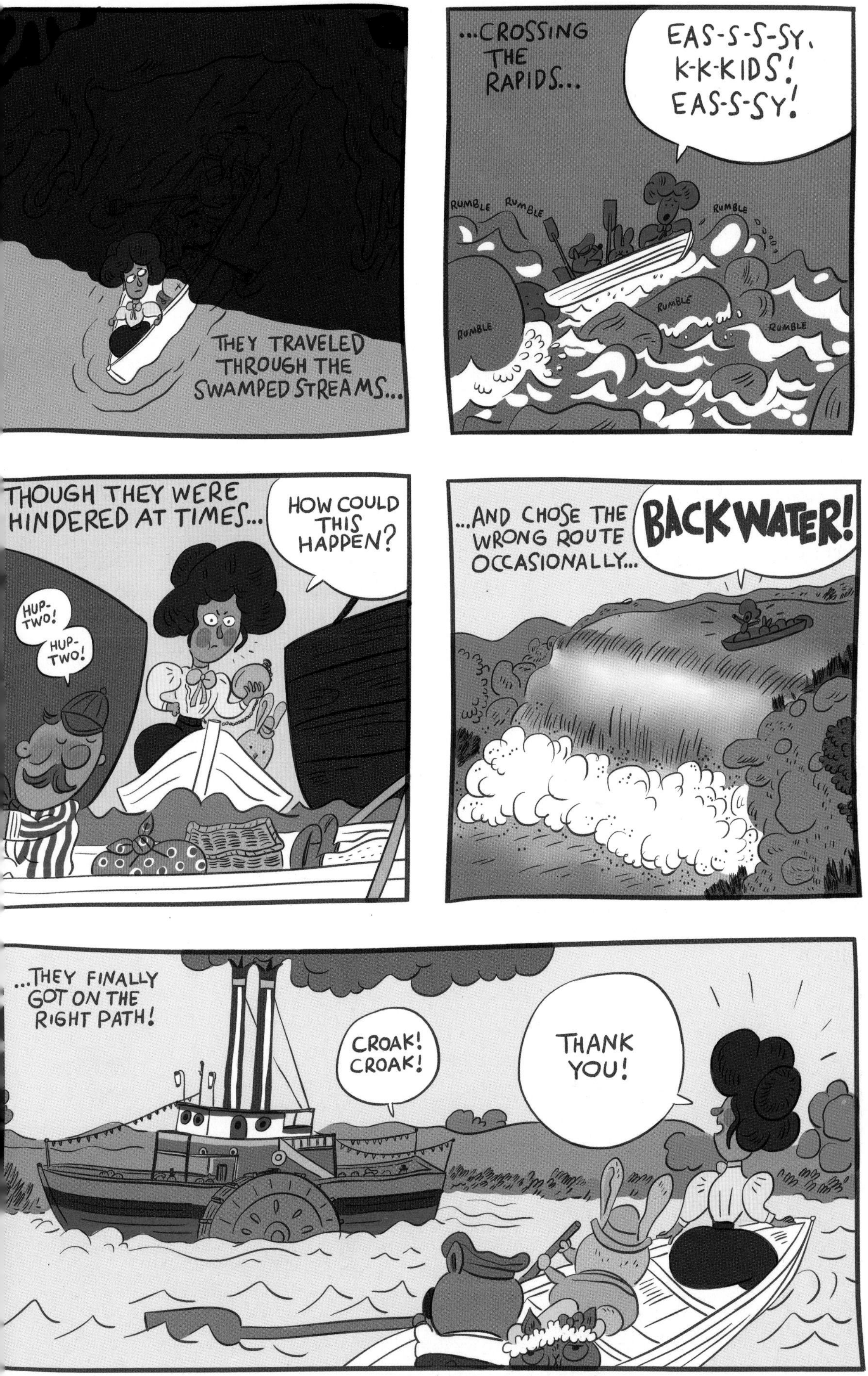
THEY TRAVELED THROUGH THE SWAMPED STREAMS...
...CROSSING THE RAPIDS...
EAS-S-S-SY, K-K-KIDS! EAS-S-SY!
RUMBLE
RUMBLE
RUMBLE
RUMBLE
RUMBLE
RUMBLE
THOUGH THEY WERE HINDERED AT TIMES...
HOW COULD THIS HAPPEN?
HUP-TWO!
HUP-TWO!
...AND CHOSE THE WRONG ROUTE OCCASIONALLY...
BACKWATER!
...THEY FINALLY GOT ON THE RIGHT PATH!
CROAK! CROAK!
THANK YOU!

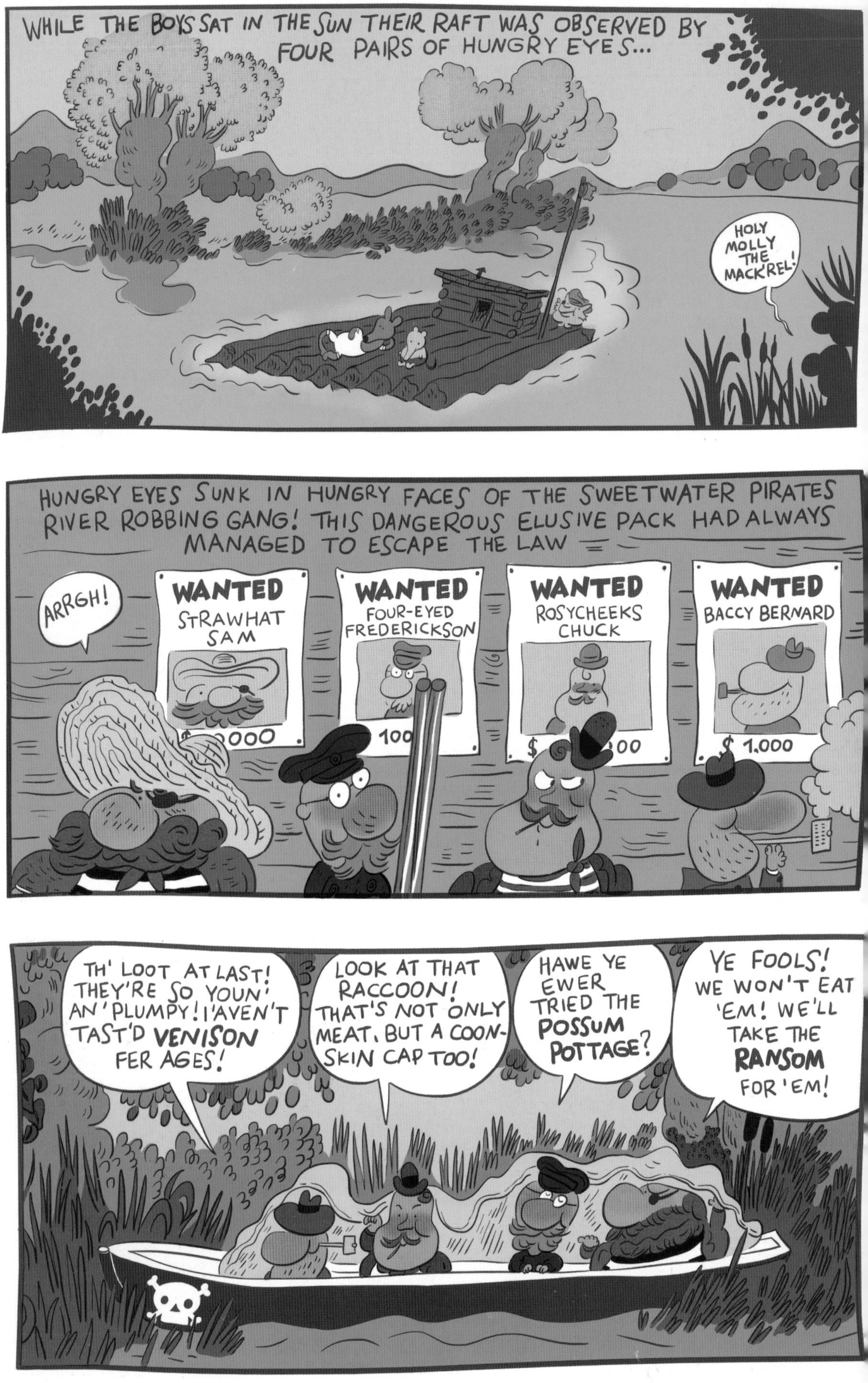
WHILE THE BOYS SAT IN THE SUN THEIR RAFT WAS OBSERVED BY FOUR PAIRS OF HUNGRY EYES...
HOLY MOLLY THE MACK'REL!
HUNGRY EYES SUNK IN HUNGRY FACES OF THE SWEETWATER PIRATES RIVER ROBBING GANG! THIS DANGEROUS ELUSIVE PACK HAD ALWAYS MANAGED TO ESCAPE THE LAW
ARRGH!
WANTED STRAWHAT SAM
WANTED FOUR-EYED FREDERICKSON
WANTED ROSYCHEEKS CHUCK
WANTED BACCY BERNARD
$ 1,000
TH' LOOT AT LAST! THEY'RE SO YOUN' AN' PLUMPY! I'AVEN'T TAST'D VENISON FER AGES!
LOOK AT THAT RACCOON! THAT'S NOT ONLY MEAT, BUT A COON-SKIN CAP TOO!
HAWE YE EWER TRIED THE POSSUM POTTAGE?
YE FOOLS! WE WON'T EAT 'EM! WE'LL TAKE THE RANSOM FOR 'EM!

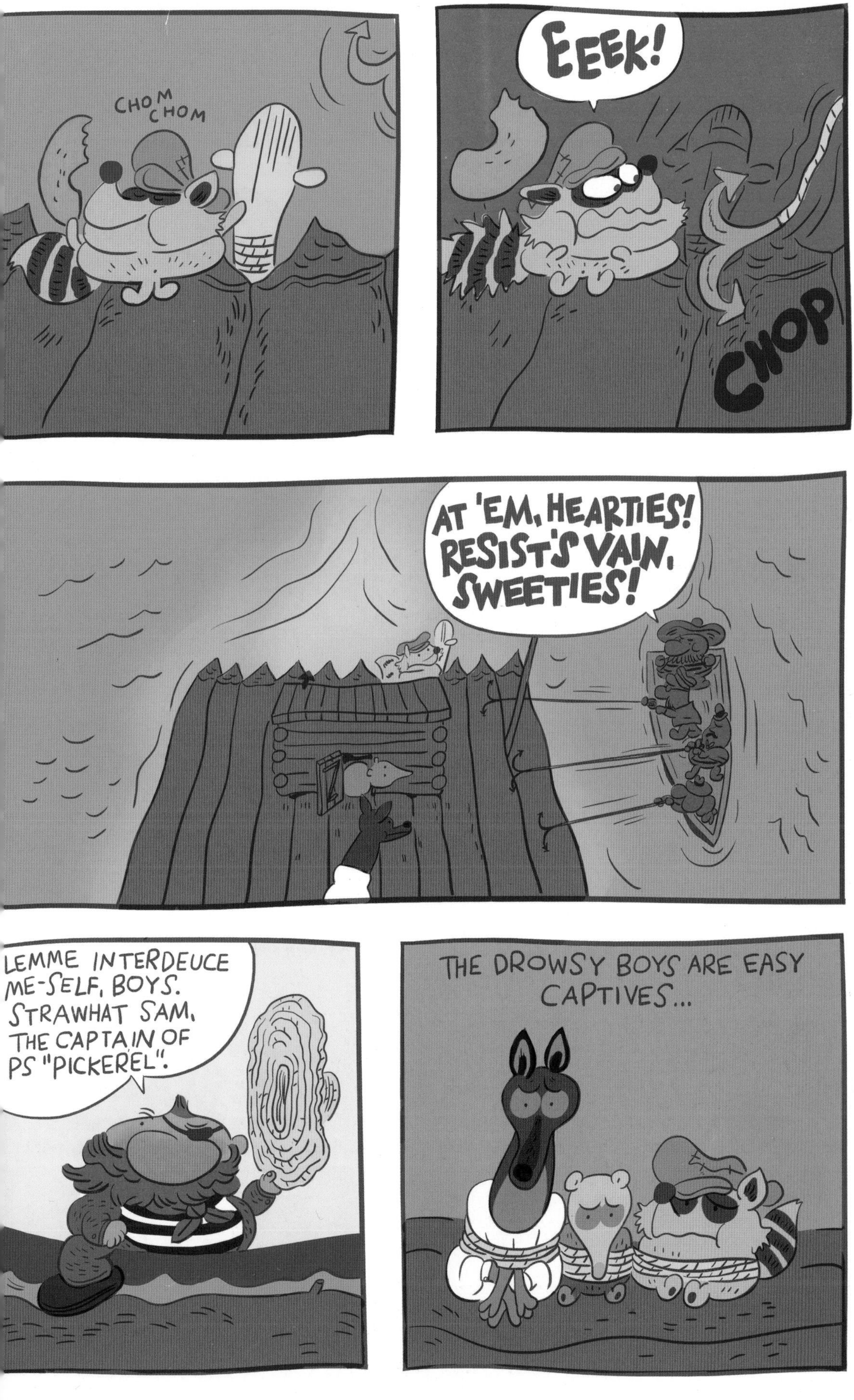
CHOM CHOM
EEEK!
CHOP
AT 'EM, HEARTIES! RESIST'S VAIN, SWEETIES!
LEMME INTERDEUCE ME-SELF, BOYS. STRAWHAT SAM, THE CAPTAIN OF PS "PICKEREL".
THE DROWSY BOYS ARE EASY CAPTIVES...

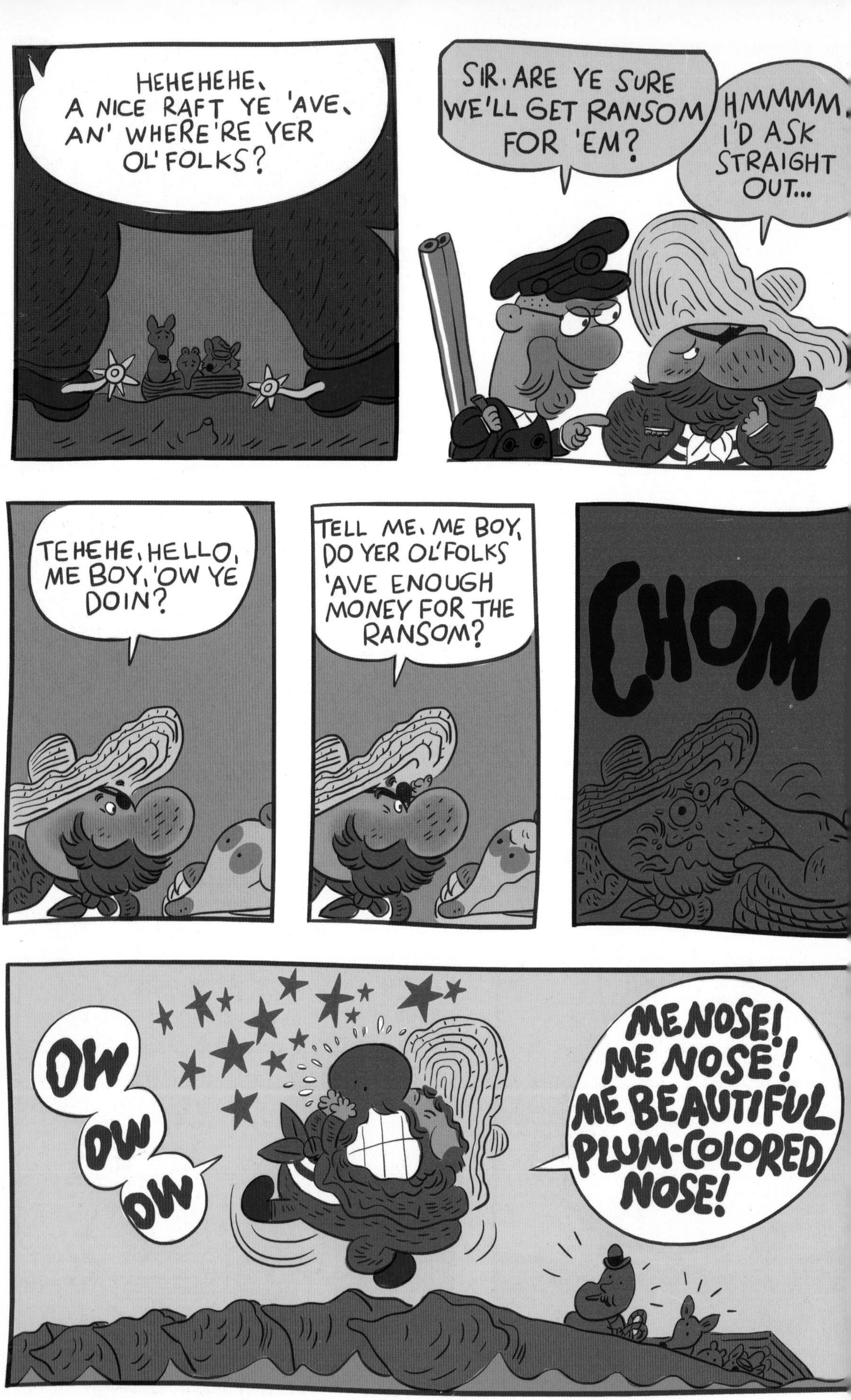
HEHEHEHE, A NICE RAFT YE 'AVE, AN' WHERE'RE YER OL' FOLKS?
SIR, ARE YE SURE WE'LL GET RANSOM FOR 'EM?
HMMMM, I'D ASK STRAIGHT OUT...
TEHEHE, HELLO, ME BOY, 'OW YE DOIN?
TELL ME, ME BOY, DO YER OL' FOLKS 'AVE ENOUGH MONEY FOR THE RANSOM?
CHOM
OW
OW
OW
ME NOSE! ME NOSE! ME BEAUTIFUL PLUM-COLORED NOSE!

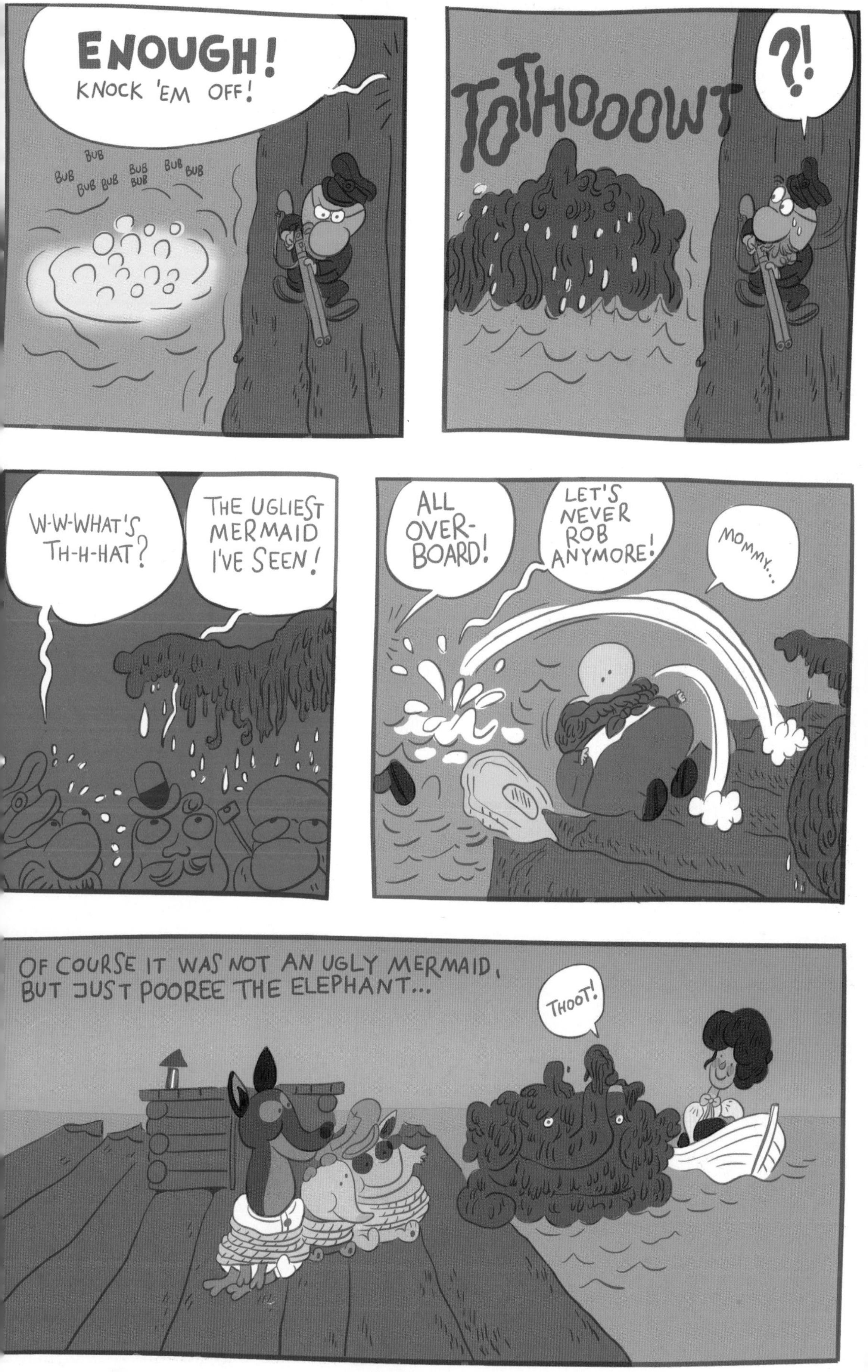

ENOUGH! KNOCK 'EM OFF!
BUB BUB BUB BUB BUB BUB BUB BUB BUB
TOTHOOOWT
?!
W-W-WHAT'S TH-H-HAT?
THE UGLIEST MERMAID I'VE SEEN!
ALL OVER-BOARD!
LET'S NEVER ROB ANYMORE!
MOMMY...
OF COURSE IT WAS NOT AN UGLY MERMAID, BUT JUST POOREE THE ELEPHANT...
THOOT!

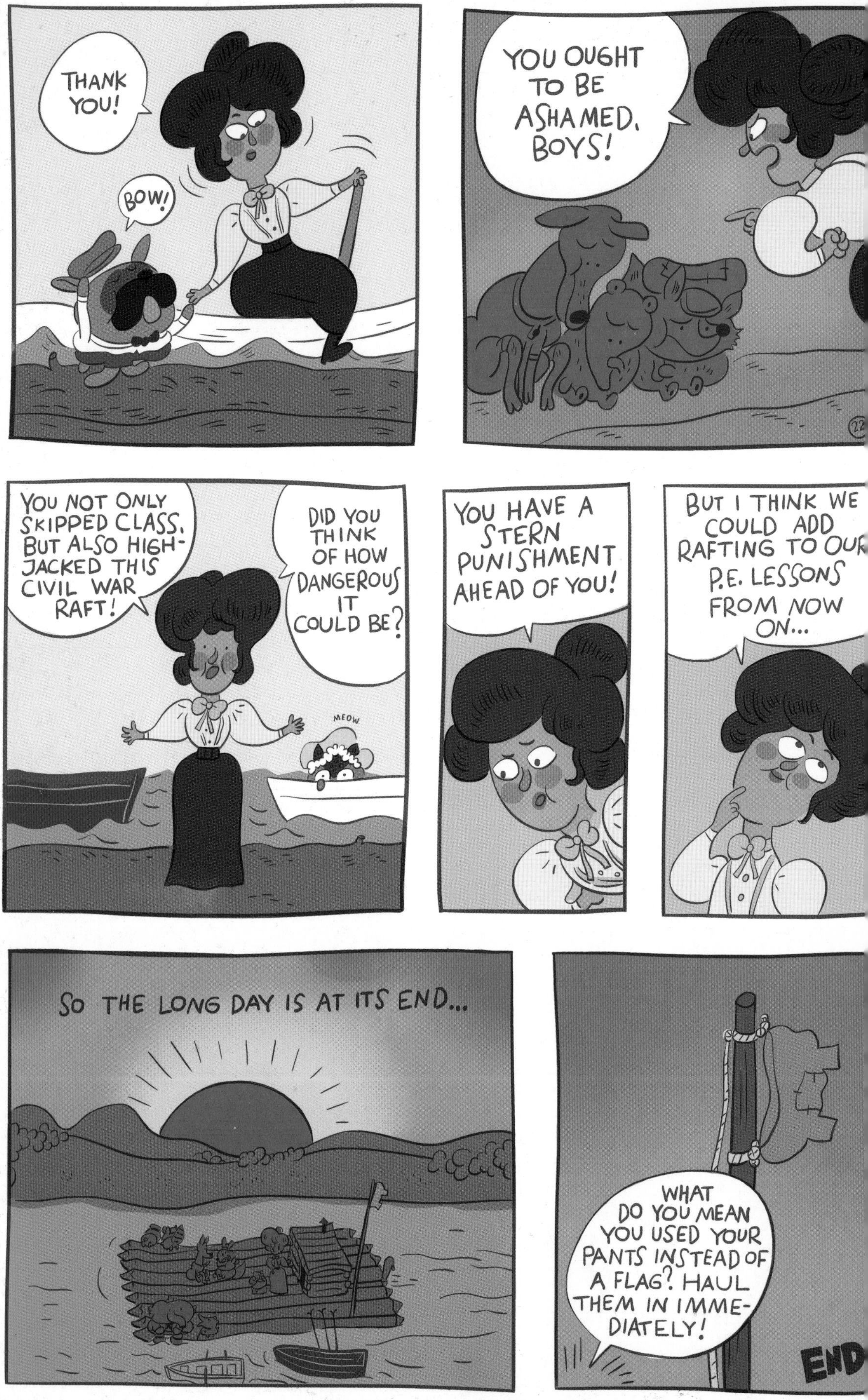
THANK YOU!
BOW!
YOU OUGHT TO BE ASHAMED, BOYS!
22
YOU NOT ONLY SKIPPED CLASS, BUT ALSO HIGH-JACKED THIS CIVIL WAR RAFT!
DID YOU THINK OF HOW DANGEROUS IT COULD BE?
MEOW
YOU HAVE A STERN PUNISHMENT AHEAD OF YOU!
BUT I THINK WE COULD ADD RAFTING TO OUR P.E. LESSONS FROM NOW ON...
SO THE LONG DAY IS AT ITS END...
WHAT DO YOU MEAN YOU USED YOUR PANTS INSTEAD OF A FLAG? HAUL THEM IN IMMEDIATELY!
END

COVER
GALLERY

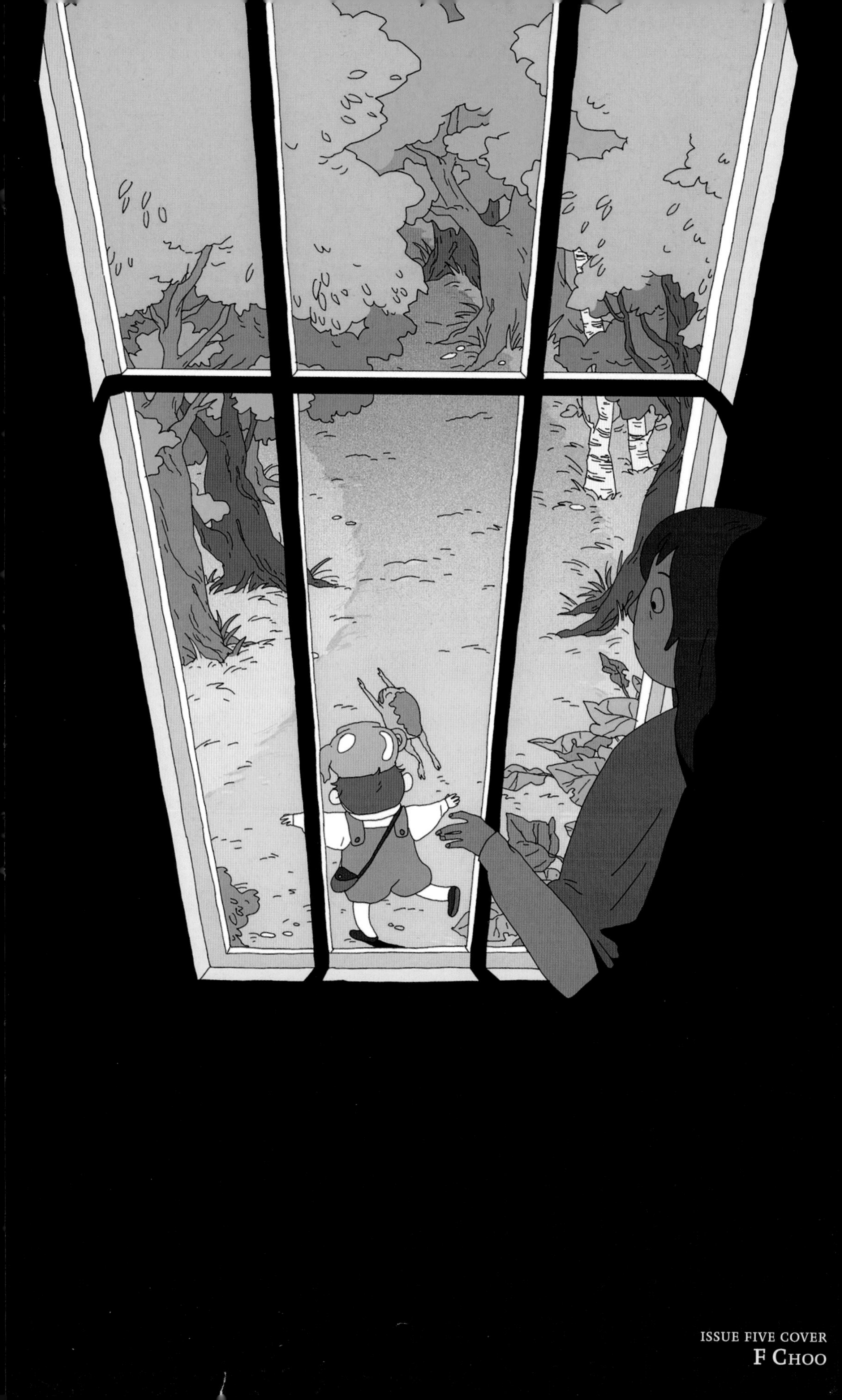

ISSUE FIVE COVER
F Choo

ISSUE FIVE SUBSCRIPTION COVER
JEN BARTEL

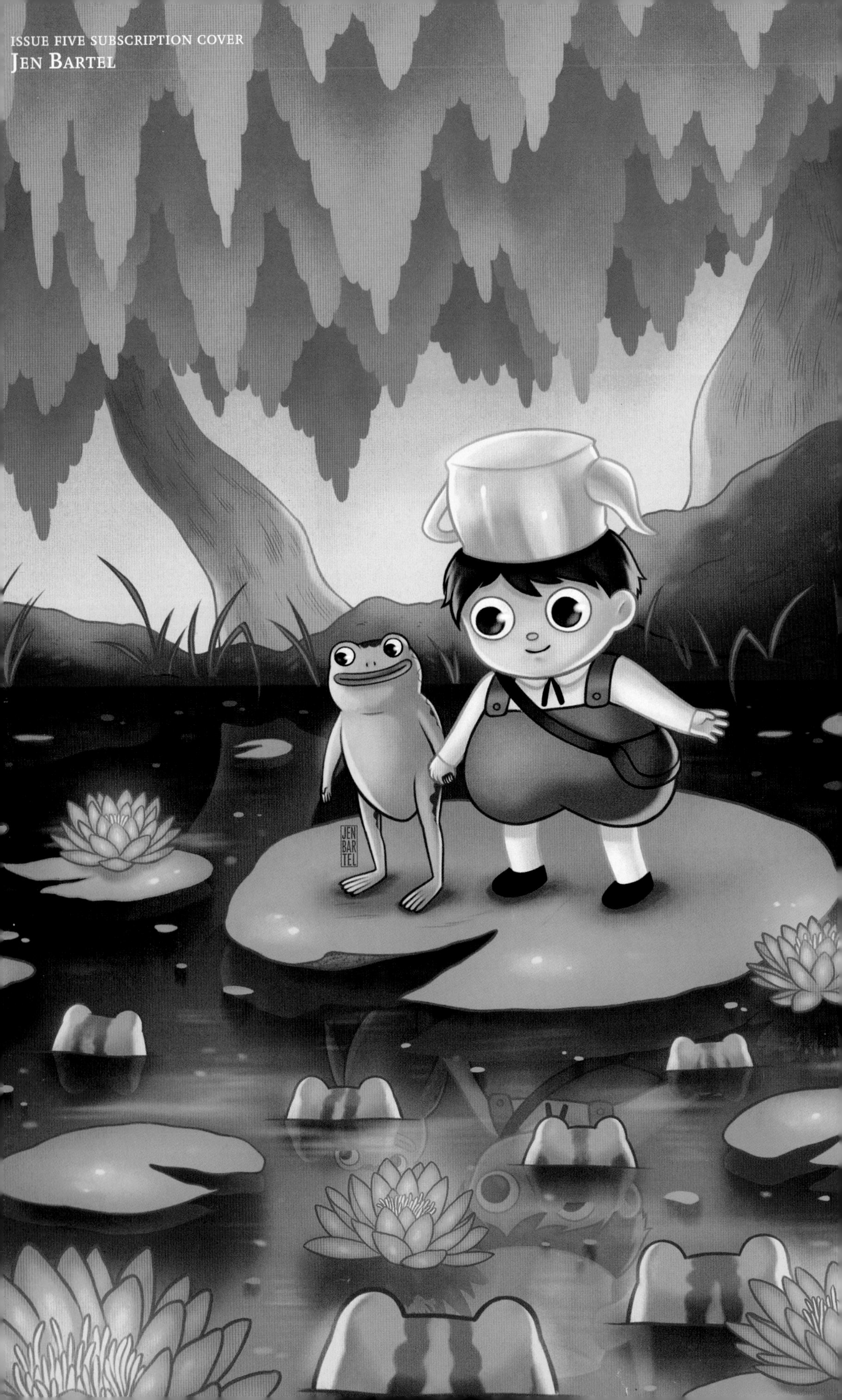
JEN BARTEL

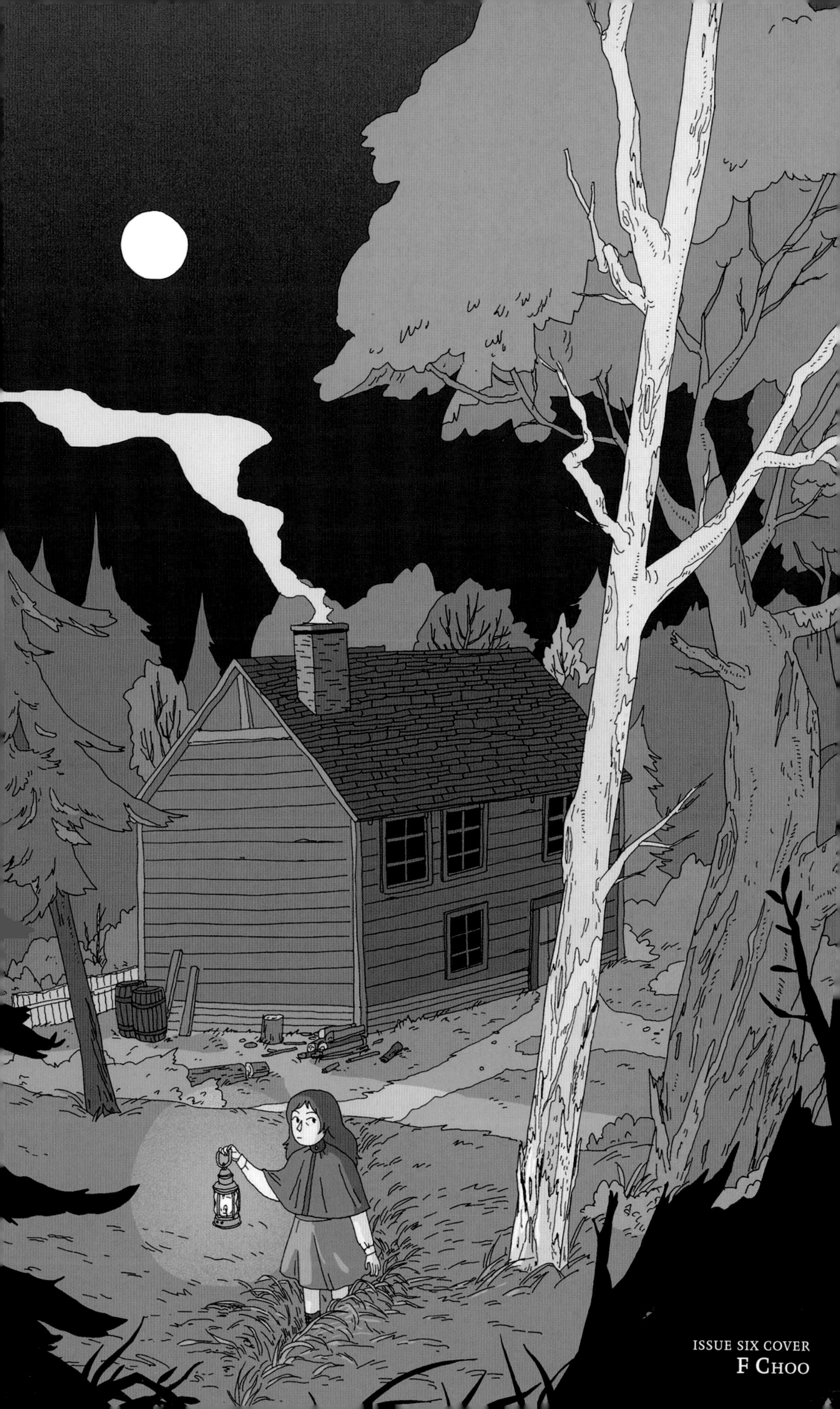

ISSUE SIX COVER
F Choo

ISSUE SIX SUBSCRIPTION COVER
AYME SOTUYO

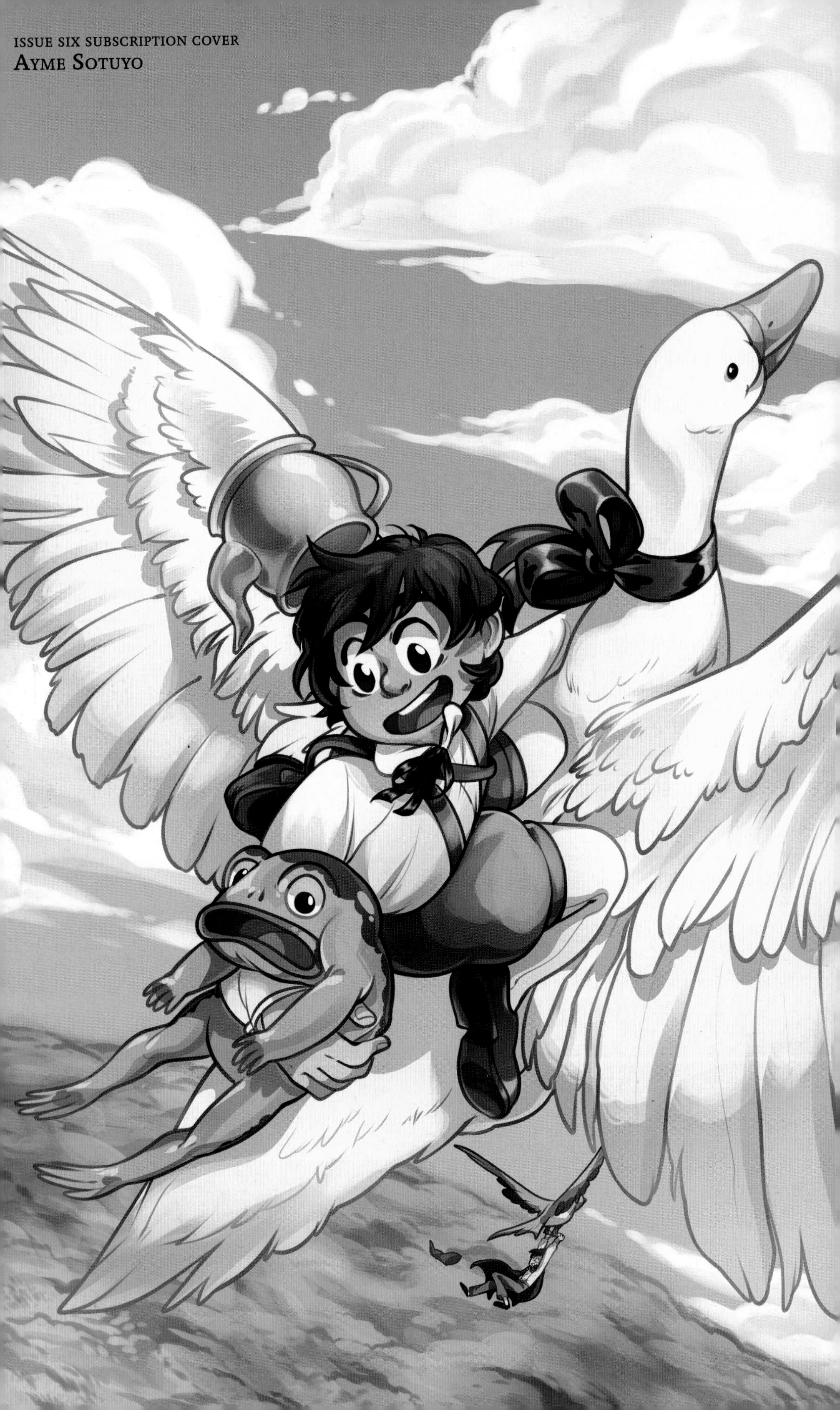

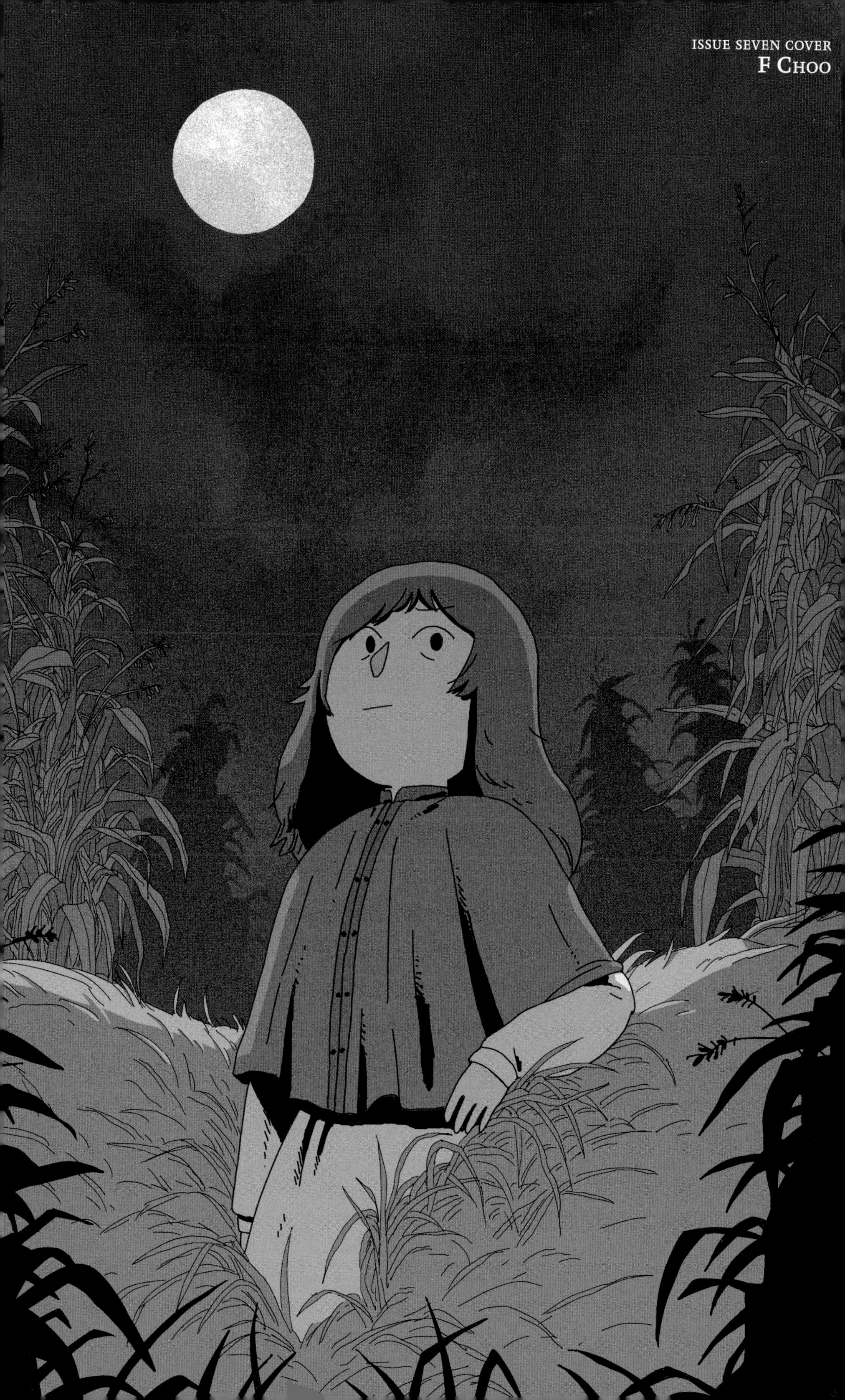

ISSUE SEVEN COVER
F Choo

ISSUE SEVEN SUBSCRIPTION COVER
MYRA HILD

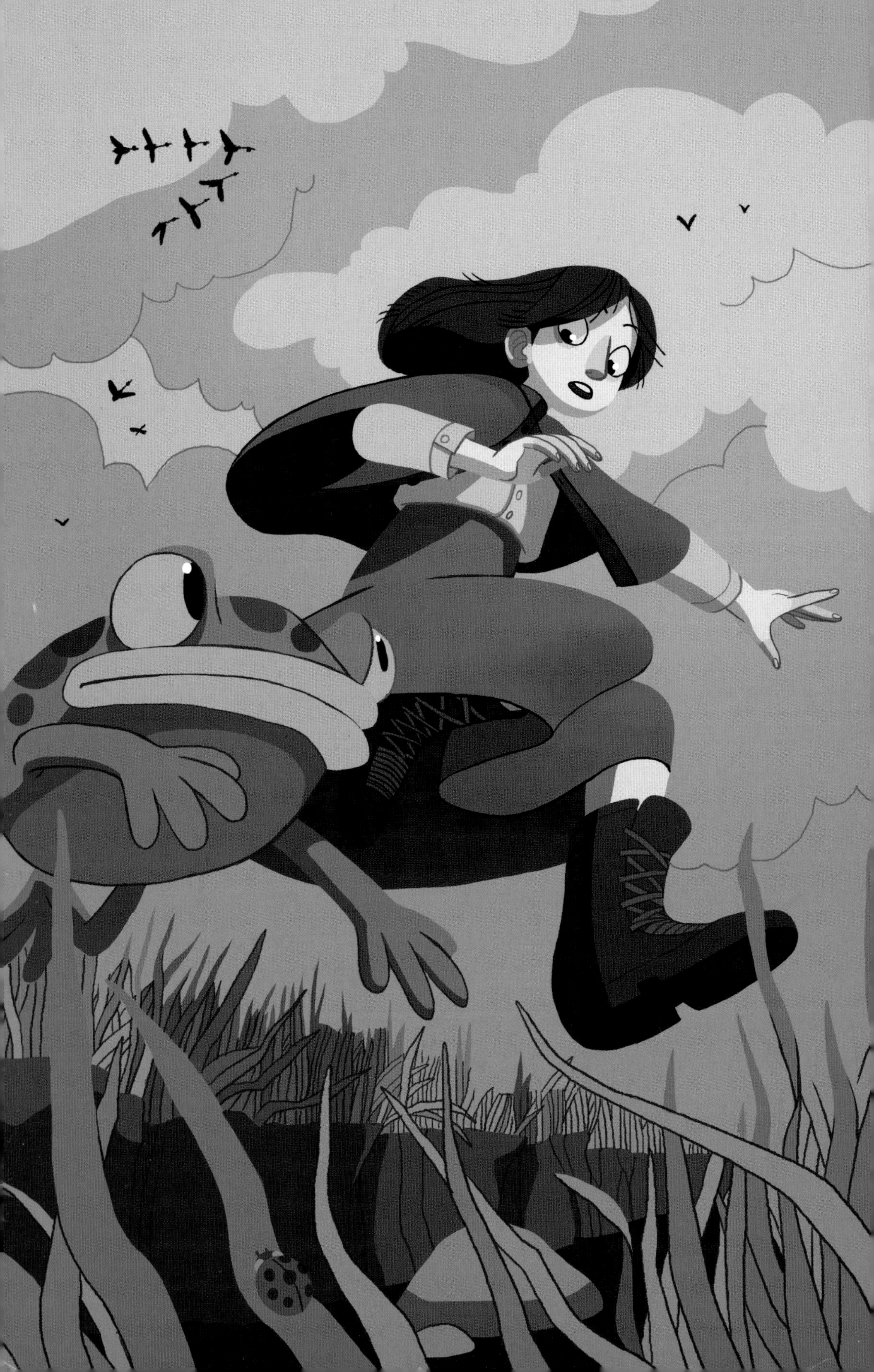

Issue Eight Cover
F Choo

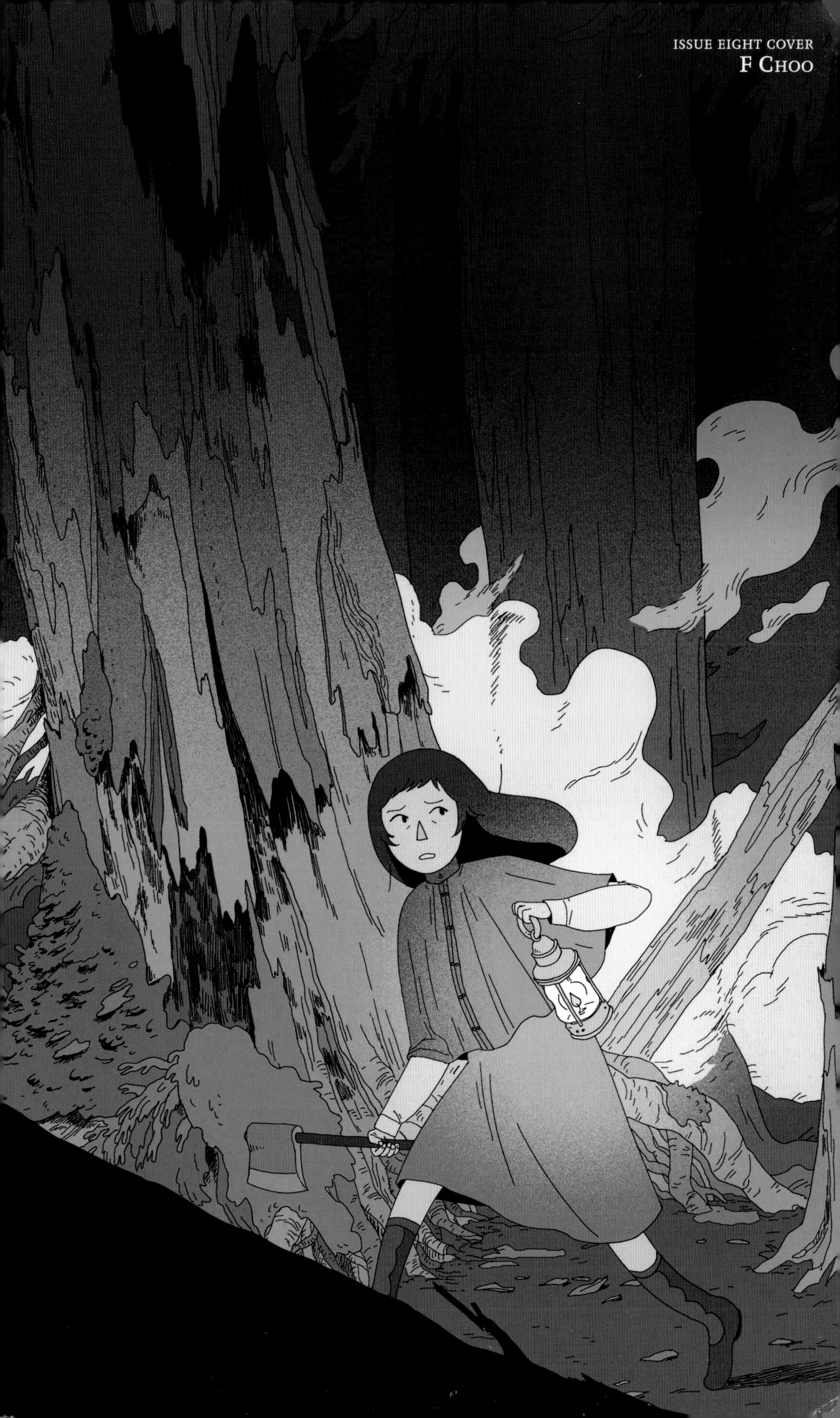

ISSUE EIGHT SUBSCRIPTION COVER
GANG YI

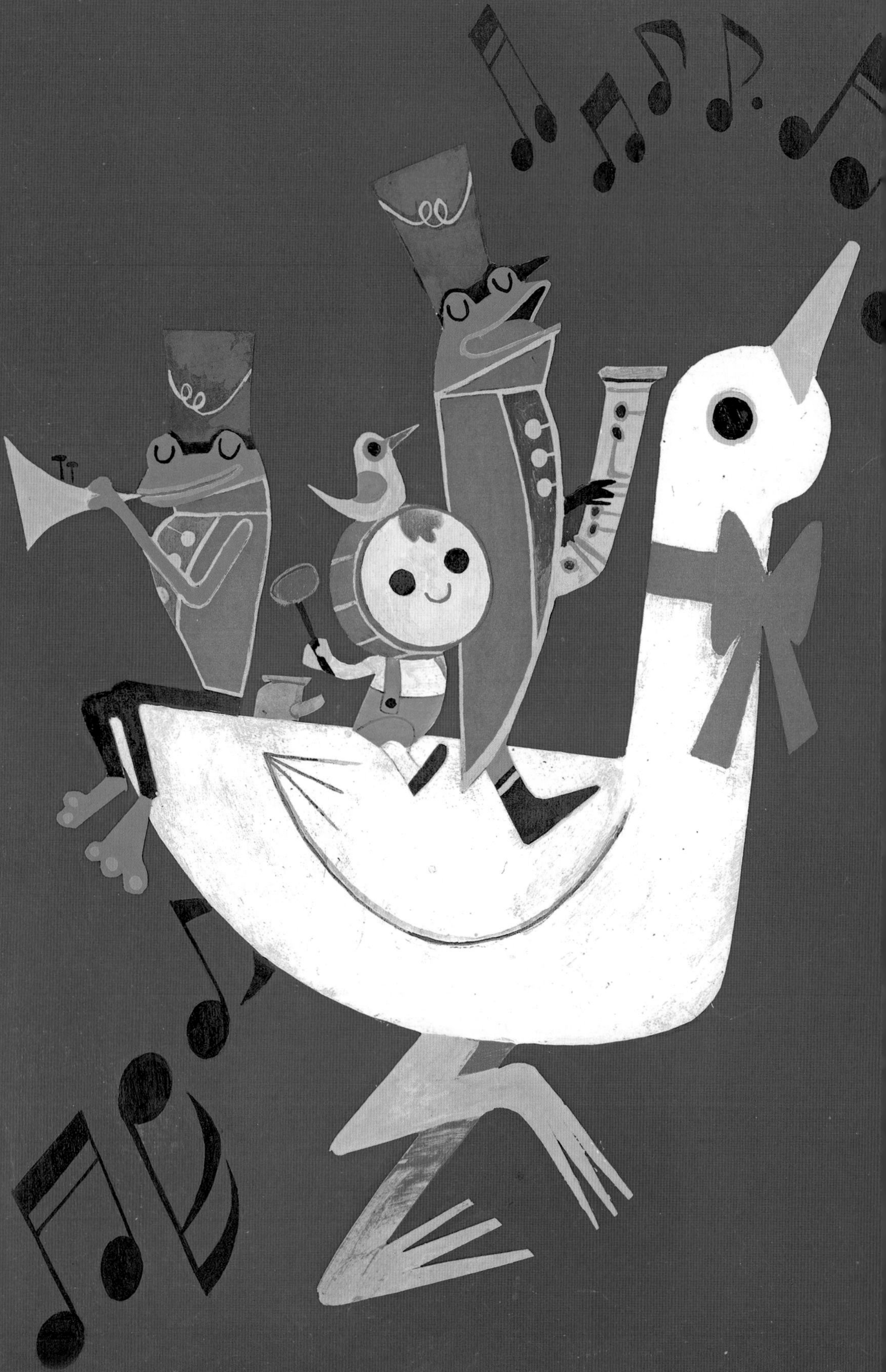

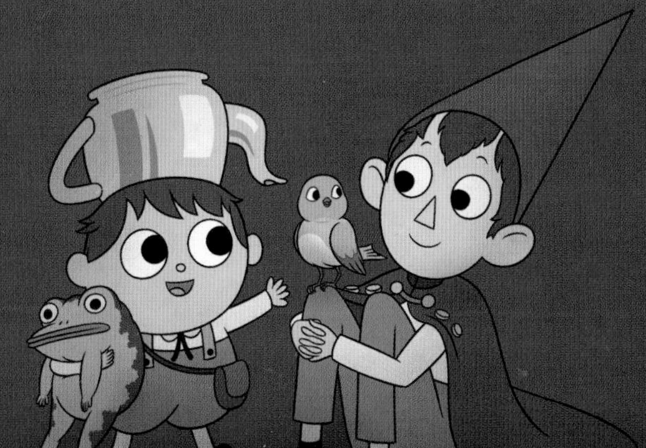

DISCOVER
EXPLOSIVE NEW WORLDS

Adventure Time

The Amazing World of
Gumball

Steven Universe
Volume One

Over the
Garden Wall

Garfield
By Jim Davis

Charles M. Schulz
Peanuts
Schulz

AVAILABLE AT YOUR LOCAL COMICS SHOP AND BOOKSTORE

To find a comics shop in your area, call 1-888-266-4226

WWW.**BOOM-STUDIOS**.COM

Adventure Time
Pendleton Ward and Others
Volume 1
ISBN: 978-1-60886-280-1 | $9.99
Volume 2
ISBN: 978-1-60886-323-5 | $14.99 US
Adventure Time: Islands
ISBN: 978-1-60886-972-5 | $9.99

Regular Show
J.G. Quintel and Others
Volume 1
ISBN: 978-1-60886-362-4 | $14.99
Volume 2
ISBN: 978-1-60886-426-3 | $14.99

Regular Show: Hydration
ISBN: 978-1-60886-339-6 | $12.99

The Amazing World of Gumball
Ben Bocquelet and Others
Volume 1
ISBN: 978-1-60886-488-1 | $14.99
Volume 2
ISBN: 978-1-60886-793-6 | $14.99

Over the Garden Wall
Patrick McHale, Jim Campbell and Others
Volume 1
ISBN: 978-1-60886-940-4 | $14.99
Volume 2
ISBN: 978-1-68415-006-9 | $14.99

Steven Universe
Rebecca Sugar and Others
Volume 1
ISBN: 978-1-60886-706-6 | $14.99
Volume 2
ISBN: 978-1-60886-796-7 | $14.99

Steven Universe & The Crystal Gems
ISBN: 978-1-60886-921-3 | $14.99

Steven Universe: Too Cool for School
ISBN: 978-1-60886-771-4 | $14.99

Peanuts
Charles Schultz and Others
Volume 1
ISBN: 978-1-60886-260-3 | $13.99

Garfield
Jim Davis and Others
Volume 1
ISBN: 978-1-60886-287-0 | $13.99

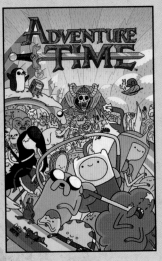

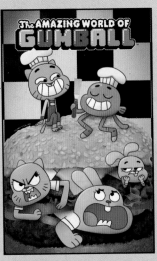

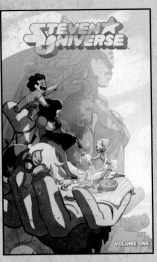

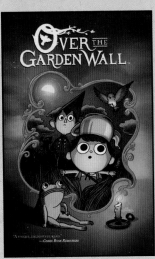

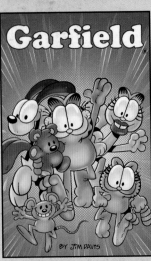

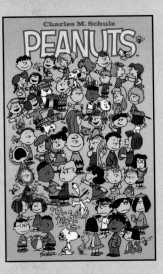

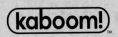